TW
Flatline

K. Kingsman

Cover by Kim Ramirez

ISBN: 978-0-9996949-0-9

DEDICATION

Is it selfish if I dedicate this novel to myself?

cuz that's what imma do

ACKNOWLEDGMENTS

A.M. – You were my first friend, even though you were closer to Luzio back then and I was a little jealous. Thanks for telling me when my ideas were bad and I should change things. You da MVP and imma buy the CRAP out of your book when it comes out.

K.R. – You are there for me without question or hesitation, I literally cannot thank you enough for helping me bring this to publication. Let's go get some happy hour tacos.

S.L. – Never forget 7th grade geometry class.

L.G. – For everything else

And also the Flock

-16-

I couldn't tell if he was dumb, or audacious. I watched him with careful eyes, smoke wafting up from the cigarette between my fingers. His hands didn't shake as he held the gun. His lips didn't tremble as he spoke, "I'll give you one last chance." His voice was steady. Calm. Collected.

An act.

I almost smiled. Despite his poker face, I could see the small beads of sweat forming at his hair line. His eyes were dilated. His face was flushed. Goosebumps dotted his arms. His body was giving him life-saving commands that he took great effort to ignore. They call that fight or flight, and yet he did neither. I couldn't tell if he was dumb, or courageous.

His heart beat through his chest. Frantic. Terrified. I glanced back up at his face, but it still held the same blank look, almost as if he were bored. I couldn't tell if he was dumb, or just very good at bluffing. His hand tightened around the metal and, under the dim yellow light, the revolver shone brilliantly against the blood splattered walls. He was going to die, but he didn't know it yet.

Or maybe he knew and didn't want to believe it.

Or maybe he didn't care.

Men much older than him had shed tears at this point. I would certainly miss his company. He spoke again, feigning confidence, "Going once." Unless he wasn't bluffing. "Going twice." My eyes narrowed. "Last chance." I couldn't tell if he was dumb, or a genius.

I tapped cigarette ash on the table. The seconds turned to minutes. My mouth was dry as I answered, *"I'm afraid I'm going to have to pass on the offer."*

He simply shrugged. His nonchalance sent chills racing down my spine for the first time in years. I broke eye contact, momentarily, but when I looked back, a sly smile had plastered itself on his face. Cocky. And yet, he was still going to die.

I couldn't tell if he was dumb, or completely insane.

He answered my thought aloud, "I prefer the term high functioning."

How bold.

"Then what are you waiting for?"

Pull the trigger.

My name is Ricky Schenk.
This is my scratch.

-1-

In any situation, if anyone ever asked, "Do you want to see the pictures from last night?"

The answer should always be no.

My head was down and resting on the cold conference table when Samantha, ASB Vice President, slid her phone to me from the other side of the table. Sweat stuck to my forehead like Louisiana heat in August.

I honestly had no idea how I managed to make it to school. Thirty minutes ago I could barely walk without vomit catching in the back of my throat. At least it was just an ASB meeting and the rest of the council was also nursing hangovers. We'd dragged ourselves in, shut the blinds, and collectively collapsed around the table for forty minutes. It was a great way to start the day.

I reached for Samantha's phone, dimmed the brightness, and immediately regretted looking at the pictures from last night. "I looked like shit."

Samantha grunted, face planted into her elbow. "You look like shit now."

Point taken.

Last night was a fucking mess. From the moment I woke up, the room never stopped spinning. My body was twisted on someone else's couch in an elegantly decorated living room, now covered in red solo cups and half empty bags of Hot Cheetos. I lifted my hand to grab my forehead, finding my fingers cold and wet.

I moved to wipe my hand on something - or maybe just I just fell over, hard to tell - and it landed in a poof of hair.

The who: A redhead. Curly hair. Smelled like cucumber. If my head wasn't splitting open, it wouldn't have been so bad waking up to Samantha Yeager, ASB Vice President, swim team co-captain, and ranked 24th in our senior class for academics, 103rd for looks, and around 230ish for personality. Out of a class of 350 students, that wasn't too shabby. Samantha's upper lip was slightly poutier than the bottom, and her mouth hung open to drool on the couch pillow I was laying on. Her face looked peaceful, with the exception of the giant dick drawn in Sharpie across her cheek.

The what: I managed to untangle myself from Samantha's freckled limbs and sit up. Jensen's house party, Sunday night into Monday morning. BYOB, except since we were all underage, most of us didn't and mooched off his family's alcohol cabinet.

Jensen's family wouldn't mind. They had gone on a Caribbean cruise for the week without him, probably oblivious he wasn't on the deck tanning with them. I didn't remember the specifics of their vacation. I didn't actually care.

The when: I dug around in my pocket for my phone. The screen was cracked and I had eleven new emails, twenty seven texts, and two voicemails. It was 4:48am.

By some miracle, I didn't have alcohol poisoning, despite the two shots, four and a half mixed drinks, and whatever was in that Satan's creation called jungle juice I chugged the last few hours. So, I wasn't feeling anywhere near the top of my game, but I was coherent. That was a win in my books.

I stood up, hanging onto the edge of the couch until the swirling slowed down. "Blake?" I called, but my voice was strained and weak.

We had school today.

Someone was passed out on the loveseat, makeup smeared down her cheeks. A black lacy 32B bra dangled from the ceiling fan, rocking back and forth from its shoulder strap. We had school today. Shit. Chips and candy wrappers crunched under my shoes. I passed through the kitchen where Jensen lay curled against the dark wood island, cuddling an empty Malibu bottle.

"Jensen, get up. We have an ASB meeting in an hour."

He mumbled something along the lines of "Shut up and leave me alone." His hair was the same color as the light bamboo flooring. I moved the bottle that held up his head and his face slapped the floor.

Ignoring Jensen's groaning, I continued on. "Blake?" Where the fuck was he? My feet scuffed along the hardwood. "Blake?" I wished I could boast that it was a pretty legendary party, but it was actually about the same as always. The usual drunken shenanigans of a bunch of teens that didn't have much else to worry about.

I stopped at the base of the staircase, only 10% sure I could lift my feet high enough to make it to the second story. "Blake?"

"Ricky?" replied a shaky voice from a bathroom.

Downstairs. Thank God. I held onto the wall as I followed his voice down the hallway. The bathroom door was wide open. Blake's gaunt frame leaned forward on the marble sink, his nose two inches from the mirror, observing the bright purple and red hickeys dotting down his neck and shoulders.

Well.

I rested against the door frame, swallowing back the saliva pooling around my tongue. "Looks like you had a fun night."

Blake turned away from the mirror, his eyes red and blue like a police siren, bloodshot from either booze (unlikely), lack of sleep (more likely), or crying (most likely). "Ricky. What. Happened. Last. Night?"

"You're asking the wrong person. Come on, we should –" I paused for a dry heave. "Go." I reversed back into the hallway.

Blake stepped away from the mirror, darting out of the bathroom after me. "No, really. I don't remember anything."

I led the way to the front door, Blake whining behind me. I wasn't even sure why Blake accompanied me to these parties, he didn't drink. He would float around the crowds for hours, mingling and making jokes and politely turning away poorly mixed vodka sodas. All the while wishing he could instead throw on a pair of sneakers and run to the top of a hill where he could watch the sunset, sweaty but elated.

Maybe he came to the parties for me. Or the girls. Hard to tell.

Blake continued talking, white noise to the back of my head. To Blake, drinking alcohol would be breaking a personal promise he made to himself, that we all made to ourselves, back in elementary school. We stood up in the assembly room, hand over heart, and repeated after a cartoon lion that we would respect others and lead a life free from dangerous behaviors.

Or some shit.

Blake nudged my arm, the fate of his life depending on whether or not I heard his accounts of the past night. "Then nothing," Blake continued. "Do you think, I don't know, do you think something was in the punch?"

Blake didn't want to become a statistic. As dramatic as that sounded—I stepped over a girl missing one of her fake eyelashes—Blake made a compelling argument. Plus, he had personal reasons.

It was all very understandable. I just wished he would calm down. "Ricky, please tell me that drink you gave me wasn't spiked."

I gave him the answer that wouldn't send him spiraling into manic self-punishment. "That drink I gave you wasn't spiked."

"Are you sure?"

"I'm sure."

Blake moved in front of me, grabbing both my shoulders and staring into my eyes with a firm frown. "Are you. Sure?"

My mind swam with blurry images of orange ping pong balls bouncing off the rim of beer cups and someone hunched over the backyard rose bushes, puking something that smelled like rancid cheeseburgers, but I had no memory of giving him a drink.

"Completely sure."

Blake squinted at my answer, but reluctantly accepted it, as he usually did.

Once outside, I fished around in my pockets for my car keys. We had about an hour until I needed to be at an ASB meeting before school. I figured it probably wouldn't look too professional for the President to show up late for the first official meeting of second semester.

I had a decent running pickup truck that I had to 'earn,' which equated to vacuuming a couple times. My parents bought the truck from a used car dealership as a surprise, but they called me during the process to confirm if it was a good deal. It was a silver 2008 Dodge Dakota and better suited for a fifty year old man from Vidor, Texas, but it was in good condition and it got the job done.

As soon as I had taken out my keys, Blake had already snatched them out of my hands, climbing into the front seat to drive. "No drinking and driving."

"I'm not—"

"You heard me."

"Whatever." It was a waste of time to argue. "Let's just go before Jensen's parents get back."

"They get back from the Bahamas today, right?"

I didn't know. "Sure." I didn't really care.

Blake parked on the curb and not in the driveway, an unspoken rule if we ever stayed out all night. My father would be leaving in exactly—I checked my cracked phone screen—thirty-eight minutes, so there was no point squeezing in behind his black Mazada, which was not only looked professional parked outside of a courtroom but also got thirty-five miles per gallon. Efficient for what it was. Just like my father.

We followed standard procedure of sneaking into my bedroom window. My parents planted the Elm tree a few months after they first bought the house, a little reminder of their apartment together back East. "Also," my father cited as he shoveled a hole in the backyard, "Trees help block roadside traffic noise." Dual purpose. Efficient.

Blake crawled in through the window first, immediately stripping down and headed for the shower. Something about feeling unclean and tainted. I slugged my body through the window after him, letting it fall to the carpet. And there I stayed.

The smell of thick-cut bacon wafted upstairs, along with whole grain toast and local strawberry jam from the Farmer's Market. My mother was already downstairs making breakfast, even though no one ever ate it except Blake. Whatever made her feel needed, since she couldn't continue her latest hobby of painting the nursery.

My backpack was already packed, but I pulled it towards me to take a look at my agenda. ASB meeting, tutoring at lunch, grading freshman biology papers for my TA period, tutoring after school, SAT tutoring after that, then my own homework. It was a light day.

Blake returned in a towel, creating a trail of little wet pitter patter footprints to my closet.

My energy didn't quite reach the level needed to raise my head, so I spoke into the carpet. "Did the hot water run out or something? That was fast."

Blake looked over his shoulder at me, blond bangs clinging to his forehead. "I thought you might want to take a few extra minutes today."

The shower didn't help me feel better on the inside, especially since I threw up and watched vomit swirl between my feet, but with a clean face I could fake feeling better on the outside. We walked downstairs to the kitchen, more or less just like any other day.

Enter stage left, a forty-three year old housewife with the annoyingly astounding ability to small talk for hours. Mrs. Schenk looked up from the cast iron skillet, giving a smile worthy of a Colgate ad. "Morning boys! I was just making breakfast."

The usual.

Our entire house was strategically decorated. Since our kitchen was only separated from our living room by a breakfast bar, both rooms were bright with natural light. The windows faced east so that the sun was always welcome to bring in fresh energy. Mirrors and air cleansing plants lined the walls, to balance the chi or spirits or something. My mother only started practicing Feng Shui a few months ago and she still didn't know what she was doing if it wasn't in a Pinterest post.

"It smells delicious in here!" Blake said, plopping down at his seat at table, waiting for my mother to fix him a plate. The usual. "How's your morning so far?" Blake asked. I resisted the urge to gag from the bacon oil and poured myself a glass of orange juice.

"My morning has been productive, thanks for asking, *Blake*." She flipped the bacon over in the pan, then moved over to scoop scrambled eggs onto a plate. "You two are down for breakfast a bit early." She glanced at the clock. "What was it you have today, Ricky? Some sort of leadership conference?" Her brown curls bounced with each carefully pronounced word.

I didn't bother correcting her. "Something like that, yes." I grabbed two slices of bread out of the bread box on the counter and dropped three aspirins in my orange juice that tasted like vodka.

My father would be downstairs soon. He had been working on a new case and the first court date was today. He was a tech lawyer at a company in the city. Not exactly what he went to school for, but it paid the bills.

My mother shook her head at the pan. “I don’t know why they insist on making those things so early.” She added the bacon to Blake’s plate. “You boys look tired, did you not sleep well?”

“Something like that.” I put the bread in the toaster.

She filled the plate with hash browns, then rounded the meal off with a nice tall glass of milk and sat it in front of Blake. She watched him like a hawk until he took his first bite, then, satisfied at feeding at least one person, she returned to the stove.

“So,” she cracked another egg against the counter, the shell splitting like a skull against asphalt. “What were you boys up to last night? I could hear a lot of *commotion* downstairs, then it got awfully quiet.”

Blake looked at me. I shrugged, watching the red glow of the toaster. Blake took a forkful of hash brown before throwing together a lie. “I just came over to study. We had the TV playing in the background for a while, so that must have been the noisy part.”

“*Studying*?” She eyed the bruises painted across Blake’s neck, too high for his turtle neck to conceal.

Blake shoveled eggs into his mouth. “Mhm…studying.”

My mother’s eyebrow raised in my direction and I shrugged at her too, turning back to the toaster. “Something like that.”

She held eye contact and I could see the mix of suspicion and confusion cross her face, scrambling more eggs as she pried, “Must have been a pretty boring night then?”

“Oh you know.” The toaster dinged. “The usual.”

On cue, my father clunked down the stairs, juggling his briefcase, suit jacket, and the ever pressing dilemma of red tie vs blue tie. My mother and Blake gave him a look over, suggesting the blue tie, knowing he was going to choose that one anyway. "Thanks," he wrapped the tie around his neck, dumped his work at the table, then stole my toast.

I couldn't stomach it anyway.

My father ruffled Blake's wet hair. He frowned and looked for a towel. "Blake, you're still here? I didn't hear you last night, so I assumed you left."

"They were *studying*, Robert." She flipped another piece of bacon.

Mr. Schenk gave Blake a pat on the back and simultaneously dried his hands. Efficient. "That's great. Education first." My mother took time out of her busy housewife schedule to help with his tie. He spoke between bites of my toast. "Keep at it and someday, with any luck, you'll be—" We all looked at the clock on the wall. "—late for work. Like me. See ya, Honey." Cheek kiss. "Bye boys." Head nod. He pulled his jacket on and picked up his briefcase.

"Bye," Blake wiped the milk moustache off his face. "Good luck with your case today."

"Thanks." Keys jingle.

My mother went back to cooking bacon, for some reason. She called over her shoulder to her husband, "Oh, and Rob, you're not going to be late tonight, right? I was going to make your favorite for dinner, I'm sure in *celebration* of the first hearing?"

The flirting went right out the front door. "Thanks, Hon." Cell phone ring.

I dumped my orange juice out, also calling after him. "I threw up in the shower this morning."

My mother shot me a disapproving look, but Mr. Schenk was already halfway out and talking to his assistant on the other line. "Yeah, thanks." Door shut.

The usual.

-2-

My father always kept a bottle of scotch in his office. There wasn't anything particularly special about the bottle, aside from the fact that it was the only alcohol present in our house. It was always a small bottle, tucked into the dark wood bookcase against the wall. It was always the same brand, in the same classic shape with the same rich yellow as dehydrated pee. On rare occasions, when a colleague or old friend would visit, they would sit in his office, pour themselves quarter glasses, and have deep laughs about mundane half topics of the past.

Do you remember when?

Whatever happened to her?

That would've been something.

Can you imagine if?

But never a complete thought. And never a current event. They would always linger in the past, telling the same tidbits of memories over and over. There was a time I believed if I listened to enough half stories, I would be able to eventually follow along. I sat outside that office door, munching on pre-cut apple slices, peeking through the crack that was always left open just enough to see the chocolate soles of their shoes pointed toward each other.

My father never drank alone, so for most of the year, the bottle would go untouched, just another golden award on his shelf.

When I was eleven, however, the bottle had changed. The shape was the first to catch my eye. "Blake," I tugged on his sleeve, drawing his attention away from rummaging through my father's desk drawer.

"Hm? Did you find the scissors?"

"It's different." I picked up the bottle in my hand, now a short stout bottle. The color had changed as well, to a roasted amber color, like caramelized honey.

"What?" Blake asked again, this time looking over my shoulder. "So?"

"It's never been different before." Which must have meant it was significant in some way. Nothing ever changed in my house without a significant push. My father was a smoker until the day my mother announced she was pregnant. As the stories would have it, he used to smoke about two or three cigarettes a day, which wasn't at all record breaking, but it was still smoking.

One at his morning break, 9:30. He would quickly duck out of the office for his first inhale of the day and an ergo stretch. His second, after he finished a late lunch. He always ate lunch later because his colleagues were eager to head out and he could stay behind and wrap up whatever they were working on while also avoiding lunch traffic. It was an easy way to gain their respect and gratitude. If he had a particularly busy or stressful day, he would mull over work at home in his office, exhaling a drag towards the open window in the room. He used to say it made him feel balanced, not necessarily good or bad, but balanced. Focused. Calm. He didn't mention a feeling of clarity, but that was what it sounded like to me.

However, second hand smoke was bad for babies.

Newton's first law of motion stated that every object (my family) would remain at rest or in uniform motion in a straight line unless compelled to change its state by the action of an external force.

"What do you think changed?" I asked, turning to Blake.

Both of his eyebrows were pulled up. "What? Whaddya mean, you just said the bottle changed, right?"

"No, I mean what happened to make him change the bottle?" What external force had acted upon my family to make such a drastic change of state?

Blake blew his lips out, "I dunno, maybe this one was on sale."

I felt the weight of the bottle in my hand. The weight of change. "I should drink it, right?"

"What?" Blake quickly covered his mouth, then moved to cover mine. "Don't say things like that!"

I swatted him away. "Think about it." I sat down on the floor, planting the bottle between my legs. It had already been opened, the seal broken, but the last time my father had someone over for scotch, they had shared the old brand. The usual brand. This one was new, and already opened.

"Think about what?" A beat behind, Blake plopped on the floor next to me, looking over my shoulder towards the partially open door. "I don't think you should—" But the top was off before he could stop me.

Acceleration (excitement) would be produced when a force (alcohol/or frankly any new experience) acted on a mass (myself).

I wanted a change too.

I lifted the bottle to my nose, sniffing the lips.

"What does it smell like?" Blake's eyes were wide now and his hands clutched his knees.

"The nurse's office." Was the best way I could describe it.

"Please don't drink it. It's not good for you. Bad stuff can happen," he warned, just a whisper compared to everything in my head telling me otherwise. Bad stuff made life interesting.

I kissed the bottle, tilting my head upwards like in the movies. My father always used a glass, but maybe a new bottle meant new rules. The taste of burnt cardboard covered my tongue like vinegar, but stronger. I had to clasp my hand over my mouth to keep from immediately spitting it back out. The liquid pinched the lining of my throat, its sharp nails dragging all the way down.

The greater the mass, the greater the amount of force required.

The third law stated that for every action in nature there was an equal and opposite reaction.

I shifted my eyes from the slowly ticking wall clock to the whiteboard straight ahead, though I didn't bother copying down the notes. My teacher faced the board as she wrote down AP Statistics formulas in blue dry erase marker, probably second guessing her decision of changing her major to education. I was still recovering from last night. My classmates were too busy tweeting to even pretend to pay attention.

No one wanted to be here.

"Hey."

Well.

"Hey, Ricky."

Except Blake.

"Ricky! Hey."

I sighed, taking a long three seconds to blink and slowly turn my heavy head toward him. "What?"

Blake's grin was so radiant I would probably get melanoma. "You wanna work on our project at lunch?" I waited. Blake took my silence as a sign for him to continue. "Okay, so I know you probably don't want to, but since you'll be busy this weekend, planning for the Valentine's dance and all, I was thinking we could get a head start on brainstorming for." He said more, but I stopped paying attention after that. School work was too boring, too ordinary, too expected.

"Sure," I finally replied to Blake, assuming my response would fit with the context of whatever he was talking about.

Blake grinned wider, continuing to whisper to me. "So I was thinking we take a survey of blah blah blah blah."

His words blurred together as I tuned him out again. Over Blake's shoulder, I locked eye contact with a girl before she fluttered her eyelashes and quickly looked down.

I really hated when girls fluttered their eyelashes.

Wavy black hair to her shoulders, and black circle eyes like a snowman, hidden behind choppy blunt bangs. She was bouncing one knee up and down, the other folded under her. My guess was 5'2", but her thick combat boots were throwing off my perception.

The boots were from a Nordstrom sale last year.

Her fingers played with the edge of her long sleeve shirt, and she kept her focus locked on the blank paper on the desk. I had seen her before, waiting outside the counselor's office, hunched over in one of the chairs, kicking at the speckled carpet.

"Blake," I shifted my gaze between him and the girl over his shoulder. "Who is that?"

Blake stopped mid-sentence, glancing over his shoulder. "Who is who?"

"That one girl."

He used his hand as a telescope over one eye. "You are being incredibly specific."

"The girl with the boots."

"Specific."

"I'm sorry, Inspector Gadget: black hair, red and black plaid shirt, faded headband, distressed jeans from the downtown swap meet, medium wash. Last night, at 7:54pm, she was spotted in her kitchen eating a peanut butter and nutella sandwich—"

"Oh, right, the sandwich, that did it." He made an event of yawning loudly over his shoulder as he checked again. "Oh." Blake laughed a little, turning back to me. "Her name's Heidi, dude, she's gone to this school since freshman year."

"Heidi?"

"Yeah."

"Then how come I've never heard of her?"

"Because you're rude."

After class ended, Blake gave me a wink when I told him I was bailing on our lunch plans to talk to Heidi. I slid my notebook into my bag, trying to keep the same pace as her pack-up routine, which was painfully slow. As soon as we stepped outside, I cleared my throat and gently tapped her on the shoulder. “Heidi?”

She stopped, half-way turning so she could look up at me. “What?” The sun made her squint.

“Hey, I just wanted to talk to you.” I got a better look at her face this time, but nothing particularly stood out.

“Wait, what.”

“You know, talking. Conversing. Exchanging friendly banter.”

“No, not that, I know what talking is.” Her thick eyebrows pulled together. “What did you call me?”

My eyebrows pulled together. “Heidi?”

“Yeah. My name is definitely not Heidi. Nice.” She gave a polite, though confused, smile and faced the ground as she walked away.

Blake, that little shit.

I quickened my pace to close the distance. “Well, a pleasure to meet you, Not-Heidi. I’m Ricky.”

“I know.”

“Well, that’s a little weird. You know my name, but I don’t know yours?”

She barely looked at me. “You’re the class president and probably one of the smartest people in school.” I shrugged. “And you’re on the weekly announcements every Monday. I’d be kinda dumb not to know who you are.” Her eyes then went straight back to staring at her boots as she walked, her fingers once again pulling at her sleeves.

We walked in silence until she made a turn for the front office. “You’re not going to lunch?” I asked, still following her. I noticed her speed had quickened, but all I had to do was take longer strides to keep up.

“Oh, no, I have. I have to talk to someone in the office.”

Her sentences were choppier than Caribbean waves during hurricane season. It was off-putting, to say the least. "The counselor left early today. Something about her son having chicken pox."

"She doesn't have a son."

Not many people knew that much about the counselor. She didn't have a son, true, but she did have a runt German Shepard named Cheese with a bent ear whom she loved just as much. "You're right, dogs are better." That made her laugh, though it barely passed as a joke. High school girls laughed at anything. "She really is gone though. What did you need to talk to her about?"

"Oh just this thing called nunya."

I held in a sigh and let her have the victory. "Nunya?"

"Nunya business."

"Funny." She laughed at her own joke (case in point), then resumed looking at the ground. "But you know," I continued, "As your president, I am obligated to helping my constituents." I waited, but she kicked at the dirt. "Really, anything. You name it."

"Could you maybe get me a front of the lunch line pass?"

Probably, actually. I had given Blake one, completely illegitimate, but no one questioned a piece of cardstock with the principal's stamped signature on it. "I'll have my people work on it."

"I'm gonna take that as a no."

"So you have been paying attention in Government."

"AP Gov," she corrected, as if that made some type of difference. "I usually sit in the back though, so, that's why you probably never see me." That wasn't why I never saw her. Hana squirmed under her curtain of hair, which was almost cute. Attention was more effective on those not seeking it. "And it's an AP class, so. I kind of have to. Pay attention I mean."

Arguably the easiest of advanced placement classes, but I didn't bring it up. I switched the topic back. "If you ever need someone that isn't a counselor to talk to though, about anything really, I can always pencil you into my busy and hectic schedule."

"Thank you Mr. President. Uh, I guess I should like, go now though, since yeah."

"Sure."

"Yeah."

I closed my eyes, slowly opening them again. She was still there. I held back another sigh. She wasn't going to end the conversation first. I started walking backwards, still time to grab a sandwich before my next class. "I'll talk to you later." She nodded, also walking backwards. "Right, okay. See ya later, Ricky."

"Wait, what's your name?"

She smiled, shoving her hands in her back pockets. "Not Heidi." Then she disappeared behind a corner.

That was awfully witty for someone as seemingly uninteresting as her. I stared after her, not quite expecting her to come back, not necessarily wanting her to either. She didn't. It was something unusual.

She didn't cross my mind for another two weeks, when she was brought up at our next ASB meeting. Jensen had offered to host the meeting at his house on Saturday, featuring his hot tub and the lazy afternoon sun.

Jensen was the ASB events and publicity coordinator, and he was the perfect candidate for the job. His list of acquaintances covered multiple education districts, with connections varying from city hall to school boards to local store owners. His parents held substantial influence in the community, and if all else failed, Jensen could try to buy someone's agreement.

Jensen reappeared in the backyard, balancing a serving plate of chips in one hand and salsa in the other. "So, good news guys," he started, placing the chips on the backyard bar and shaking out his hair. "I was able to book the concert hall downtown for the dance, so that's more than enough room. I know, I'm amazing, thank me later."

Samantha, the only one fully submerged under the warm bubbles of the hot tub, gagged.

Our secretary, Katie, helped herself to the plate of food. "And how'd you do that Amazing Jensen?" She asked, between chewing and hopping up on a bar stool. A solid half inch short of 5 feet, Katie Nguyen was one of the smallest girls at school with jet black hair and a single Monroe freckle.

"Nothing I can't handle," Jensen kicked off his sandals and joined Samantha in the hot tub. "I called a few friends, traded in a few favors."

Samantha scooted two inches away. "So all those blowjobs you gave finally came in handy?"

Katie snorted at the word handy.

"They did, actually. I was able to trade them in faster than you because mine are worth more."

I sat at the edge of the tub with only my legs in, my jeans rolled up to the knee, but Jensen's entrance into the hot tub made the water splash up to my thigh. "Good," I started, pulling my jeans up higher. "We have the location covered. Samantha, how are we on decorations?"

She sunk lower, so that her chin floated above the water. "Um, yeah, so I got in contact with the party store and they were willing to donate a few things, and I found a bunch of stuff at—" I stopped listening.

Dances were perhaps the least important part of high school and held no significance to my resume. At least when we fundraised for the dances, it typically involved some sort of marketable charity event that made me sound like a decent human.

Jensen adjusted himself in the water, continuing whatever conversation they were having. "Uh, I think? Greg and Eric maybe?" He looked at me for confirmation.

"Sure."

Samantha looked over her shoulder at Katie. "Are they hot?"

"The junior, yes. Greg is alright at a distance."

"Good enough." Samantha sunk back into the water. "They're booked. DJs," she finished her sentence by drawing a check in the air with her finger.

Katie walked over holding the half-empty platter of chips. "And what about chaperones? Should I send out a letter to the parents for volunteers or something?"

"No," I dipped my hand in the water, "No one's going to want their parents at a dance. I'll talk to the faculty about it on Monday."

"Hey, but only the cool teachers, like—" They all chimed in suggestions, their voices melting into the sounds of the bubbling hot tub water. These people had become my friends. Friends in the sense that I voluntarily spent the most time with them, but what else did we have in common besides alcohol consumption and similar class schedules and ASB responsibilities and IVY League expectations and career aspirations?

Very little.

I nodded to whatever was said, "Right, I'll take care of that. How are the ticket sales, Katie?"

She sat down next to me, bunched her chiffon skirt between her legs, and stuck her feet in the water. "Pre-sale is going really well! I mean, it's only the first week but we've already—oh hi Blake!"

Finally.

Blake wasn't an official ASB member, but wherever I went, Blake was my +1. He was still in his Pizza Palace uniform and carrying three pizza boxes. "Hey guys, sorry I'm late. But you'll never believe who I delivered to today." He handed the pizza boxes to Katie, who graciously opened them and helped herself to a pepperoni slice. "Are you guys almost wrapped up?"

I shrugged. "Mostly, I guess. We're basically done."

Blake shook out his hat hair, combing his fingers through it as he kicked off his shoes. "What's the theme again? Please don't tell me it's the 50s."

"No, I was luckily able to talk this pesky one—" Jensen pointed at Samantha, who slapped his hand back under the water, "—And Katie out of the idea. I hate the 50s."

"So did every non-white inhabitant of America," I added.

"But there were pin up girls." Samantha pouted.

Katie finished off her first slice of pizza, using the hot tub water to rinse off her fingers. "The new theme is better anyway."

Blake balled up his socks and stuck them inside his shoe, tapping his chin while he wiggled out of his slacks and draped them across a lawn chair. "Hm okay, let me guess," Blake went on, about to strip off his shirt. I noticed the grapefruit sized bruise under his ribcage though, and when we made eye contact, Blake quickly lowered his shirt. "But um, anyways," Blake recovered, "What's the theme? Is it sexy rough alley cats?" He dipped his feet in the water.

Samantha slapped Blake's thin leg. "What's up with the shirt? You need all the sun you can get."

"Look who's talking. Top o' tha mornan to ya, O'Sammy," he laughed, scooting away from her aggressive leg slaps.

Katie was on her fifth slice and she spoke between chewing. It was amazing how she managed to keep it all in her mouth. "No, no cats. Not after the last dance."

"I didn't know they were real prostitutes, okay?" Jensen rolled his eyes.

"Is it based on a movie? Like Casablanca or Twilight or Alice in Wonderland something?"

"Oh my God, Blake, no, you're way off." Katie stifled a burp, then continued. "We're doing a county—"

"Masquerade?" Blake interrupted, slipping into the hot tub with his shirt still on. "Oh, sorry, that was the last one, promise. Go on."

"Thank yo—actually, wow, masquerade sounds really cool. Darn it, we were just gonna go with a country barnyard theme. But dude, masquerade would be a lot cooler." Katie trailed off, opening her eyes really wide at me. "Do we still have time to change? I mean, we haven't officially announced it, right?"

Well, the flyer posters had cowboy hats on them, but whatever. "We could still change it." Change kept life interesting.

I looked at the pizza. "Jensen, do you have any napkins?" He nodded, then hopped out of the tub to go get them. It would have been polite to add please, or even more offer to grab them myself, but why bother when he was already so willing to jump.

Blake pointed his big toe in my direction. "Who did you ask to the dance?"

Samantha snapped her head toward me so fast I swore I heard her neck snap. "I didn't know you wanted to go to the dance."

"I don't, actually."

"Why not, Ricky? Too embarrassed by your own event?" Katie gently pushed my arm, but her slick fingers slid right off with their greasy lubrication.

I tried not to make a face. "Mostly, yes." She laughed as if I were kidding. Plus, we didn't get in free. With my only sources of income depending on whether or not I took out the trash every week and tutoring, I wasn't inclined to spend my money to dance in a decorated building with decorated people.

Katie caressed my arm with more grease. "Oh, I get it. You're just too nervous to ask a girl to the dance. I'm sure plenty of girls would want to go with the Amazing Ricky."

"I heard my prefix Amazing?" Jensen was back with napkins.

"We're talking about Ricky." Katie reached for me, but I dodged her greasy touch. "He's too shyyyy to ask a girl out."

Jensen dropped a few napkins in my hand, then put the rest on a closed pizza box. "Aw, too soon for you to get over Andrea?" He grabbed a slice of pizza and slipped back into the hot tub.

"Ha, no," but the others coo'd and made baby noises at me anyway. Katie looked away and stuffed an entire slice of pizza in her mouth. Andrea, my ex, moved to Idaho last school year. "I just don't have anyone to ask, I guess."

Samantha noticeably stuck her chest out more. "I don't have anyone to ask me."

I ignored her. "Who are you going with, Katie?"

"I'm just going stag with Lauren." Her new best friend. They did everything together now. As usual.

Blake reached for a pizza slice. "I heard Lauren was going with Eric."

"Are you serious? That bitch, she was supposed to be my date." Katie finished off the first box. The mental image of what her arteries might look like in five years was scarring. "What about you, cutie? Who is the Amazing Blake taking out for Valentine's Day?"

Jensen frowned. "You really like to overuse amazing, don't you?"

Blake passed over a pizza box. "I don't know yet." The conversation blended into the hum of the hot tub machine. I leaned my head back towards the sky as he talked. "Maybe I'll ask someone random from class, get to know them better, yanno?" His eyes lit up, and he smiled at me. "Speaking of, Ricky, why don't you ask Heidi?"

"Which Heidi?" Samantha looked too interested in her pizza, though her ears were still perked, waiting for a response.

"Oh, right." I generally didn't look towards the back of the classroom, so I hadn't seen her. "But, her name's not Heidi."

"I know," Blake laughed, "You needed conversation starter. Her name's Hana. Hana Patel."

"Hana Patel?" Jensen joined in the laughter. "She's literally been in our grade since forever."

"So I've been told." I took off some of the pizza oil with my napkin. "Does she have a date to the dance?"

"Hopefully," Samantha muttered. "I heard there's something wrong with her."

Katie moved closer to the pizza box next to Blake. "Hana's nice, I worked on a project with her once. She has really pretty handwriting."

"You hear that? Pretty handwriting. Don't miss your chance." Blake and Jensen laughed again.

"Yeah, maybe." Though, it would be something different. My veins dangerously itched for a change in routine.

Hana Not-Heidi was a tempting scratch.

-3-

Technically, I wasn't supposed to be in the counselor's office. Technically, I was supposed to ask for the keys to the office room so I could use the twenty year old printer that smelled like expired technology and ink that had turned to powder. If I didn't want to wait for the keys, or if time was of the essence, I was always welcomed to go off-campus to a printing store and have the new school dance flyers printed there. Technically, the counselor's office was to remain closed while she was out for lunch and anyone waiting for her (or her fancy new printer) was to be notified of her absence and asked to come back at a later time.

Technically though, I didn't care.

I was about halfway through printing, just a stack of dance flyers and a couple of university entrance statistics for the junior class president, when there was a knock on the door, then the creak of it slowly opening. I turned around, already prepared with a fairly usable lie as to why I was in the office, when I saw it wasn't the counselor or anyone else with authoritative power.

I smiled, and turned my attention back to the printer. "What's up, Not-Heidi?"

"Oh, right, I forgot about that. Hey, Ricky." She stayed close to the door as she surveyed the office. "Yeah, I was just. I needed to talk."

"So talk."

"No, I mean, to a professional."

"I'm a pretty professional person."

She hesitated, but then sighed. "No, it's okay, I'll just come back later." I looked up, expecting her to leave, but she didn't.

"I'll tell her you stopped by," I added.

She nodded, but still didn't leave. I looked at her closer. Tears swelled in her waterline, threatening to spill over. Her sleeves were pulled tightly over her balled up fists. She was either angry, scared, sad, or hyped on meth.

I didn't have anything better to do. "Hana, what's wrong?"

"Nothing, I mean, it's not really your business." But she still didn't leave.

"Ah yes, more nunya to discuss." I checked the printer to make sure it was still running, then walked over to her. "Whatever you say, but I'm just trying to help. You can talk to me."

"It's kind of personal."

"Okay, guess I can't help you then. See you later." But she didn't leave. I thought so. "It just helps to get things off your chest. You don't even have to tell me the whole story." I sat down in one of the student chairs against the wall, then patted the one next to me. For encouragement. Some meek minded people needed a push off the ledge.

She inched over, but instead of sitting down, she leaned against the counselor's desk. "Okay, like, have you ever had a kind of embarrassing personal problem, and it really shouldn't be that embarrassing because tons of people go through it at some point but it's still weird and uncomfortable and you just feel ashamed that it's happening to you?"

"Is this a period thing?"

"What? No," she frowned. "I'm just talking about like, the general feeling."

"Sure."

She continued. "Right? Yeah, so. That's kind of what I'm going through now, if I leave out all the other stuff."

"Huh. I wish I could help."

"Me too."

We stared at each other in silence for a few long seconds, then she looked down at her hands, still balled by her sides. What made her clench her fingers into fists and what made her eyes red and her knee nervously bounce up and down and filled her with so much emotion it gave her the need to see the school counselor on a weekly basis?

What change was she going through?

"Hana, if you need someone to talk to, someone your own age who could understand where you're coming from, I promise to keep everything confidential."

"Wow, such a gentleman."

"One of my many presidential duties."

She laughed a little, still looking down at her chunky boots. "Thanks, but ah, I don't want to put all my baggage on you."

"I don't mind. In fact, when I was younger, I really wanted to be an airline attendant just so I could help others with their baggage."

Hana laughed a little harder, finally lifting her eyes to me. "Yeah, okay, Mr. Harvard. What do you really want to be? A big shot lawyer? A neurosurgeon? Some kind of astrophysics engineer?"

"Yes, to all of them obviously, but also a private investigator, actually."

"Wait, seriously? Why?"

"Seems exciting."

"Spying on someone's cheating husband sounds exciting?"

"No, not trivial boring cases. I would only accept mindboggling cases with clever criminals and puzzles and intricate plans and foolproof schemes that only I will be able to solve."

"You sound full of yourself when you put it that way."

"I am."

"Now you sound like an actual president." She smiled, pushing her bangs out of her eyes, still red but considerably less on the verge of Niagara Fall tears. "But that sounds cool. Kinda like a Sherlock Holmes kind of thing."

"Something like that." I offered a smile. "But before, I definitely wanted to take people's baggage."

She smiled back, but her eyebrows bunched together. It was a strange combination of facial expressions. "Ricky, why are you being so nice to me?"

I shrugged. "Because you look nice with a smile." Mostly because I was bored though.

Hana bit her lip, but her smile grew. Smoothly timed but unexpected compliments could work wonders. "Please, just let me try to help." I folded my hands on my lap. The printer finally finished the flyers. "I won't judge or tell anyone if you don't want me to. Well, unless it's a case of child abuse, but that might only be mandatory for the actual employees at the school—"

"It's not child abuse."

"What is it then?"

She sat down in the chair next to me, but avoided eye contact. "So, I have a. Ah."

"A problem?" My favorite pastime. The most fascinating stories originated with a problem. If it wasn't so socially unacceptable, I might have rubbed my hands together and chuckled with excitement.

"Um, yeah." She hung her head. I waited, my ears burning to hear more. "It's hard to. Say. I don't know. It's just."

"Just what?" I urged. Hana shook her head, sniffling to keep back tears. I wrapped an arm around her shoulders, but she tensed, her shoulders clinging to her earlobes. I slid my arm to the back of her chair instead. "It's alright, take your time." Though, we only had eight minutes until the next bell rang.

"I. I can't say it." Her words were shaky, with most of her mental strength holding herself together. She leaned into my armpit with a deep sigh. I could either push her off the edge or build her trust and get what I wanted later, avoiding any potential burned bridges or awkward encounters.

"That's okay, you don't have to tell me." I gave her shoulder a pat, relaxing in my chair by example. She wiped her nose with her sleeve, keeping her chin tucked into her chest, hair hanging over her face. "Inhale," I instructed, taking my own deep breath. Her shoulders dropped a half inch from her ears, her head raising with the inhale. "Exhale."

Breathing helped with 70% of life's problems.

"Besides, I'm wayyy too busy anyway, you know, busy waiting on my flyers to cool down a little before I pick them up." She responded with another nose wipe. "Really though, I've helped friends through tough things before, if you ever eventually need a not-counselor to talk to. Like I said, aspiring baggage carrier."

She smiled, but not at me. Her eyes followed the moving hands on the clock that filled the silence with the whisper of a ticking bomb. "Um, thanks."

"My pleasure."

She let her body fall back in the chair with a sigh. "No, I'm sorry, I didn't mean to do the drama thing, I just..."

"Very inconsiderate on your part, but I'll let it slide."

Hana laughed, then sniffled again. She seemed like a really snotty crier. Those were always the most unattractive. "This isn't going to make things awkward or anything? Like, I mean, I've barely talked to you after, what, like ten years of being in your class, and now I think I crossed the friendly acquaintances line."

"Just a little." I gave her another light shoulder pat, and when she didn't pull away, I let my arm drape over them. Her skin was cold to the touch. "I guess that means we're friends now?"

"Wow, this is all so sudden. Shouldn't you ask me about my hobbies first?"

"Do you happen to like putting up flyers in your spare time?"

"That's actually one of my favorite things to do, how'd you know?"

"We're just so connected. I think my friendship bond with you is growing. Can you feel it?" She laughed, and I took the moment to go grab the flyers. "Are you going to the dance, by the way?" When I looked back at her, she was standing with her hands folded high over her chest.

"The dance? Um, I don't think so. My friends are going, but I don't want to be an awkward seventh wheel."

"What if I went with you?"

"I think you're starting to move out of the friendship zone a little."

"As your president, of course."

She noticeably avoided eye contact. "I'll think about it Mr. President."

I handed her a couple flyers and a roll of tape from the counsellor's desk. "Just tape them up anywhere."

"Does it matter how I tape it?" She moved her hand in the air to demonstrate. "About eye level or a little higher?"

"Sure," I gave her a thumbs up and a grin.

"Thanks, Ricky." She nodded exactly six times, then waddled out of the room, almost tripping over the folded corner of the door mat.

I dropped the grin, opening the bottom drawer of the file cabinet under the desk. The counsellor conveniently kept all of her student files in one place, locked of course. Everything ranging from transcripts to letters of recommendations to contributions to Back to School Night. Technically, I wasn't allowed to look.

Technically though, I had a key.

Sometimes, just for fun, I would cruise through random classmates' grades, updating my mental roster. Detention and suspension records were also juicy, but more subjective. My fingers walked along the name tabs in the second to bottom cabinet, looking for Hana Patel.

Her folder was about as thick as I expected. No extra classes on her transcript, and very few extracurriculars. I skipped the boring stuff, opening the folder to a mental health evaluation from the school nurse, dated two years ago.

She was 5'2", on the border of pre-diabetic, and a slight tendency to self-harm.

Cutting, specifically. I ran my tongue across my teeth, looking for more details, but finding none. The note was specifically vague. What did she cut with? Why? I didn't know much on the subject of cutting, other than it was common enough.

Did it feel like clarity?

I ran my finger along the edge, wondering how hard and fast I'd have to slide it to get a paper cut. It made sense why she had regularly scheduled visits with the counselor, but the counselor wouldn't have missed an appointment without telling Hana first. It must've been an emergency drop in. An emergency need to scratch.

I closed her folder, returning it between Pate and Patin.

Later that night, I knocked on my father's office door, the hollow tap resonating down the dark hallway. He mumbled for me to enter.

My father looked away from his computer screen, making his glasses slide down his nose and he straightened his posture. "What do you need, Ricky?" He scratched at his head with a sigh, pushing away from his desk. Papers and textbooks were scattered in front of him, sticky notes and scrawled red pen decorating the pages.

His fingers ran through his chestnut hair whenever they sat his pen down, unable to keep idle. They moved from his hair to the objects around him to his chin stubble, in an endless cycle, both his body and his mind occupied.

It was a weird thing to become obsessed with, working, because it induced stress. Maybe the benefits from accomplishing something outweighed the possibility of hair loss.

Or a premature death.

I leaned against the door frame, gesturing my head toward his desk. "How's work going?"

He frowned, then pulled another file from his briefcase. "It's going. Just a lot of reading, writing—"

"Rithmatic."

"Exactly."

The usual.

I waited, thinking he might go on even though he never did. I stared at the scotch bottle on the shelf, my mouth parched. "Is there anything I can help you with?"

"Unless you can suddenly become the judge by tomorrow, I don't see how you could help."

"I'll get right on that."

My father 'mmmhm'ed, turning back to his desk. His allotted family time was up and he needed to resume working. The back of his head was outlined by the glow of his monitor screen. "Thanks, Ricky." He waved uncommittedly, bringing his red pen to the paper and scribbling in the margins.

I ran my fingers along the corner of the door frame, but he didn't acknowledge me. "By the way, I'm going to the dance."

"Oh really?" The sound of his pen frantic across the page was louder than his response.

"Her name's Hana."

"Ah hah." He opened another tab that was open, then began typing.

"She performs satanic rituals in her backyard."

He switched back to his previous tab and picked up his pen again. "Mmmhm."

I rolled my eyes, pushing myself off the door entrance. "Also, I'm going to borrow your razor blade real quick."

"Okay, close the door on your way out."

The usual.

My father kept his replacement blades in the cupboard under the master bathroom sink, right next to a box of tampons, two different blow dryers, and my mother's hefty makeup bag.

I pulled a case out the box, then plucked an individual razor head out, stuffing the rest back. Closing the cupboard door, I examined the razor head closely. It had five blades, FOR THE CLOSEST SHAVE EVER as advertised on the box, and a thick coating of moisturizer along the edge. That should be enough for just making a cut.

I double checked that I had locked the bathroom door and sat on the toilet seat cover, turning the razor head over in my right hand. I had accepted that it would most likely hurt a little, slightly more painful than a shaving nick, but hopefully I would get some sort of blood rush of serotonin or dopamine or adrenaline or something. That was what made the whole thing worth it, right?

That was what Google said.

I put the blade to my skin. My breathing was regular, my mind was clear, and my hands weren't shaking. I was just a rational person doing an irrational thing. A smile spread across my face as I pressed down on the blade and slid the blade across.

I winced, picking the razor up from my skin. There wasn't any blood and I couldn't even see the cut, but I had felt something. I squinted at the razor head, then threw it away in the trash bin. It made sense that it didn't cut skin very well, after all, that was what it was designed not to do. Hana probably used the single bladed razors.

An oversight on my part.

My nick had started to bleed, slightly. Just enough. It was a satisfying bleed, an acknowledgement by my body that I had actually done something. Slightly more pestering than a stinging paper cut. I pulled some toilet paper and dabbed at it, stood up and flushed it, evidence destroyed.

I flipped the faucet on and stuck my arm under the cool running water. The initial sting of the cut was replaced by relief so refreshing that I sighed in appreciation. It was a pleasant sigh. It was a start.

I flipped the faucet off, patted my arm dry with the hand towel, and left the bathroom.

-4-

Blake called me a few days later asking if I could drive him to the grocery store. On a Saturday. Morning.

It was a surprise to everyone that Blake even got a job as a pizza delivery boy when he didn't have a car. The boy had charisma.

I was only about five minutes from his house when I slowed down at a crosswalk to let a young couple cross the street. They were already halfway in the street, turning their heads to check for cars and hesitantly inching forward into the road.

Last year was the first time anyone had ever pointed out to me that I never looked both ways while crossing the street. Once upon an eon ago I listened to my parents and always checked left, right, and left again, but somewhere between then and now I had stopped caring. That was part of the reason my relationship with Andrea ended. I had just stopped caring, or at least that was my logical conclusion.

That, and she moved.

Sometimes it was better to stop caring than to care too much.

We were talking about the choices at Subway when she pointed it out. I remembered because she was wrong. Subway wasn't that far of a walk, maybe three or four blocks. November 1st, not that it mattered, and her makeup from Halloween was still visible even after sleeping in my car overnight in the park, the last remnants of her deer spots smudged across her cheeks.

I had never been very creative with costumes as it was, so that Halloween I was decked out in Andrea's dad's hunting tracksuit with a crumpled paper taped to my chest, 'hunter' scrawled across.

She had chosen the costumes to symbolize my ability to leave her lost in headlights whenever she looked at me.

"But wouldn't that mean Ricky is trying to kill you?" Someone would point out.

"That's the fun part, right?" She laughed and giggled every time she detailed the deep metaphors of our costumes, fluttering her eyelashes and proceeding to stand on her tiptoes to plant a one-sided kiss on my lips.

It was supposed to be funny, or something.

Andrea's nose was bitten red from the crisp morning cold, it was long and straight as if it were chiseled by Michelangelo. Her hair was still perfectly combed, surviving both Jensen's Halloween party and a drunk makeout session in the back of my truck, not one stray hair or flyaway. If there was one thing she perfected, it was keeping up her good hair.

Andrea was easily in the top 55 most attractive girls at school, in large part because of her soft russet brown hair that she usually wore in a high ponytail. Andrea was a boring kind of mainstream pretty though, with her prominent collarbone and white teeth and bright blue eyes and long black eyelashes that fluttered too fast whenever she was worked up about anything.

Her and those fucking eyelashes.

But I digressed.

She tugged on the sleeve of my jacket, a toddler needing to be coddled. "What? Ricky, no, they definitively don't have pickles at Subway."

I rolled my head to look at her because rolling my eyes simply didn't convey my opinion strong enough. "You are so incredibly wrong. Yes, they do."

"I think you're thinking of pepperoncini."

"No. I'm not. I'm thinking of pickles."

"Pepperoncini are pickled, you know. And they're almost the same color."

"Yellow and green are not the same color."

"Actually, yellow is just a different shade of green."

I laughed, zipping my jacket up to my chin. "You've just broken a new world record of being wrong."

"Oh my God, stop, you're just trying to make me feel dumb."

"I don't really have to try to do that."

"What?"

"What?"

She softly punched my arm, then tried entangling her cold little fingers in mine. I moved my hand out of reach before she could finish and shoved my hands in my pocket, pretending not to notice. I cleared my throat, "How about when we get to Subway, if there are pickles, you have to buy my sandwich too."

"Hah, okay, sure." She wrapped her hands around my waist instead, and I had to move my arm around her shoulders so she could nuzzle under my armpit. I should have just let her hold my hand. "But if they're aren't pickles, you have to buy mine."

"I was originally going to do that anyway."

"Such a gentleman." I shrugged and she squeezed my hand that was drooped over her. "Then how about you give me something bigger?"

"Oh yeah?"

"That's not what I meant."

"I'll give you anything you want if there aren't pickles at Subway."

"Deal! You said it, not me." Her voice continue to talk, but I wasn't listening to the words. I don't remember what I was thinking about, probably college applications, but out of nowhere, I heard my name being called, then felt Andrea grab me by the chest and pull me back.

A car zoomed by in front of us.

I looked back at her, watching her eyelashes blink like a hummingbird's wings. I couldn't formulate an elegant way to say 'I almost got hit by a car but whatever,' so I just shrugged.

"Are you serious? You could have been killed!" There was more concern in her voice than nagging, but it was all starting to sound the same to me. "Be careful, oh my God."

"In my defense, a Volkswagen that ugly shouldn't be on the road in the first place."

She huffed, and her breath made a puffy white halo around her face in the morning fog. She was upset, but I also didn't feel the need to apologize. So I didn't. Even if I had seen the car, I wasn't convinced that I would have moved anyway.

She held onto my arm again and guided me across the street like a blind man's Seeing Eye dog. Andrea scolded me for a bit more, but eventually dropped the topic since I still didn't apologize. When we finally got to Subway, she stopped me as I reached for the door. "Ricky, you said you would give me anything I want, right?"

"Granted there are no pickles."

"There aren't. So here's what I'm thinking. You almost got hit by a car and you're staying up late doing sketchy stuff with Blake and Jensen, and last night you drank way too much—"

"Not my finest moment, but it was fun." I smiled.

She didn't. "You'll give me anything, right?"

"Sure."

"I just want you to be careful." She gave me a quick hug, then I opened the door for her.

Of course, she was wrong about the pickles.

Blake's house, or rather small apartment/closet dwelling, was on the nicer side of the slums, but regrettably, still in the slums. Blake had emancipated himself from his parents two years ago and moved in at my house, but once he scored a driver's license and a job at Pizza Palace, he eventually went back to his parents because of the usual excuses he occasionally recycled.

My parents thought he lived on his own. It was easier that way.

Blake stepped outside of his apartment door, checked over his shoulder, and pulled out his keys to fumble with the doorknob. When he turned around, he had a stupidly wide grin. I unlocked the door for him.

"Hey man, thanksssssss—" He drew out the s as he climbed into the passenger seat and closed the door in one swift movement. "—ssssss again. I literally only had three slices of bread and half a boiled egg."

"I'm not surprised."

Blake buckled up, then pushed his reusable bag on the floor. "So what have you been up to, handsome? Besides serving your community and taking a friend in need to the grocery store?"

"Fantasizing about running people over." Pause. "Nothing much. The usual, I guess." I started the car and let Blake do all the talking until we got to the store. He didn't seem to mind, and even continued talking once we were inside.

There were a couple different types of people in every conversation group, all of which had their own social purpose in maintaining the balance of conversation. An excess or lack of one type would make a notable impact on the talking flow.

For example, Blake was an idea vomitter. He talked a lot and talked often, about anything and everything. Generally, gossipers, obsessively passionate fans, and mad scientists fell into this category. Too many of these types in one group, and people would start talking over each over mid-sentence. Not enough of these people and there would be the dreaded awkward silence after twenty seconds.

The second type: listeners. They listened. They also silently judged, but weren't as open about it. They were a boring, but necessary, type. Then there were the others: the one always on their phone, the attention seeker who always managed to direct the conversation to themselves, the person who waited for the opportunity to leave early. So on and so forth.

A varied mixture usually made for an engaging friend group. The advantage of the generalization was that it made it easy to identify when there was something wrong with someone.

And there was something wrong with Blake.

He was talking too much. I hadn't given a "mhm", head nod, or any sign that I was still alive for almost an hour, and he just continued down the cereal aisle talking about the benefits of added fiber.

"You see," he picked up a box, pointing to the added fiber label on the front. "Yes, they're lying. It's not the same great taste, but it's not bad. Plus, you're getting your fiber. So that's some hashtag fake news I can tolerate. Did you know 20% of Americans don't get enough daily fiber in their diet? I read that somewhere. Probably Buzzfeed." He put the box in his cart and kept going, commenting on every brand. I followed in silence.

"What do you think, Ricky?" He barely held eye contact, then his eyes flickered to the floor. "Yeah, chocolate flavored cereals were not a smart idea."

"Blake," I unlocked my phone. "Is your father back?" I had gotten Hana's phone number the other day from the school directory. When I called her house, her mother picked up and sounded too excited to hear a boy's voice on the other end of the line, then proceeded to give me her cell phone number. I glanced up at Blake, who still hadn't answered. "Is he?"

If I had to repeat the question, I was right.

He shuffled his feet. "Well, I mean, he stopped by."

"Is that where the bruises are from?"

It was completely weird for me to text Hana without her personally giving me the number. Then again, that made it more exciting. Or creepy. Depended on the wording. I glanced back up at Blake. "Is it?"

"I should really look through the peephole before I open the door."

"You should."

'Hey new friend.'
-Mr. President

It sounded lame, but I sent the text anyway. I had two texts from Samantha and one from Jensen, but I didn't open them. "So, Blake, we're going to swing by your place to pick up your homework and nightlight, then we'll go to my house." He'd probably stay for at least two weeks, maybe longer if my parents convinced him.

"So I don't need to buy cereal?"

"Unless you want to insult my mother's breakfast."

Blake put the cereal box back. "No, your mom is lovely." I shrugged. "You know what's really lovely though? Applause. You should buy it and then burn me the CD. Remember? That time? When you said you would do that for me?" He nudged me with each question mark.

"I'll get around to it."

"Sometime before you die, yeah?"

"Sure."

"Don't fucking forget, you know that's my song." He paused. "But really, what do you think of chocolate cereal?"

Dinner time rolled around and Hana still hadn't texted me back. My mother tapped her foot against the hardwood in the kitchen, polished fingers methodically tapping her fork against an untouched plate, lips pursed together in a tight line.

She kept looking between me and my father, expecting one of us to say something. My father was trying to hide the fact he was using his phone under the table, rewriting his opening statement. Mr. Schenk had many skills, but navigating uncomfortable topics outside the workplace was not one of them.

Blake also avoided her eye contact, but he could feel my mother staring holes into his face.

I took another bite of my food.

"Ricky?" She spoke to me, but kept her eyes forward to catch any change in my father or Blake. I took my time shifting my attention to her. "Well? Do you want to *say* anything?"

"The carrots taste a little overdone."

"The carrots taste fantastic," Blake hurried to speak over me, smiling and raking the orange mush into his mouth to demonstrate.

I pushed the carrots to the side of my plate. "It's not your best work."

At the mention of the word work, my father's interest suddenly sparked and he slipped his phone back into his pocket, checking in at the dinner table. "Speaking of work, the case I'm working on, things are looking promising."

Desperate to change the subject, Blake stroked the work talk. "What's the case about?"

"A security breech. Hackers," my father tsk'd under his breath.

"What was hacked?"

"I'm not at liberty to discuss."

"*Boys.*" My mother, despite her sharp tone, gently placed her fork in its proper place next to her plate. "Are we not going to talk about the *situation* here, or am I the only one who cares?"

"What situation, Honey?" My father pulled out his phone.

"The Carrot Missile Crisis is a serious threat." I poked around my plate.

But of course, Blake caved in. "Mrs. Schenk, thank you for taking me in, again. But, if it's okay with you, I would rather not talk about it." He smiled. "Can we just, do what we normally do when this happens? We don't always have to talk about it."

"But why not? Talking about things is *healthy*." I rolled my eyes and took another bite. "Blake, tell me *what happened*."

My mother must've had short term memory loss because the story was always the same. It was unfortunate, but it was never going to change. Blake was terrified of his father, but no matter what we told him or what support we offered or what restraining orders we gave him to sign, Blake was going to keep letting it happen.

So it was beyond my ability, or anyone else's really, to help. I didn't know why my mother kept pushing the subject, but it was annoying. It made my chest swell with heat, then chills raced down my limbs right after.

"I'm going to excuse myself," I announced to the zero people listening to me. They were all talkers. I stood, grabbed my plate, and rinsed it off using the soft side of the yellow and white sponge. I opened the dishwasher, and the reflective blade of a kitchen knife caught my eye.

I swallowed the lump that was caught in my throat.

Swiping the knife, I almost debated hiding it as I walked upstairs, but no one was watching me.

The bathroom door locked with a satisfying click, and I noticed my heart was beating faster than last time. Perhaps because this blade would actually cut. I closed the toilet cover and sat down, switching the knife to my right hand. The sink faucet dripped water slowly, a thud against the porcelain. I closed my eyes and listened, lightly scraping the blunt side of the blade against my left forearm. I could still hear the conversation from the dinner table, the sound of concern for poor helpless Blake. Or was it nagging?

Thud.

Blake, you don't deserve this.

Thud.

You are going to stay with us for as long as you need.

Thud.

We're going to help you through this.

Again.

Thud.

We love you.

The usual.

I turned the faucet knob all the way up to drown it out. At least this was more stimulating than boring everyday crap that everyone seemed to care so much about. It was something new. A change. The tip of the blade traced a vein running from my wrist to my elbow. Although I (probably) wouldn't immediately bleed out and die if I cut through it, it was better to avoid hospital trips. I wasn't suicidal. I didn't have a problem. I didn't need help.

I just needed something.

A scratch.

The knife chose a spot on the lateral side of my forearm, closer to the elbow. It just felt right somehow, like it would cut well. I would have to ask Hana later if there was such a thing as the best cut, or maybe that would be insensitive.

The blade pressed down harder, the pressure needed to break skin was greater than I expected. I clenched my jaw, a little red jewel bubbling up to stain the tip, and then the knife dragged horizontally across my arm, as if I were slowly unzipping myself.

I fought the instinct to close my eyes against the pain, instead watching with frank fascination at how quickly the red welled up from the wound. The response was immediate.

I picked up the blade once it was halfway across, accidentally dripping onto the tile. It wasn't a violent blood spurt or even dramatically uncontrollable bleeding, which was the most disappointing. It was too short lived. The pounding in my ears started to fade, and the goosebumps had already left. The adrenaline was a nice touch, but the feeling was marginal.

What the fuck was I doing?

I slid the knife into the sink, grabbing some toilet paper and pressing it to my wound. Adrenaline. That was the trick.

That was the something I was looking for, and I needed to find a way to get more of it instead of just a taste.

I stood up, lifted the toilet seat, and threw the soiled toilet paper in. I was still bleeding a little, the extreme disadvantage to cutting. I placed my arm under the sink, gritting my teeth as the cold water hit the cut.

"Hey Ricky?" Blake called from outside the bathroom door. I had not heard him come up the stairs. I didn't even know how long I had been in the bathroom.

I turned the water down a little, pulling my phone out with my other hand. It had been twenty minutes, but Hana had finally texted me back. "Yeah?"

"Are you getting ready for bed already?"

"Oh no, I was just—" I didn't have an answer yet.

"Just what?"

I unlocked my phone, checking Hana's message. "Uh, checking my phone."

"For what? Porn?"

"No, I got a text."

'Wow! Is this Ricky? Sorry, I was at my dad's house and didn't have my phone
I don't usually get texts lol
What's up?'

I turned toward the door. "Remember Hana?"

"You're texting her from the bathroom? That's kinda weird. Are you sexting?"

"Absolutely."

"Kink kitten." I heard him start to walk away, but then he paused. "Oh, and, uh."

"Yeah, go ahead. The blankets and pillows and stuff are in the usual place." Blake would make a little bed on the floor next to mine and we would not talk about the situation. It worked for us.

"Thanks."

I shrugged, even though he couldn't see, and went back to my messages. One from Jensen, giving me a heads up of a party tonight. Samantha's text was just her looking forward to seeing me at said party tonight, winky emoji heart emoji winking tongue emoji.

I put my phone back in my pocket, turning the faucet off. I was almost disappointed, but it was foolish to have higher expectations for cutting. I could find more trouble at a party. I bent down and grabbed the Band-Aid box from under the sink, slapping one over the cut.

"Hey, Blake," I said, walking into my room. He had already made his little bed on the floor and had taken out his math book. He looked up at me, his eyes red and puffy. Blake was not a snotty crier, good for him. "You want to go out tonight?"

He sniffed, and I ignored it. "Uh, nah, I think I'm gonna, yanno, get a head start on, uh." He pointed at his textbook, looking down.

I shrugged. "Alright, well the party should theoretically be done by 3ish." Maybe not though, if I was lucky. "Could you pick me up?"

He nodded.

"Cool." I threw him the keys. Blake wasn't a puppy lost in the rain. He was old enough to take care of himself. We were past the point of pity, but I still felt guilty leaving him. "But also, hanging out would probably get your mind off things. You should come."

"Math though."

"You can copy mine."

"I'm not dressed."

"Alright Princess, well hurry up and get ready. I want you to come." Blake unwillingly picked himself off the floor and went to my closet, where most of his clothes waited regardless if he slept over or not. It happened too often to not be prepared. I was surprised my mother took the second bed out of my room. "You're still driving though, unless you're planning on drinking." Which would be a change.

"I'm never drinking."
Too bad.

-5-

One day before the dance, I skipped the final ASB meeting at Jensen's house. For one, it would be pointless chatter about how everything was 'good-to-go' and then idle gossip. Two, relaxing in bed on a Friday night was a needed change of pace for my liver. Three, I had only cut once more, with the same lackluster results.

It was frustrating. I was too big of a thinker. Aside from sawing my entire arm off, I couldn't imagine how to achieve better returns. I needed smaller ideas and for that I needed a smaller thinker.

My eyes drifted from my sleeved arm to my phone laying on the desk beside me. Cutting was a small idea. I reached for my phone, ignored Samantha's text about missing the meeting, and called Hana.

It only rang once before she picked up. Her Friday night was as uneventful as mine. "Hey, Not-Heidi," I started, then looked over at Blake getting ready for work. Pizza Palace was busy on the weekends and he practically made a week's worth of pay just from weekend tips.

"I'm sorry, who is calling?"

That wasn't Hana's voice. My mouth dried instantly. "Oh, this is Ricky speaking. Is this Hana's cell phone?"

I could hear a smile over the phone. "This is her mother."

"Is Hana around?"

"Oh, of course, right, of course," laughing at herself, she covered the phone as she called for Hana in the background. Her mother's voice returned to the phone. "Were you calling about school?"

"MOM." Hana's voice. There was some shuffling and then Hana was talking on the phone. "Oh my God, sorry about that. That was my mom."

"It was."

"Um, yeah, so what's up?"

I wanted going to ask her if there were any other methods that she had tried, perhaps more extreme than cutting. "You want to see a movie tonight?"

"What?"

"You know, a movie. A film. A motion picture shown at a public viewing area where you can also indulge in snacks and light refreshing beverages, such as a fountain drink and—"

"Okay, yes, I know what a movie is. But, like," she paused, and I tried to imagine what she was doing on the other end of the line. Pacing. Pulling at the ends of her hair. Eyeing a bottle of alcohol. Or maybe that was just me. Hana finally settled on, "You surprised me."

"So, do you want to go?"

"What movie?"

I hadn't planned ahead that far. "How about I surprise you?"

"You really like surprises."

"Aren't they supposed to be fun?"

"No, I mean, well, yes, they are, I guess, but why are you asking me?"

"Because we're friends, remember?" I sat up, reaching for my shoes. "So I'll be over in twenty minutes to pick you up. That's enough time for you to apply your lip gloss or fasten your bra straps or whatever girls do in the bathroom, right?"

She laughed. "Yeah, um. Wait, I can meet you at the movies. I think that would be easier."

"Easy is boring. I'll pick you up."

"Ah, you don't know where I live though."

"I have GPS and the student directory. I think I'll be fine. See you in twenty." I hung up before she had a chance to say anything else.

By the time I finished tying my shoes, Blake was grinning at me, tucking loose strands of hair under his uniform cap. "You have a date."

"It's not a date."

"Of course not. Uh huh." He pulled his jacket on and zipped it up. "Could you give me a ride to work though? Your house is a lot farther than where I live."

"Why don't they just let you keep the delivery car so you can stop bumming rides to work?"

"I try not to ask questions that could get me fired."

It was a miracle Pizza Palace wasn't bankrupt. "Also, Blake, on the way," I handed him my phone as I scooped my car keys off my desk. "I'm going to need you to find the nearest theater playing a movie in the next thirty minutes."

Despite popular societal beliefs, a person could not accurately be judged solely on their living arrangements. A lot of varying factors go into housing decisions, ranging from cost to location to amenities to personal preference.

I parked outside of Hana's apartment complex, in a spot labeled for guests. The grounds were well-kept with not a daisy out of place, but I noticed the fitness facility was small and only had one treadmill facing the window. Most of the cars were average and the children playing on the swings didn't have supervision.

The sun was setting, but I could still make out Hana's frame bumbling down the stairs to meet me. She lived upstairs, third floor. She hurried to my car and opened the door gently, squeaking hello from outside the car. I waited almost ten seconds, but she just stood there, shuffling inside her sweater.

"You can get in."

She got in the car, quickly buckling her seat belt before making eye contact. "Um." The sweater was long sleeved. When was the last time she cut herself? Where did she cut? Arm? Stomach? When was the last time she was tempted?

"You look nice." I smiled, then turned away to start the car.

"Oh, thank you. You too."

"I try my best." I moved my arm around the back of her seat to reverse and she tensed.

The movie was a disappointing, a two hour long gore-infested thriller. Very predictable, almost enough topless scenes to apply for a low rate porno, and barely decent acting. But it was the only thing playing on such short notice. The movie also didn't help with Hana's nerves. She hadn't said a sentence longer than four words since we stepped inside the theater. "So, how'd you like it?" I asked, driving out of the theater parking lot.

She'd mm'd under her breath, "I don't really like scary movies."

"Why not?"

"Because they're scary."

I looked away from the road and she was frowning into her lap, genuinely shaken by the B-list movie that used grocery store paint for blood. "I'm sorry, why didn't you tell me?"

"It could've been amazing, I don't know."

"Next time I'll hold your hand, okay?" Her eyes reached up to mine. I took the shot and laced my fingers into hers. I really disliked the concept of holding hands, but it seemed to make girls feel better for some reason. It may go back to a primal feeling of protection from the person holding their hand. Or girls protecting what was 'theirs,' as if my hand was a Birkin bag.

Hana's eyes widened, but she didn't pull away. "Okay."

"Are you hungry?" I changed the subject, looking back to the road. "I assumed you hated popcorn, but now I realize you just hate good movies."

"That was not a good movie."

"You're biased, Hana."

"Even if I liked scary movies, that would not be considered one of the better ones." I could hear the animation creeping back into her voice. "Also," she held up a finger, "I actually do hate popcorn."

"Oh come on, it's corn and it has butter. What is more enjoyable than that?" I pictured slicing into my arm, Halloween paint slowly welling up at the cut.

"It always gets stuck in my teeth though!"

"Excuses."

"Um, I am hungry though, if that's alright."

"What are you in the mood for?"

"Anything."

"Anything? Really?"

"Yeah."

"Alright, we're going to go to the popcorn buffet downtown then."

We ended up going to the closest fast food and eating in the parking lot. "How's your popcorn?" I asked.

Hana turned her burger over in her hand, "Strangely, it's a little meaty."

"They always mess up the order here. You want me to take it back?"

"Oh no, its fine, I don't want to cause a scene." She laughed, dipping her hand into the bag to pull out a fry.

"So, Hana. The Valentine's Day dance?" I leaned back into my seat, resting my arm along with driver's window. One of my earlier cuts still stung from pressure.

"Oh. Well I mean, if you want to join our group, that would be cool, if you want." She spoke into her fry bag.

"Yeah, I think I'll do that. What time should I pick you up?"

She stared even harder at her burger. "My friend's dad is a limo driver and he was going to drive all of us. So everyone's just going to meet at her place."

A limo? For a Valentine's Day dance? I swallowed my judgment. "Right. So what time should I pick you up to meet at her place?"

She finally looked at me. "Um. Maybe like an hour before? I think that would be fine. In case they want to take pictures or something."

"Do you want to take pictures?"

"Not really," she laughed, then stuffed her face with fries to avoid talking.

"Why not?" I prodded, finding a path to the point of this impromptu hang-out.

She took her time chewing. "Well, I mean, I'm a little self-conscious in pictures," she sighed, putting her burger down. "Can I just tell you something?"

"Please do."

"So I did this thing." She clenched her teeth together. "Cutting. A little. It wasn't a big deal or anything but okay yeah." She spoke fast, rubbing her hands together. "Is that weird?"

It was the only reason I talked to her. I smiled, "No, it's pretty normal, I think. Nothing to feel ashamed about, but I understand your hesitation. Are you okay?"

"Yeah, I'm fine, it was just, a thing, I don't know. It's dumb." She huffed, looking at me. "Forget it, it was a long time ago. Anyways, my dress doesn't have sleeves. And everyone in the group is a close friend and they already know about the—"

"The cutting," I continued for her.

"Uh, yeah. But. I don't want it to be so permanent. An open. Like on camera. Forever in a dorky facebook album and tagged on Instagram. It just looks so ugly."

My own arms bared a few new cuts, but they weren't deep, already fleshy pink and starting to fade. Plus, I wasn't going to make any more. "The important thing is that your arms won't be the focus of the picture. You will. And you will be beautiful."

Her mouth twisted into a weird half-frown, "Beautiful?"

Maybe about a six. "Yeah." I smiled, then reached into her food bag and stole a fry. She rested her head against the back of the seat, looking up. I let the silence linger for a while, but my brain was itching. I needed another way to scratch. "Hana," I started, my throat dry. "Have you only ever cut yourself?"

"What?" Her eyes darted toward me.

I eased off a little. "I just care about you."

Thankfully, her face softened. "I appreciate the, um, care, but I'm doing a lot better now. Talking about it helps. At least for me." She paused, looking toward the ceiling. "But, yeah, so. My mom has to take insulin shots for her blood sugar or something. One time. I've uh, given myself an insulin shot before. But, that landed me in the hospital and they found out about the cutting and stuff and I had to go to therapy. So, yeah."

"What did it feel like?" Unfortunately, neither of my parents had diabetes, but it was a creative idea. Creativity wasn't my strongest attribute.

"I couldn't stop shaking. Like, my hands, my legs, everything was jittery and my heart was pounding really really hard. I went to my room to lay down…then I woke up in a hospital bed. My mom said I collapsed, which is kind of scary to think about." She grabbed another fry. "Sorry, is this uncomfortable?"

"It's alright. If you hadn't ended up in the hospital, do you think you would have done anything else to hurt yourself?"

"Maybe. I don't know. I didn't have anything planned really, I was just doing what I thought would make me feel better. And it did, a little, for a while, but it also made me feel worse."

Disappointing.

So I had an insulin lead, which sounded kind of fun actually, but other than that, nothing. Tonight wasn't a complete waste, but I would have had more fun riding shotgun on Blake's pizza deliveries. Or getting into whatever trouble

Jensen had planned for the night. There was still time for the last option though. “Hana, do you drink?”

“Huh?”

“Alcohol.”

“Wha, oh, no, I don’t.” She raised her eyebrows with a little laugh, fishing the bottom of the bag for the last of her fries. “Where would I even get alcohol?” She looked at me, lowering her voice. “Why? Have you ever had alcohol?”

“No, never, I was just wondering.” I started the car and pulled out of the parking lot.

Rummaging through my parent’s medicine cabinet was extremely revealing. I had only expected to find my mother’s disposable toothbrush, contact solution, and maybe birth control. In reality, there were a lot more pills, and not one of them prevented pregnancy.

I took out the first bottle, turning it over in my hand slowly so I could read the label. Benadryl. My father was allergic to a large majority of nature, so I wasn’t shocked over the amount of allergy medications, but more so the fact how many different brands and varieties.

I put them all on the counter and that cleared out at least a third of the cabinet. Moving up to the second shelf was a similar bottle. Acetaminophen. Over the counter Tylenol, placed right next to actual Tylenol. A waste. I tossed it in the trash.

There was a bottle for premenstrual cramps and something about a keratin boosting serum for the natural lengthening of eyelashes. There was also one for stimulating skin cell rejuvenation, three different diet regimens, and a breast enhancement supplement. Trash.

My face twisted involuntarily into a frown upon the discovery of Viagra. I almost threw it away too, but it felt gross touching it. Plus, who was I to cock block someone?

There was a little white tube hidden in the far back, some weird brand of toothpaste. "Premarin?" In a way, my blatant invasion of privacy allowed me to connect with my parents in a strange and disturbing light. I wouldn't recommend it to anyone.

Aging really sucked.

My mother didn't have diabetes, but she did have another special medication.

Paxil.

Sounding it out in my head didn't have the looming dark cloud effect I wanted, so I tried it aloud. My voice hit the bathroom walls like an autumn leaf against the sidewalk. This was my mother's antidepressant medication.

She was diagnosed last year after her miscarriage when she basically lost all ability to function normally without breaking down into tears for no reason. Simple things triggered her 'attacks,' as her 'doctor' described them. Things like seeing the half empty paint cans from the nursery, or when my father sent back all the baby shower gifts. She melted into a heaping pile of her own waste because 'her *emotions* were *provoked*.' However vapid, at least there was a reason.

It wasn't just an unexplained itch.

A couple of months passed and she couldn't/wouldn't eat or sleep or talk (which I personally didn't mind) and couldn't/wouldn't explain why. My father couldn't/wouldn't concentrate on work and, for the first time in his life, he took a leave of absence and gave undivided attention to his wife.

Blake, that poor unfortunate soul, was no longer getting the food nor the stable family structure my mother provided for him and what he so desperately grasped for, but he did everything in his limited power to help out. He brushed her hair. He washed her face. He made sure she put on deodorant.

My maternal grandparents moved in to pick up her motherly duties and play uncomfortably loud folk music from their dusty old record player in our living room. I think someone even had the brilliant idea to have her monthly book club at our house, maybe to snap her out of the pitfall she had plummeted into. My mother started crying during the reading of Wild. We had distant relatives and community members dropping in every other day, bringing condolences and personal advice and casseroles and bible quotes.

It was real fucking annoying.

I used the palm of my hand to press down and open the Paxil bottle. My fingers were almost too big to fish out the little cotton ball at the top.

After a few months of 'attacks,' my mother's doctor questioned her medication routine, to which my father reassured the Paxil was being taken as prescribed. The usual standard procedure. My father never lied but, as I held the full bottle in my hand, *someone* did.

Because her 'condition,' as the doctor put it, wasn't improving, they moved her into a 'facility' where they could more closely monitor her recovery, prescribing her a new medication. My father wasn't neighborhood savvy enough to think of creating a cover story and soon pity was bestowed upon us.

You poor boy.

Robert, how are you holding up? You know, about…

I can't imagine anyone watching their mother go through that.

Robert is not fit be a single father.

Let's invite them over for dinner, I'm sure they haven't had a decent meal in months.

Shit like that.

My mother's pills were pink, shaped like an oval. 20mg, though I wasn't sure if it was a light or heavy dosage. I also didn't care.

My mother eventually 'recovered,' and was moved back home after a few months. For the most part, she resumed her role as house-maker quickly and soon all the pesky, nosy, and concerned family members and neighbors scattered back to their own problems.

My father hesitantly returned to work, Blake started sleeping at his own crappy apartment again, I remained the same, and everyone silently agreed not to bring up the dead fetus. Still, no pun intended, it wasn't like she was born yet or anything. She didn't even have a social security number. How could someone who wasn't even a 'someone' have such a large impact? Did I have as big of an impact?

Estelle would have been a nice name.

I swallowed a pill. Thunder didn't boom in the background nor did the lights flicker. I was a bit surprised at how easy was, especially without water. I closed the bottle and slipped it into my pocket, putting the medicine cabinet back to its previous organized mess. Pills were slow, but they'd start to kick in within the next few days.

Anticipation was part of the hype.

I left the bathroom and ran into my mother. My smile dropped.

"Ricky! What are you *doing* in my bathroom?" She seemed pleasant enough, but I had learned to read behind the plastic façade she put up.

"Sorry," I rarely apologized, so her eyes quickly softened. Too easy. "Blake was in the other bathroom and I didn't really want to walk downstairs and bother dad." I also rarely used 'dad,' which should have been a red flag, but moms loved acts of consideration.

"Yes, he's been working so hard on his case. I was just going to take a nice long bath and then head to bed. I'm really tired today."

"Oh I bet. You did cook an assumingly decent dinner." My mother frowned. The pill bottle in my pocket felt heavy. "I'm only joking. Blake texted me, he said it was delicious."

"Blake is such a nice boy."

He really was.

My mother respectfully waited until I moved out of the bathroom doorway and at least three feet away before she walked to the bathroom. That was the usual distance we kept between each other. Generally never less than three feet.

I paused at the door and she waited at the bathroom, like she wanted to tell me something. Needed to. I searched her eyes for what it was, but only found her façade back up, a barrier between her and the outside world. She wasn't going to let me in. Or anyone else.

"Goodnight," I broke the silence.

"You're a nice boy too, Ricky."

I shrugged. Not really.

-6-

I had already forgotten what the theme was for the Valentine's Day Dance. Jensen texted me two hours before asking what kind of Masquerade mask I was going to wear.

I threw on a black suit and went to the vintage boutique/drag consignment store downtown with Blake, finding a velvet hat the size of Brazil and a simple white eye mask. Good enough. Blake's costume was a lot more extravagant, with ruffles and glitter and and feathers and color coordination. And just general effort. I wondered where he found the time. Or the motivation.

Since he didn't have a car, Blake's date was meeting him at my house, prompting my mother to take out her phone and snap two or three thousand pictures. Our fireplace was adorned with fake red and white roses, the perfect background for a photoshoot. My mother coordinated our house for every school dance so pink and white streamers floated from corner to corner of the living room, lightly blushed balloons littered the floor, and my mother somehow found candles that smelled like pink Starbursts. She should have been on the decoration committee.

My mother retreated to another room in the house to grab more balloons, so Blake set up a self-timer for even more pictures. "Blake, if I didn't know better," I looked up from checking my emails. "I would say you're more into yourself than your date."

Blake's date rocked back and forth on her heels, holding her silver clutch in front of her dress. Half of her hair was pulled up into a bun, while the rest of her black braids swept down her back. Emma Jackson: ranked exactly 60th for academics, around 117th in looks, and an even 100 for personality. Quite the catch. Last year, Emma accidentally cheated on a final because the last page of her test had the answer key stapled to it. I was in the same class, AP-something or other.

Emma went after class and requested to take it again, even though she hadn't studied well for the final. Her request was granted and she came in during lunch a few hours later to retake the final. Emma flipped through binders of notes and highlighted sections of her study packet during passing period, but she never regretted her decision. She passed the retake with flying colors and during her college interviews, she explained how integrity and honesty were more valuable and rewarding than a deceitful victory. Emma was accepted into early admittance of her top choice.

She was very proud of herself, so I decided not to tell her I changed her grade on the teacher's computer after school. She had actually failed her retake.

Emma laughed, "He is definitely more into the pictures."

Blake changed poses, "I am." He looked me up and down. "Are you headed out already? Take a group shot with us."

I shrugged, jingling my keys. "I going to go pick up Hana."

Blake frowned, "I wanted to ride with you."

Emma gently nudged him. "Do you remember which one of us is your date?"

"It's just harmless flirting. Ricky's way out of my league."

"I'm not sure how I should take that."

I saw that as my exit, so I grabbed some gum and headed for the door. "I'll see you guys at the dance." My mother hurried back in to offer some variation of goodbye, but I had already shut the door.

Hana's mother, thankfully, only took a few pictures. Her mother had a red camera, one with a flip screen so she could take selfies with us as her daughter grimaced. Her mother wore bright prints and bold patterns, as if the world's happiest crayon box exploded inside her closet, but it wasn't garish.

Hana insisted we were going to be late, shooing the camera away and giving her mother a quick hug before hurrying us out the door. Hana's black dress was more modest than I was used to, no cleavage and floor length. I didn't know they still made dresses that long.

Her mask certainly made up for the plain ensemble, bedazzled with cheap jewels and cartoonish feathers shooting out of the sides. As we pulled up to her friend's house, Brittney or Tiffany or something, I turned to her and said, "Hana, your mask looks really cool."

She smiled. "Thanks, my mom made it! I think that's why she wanted so many pictures. I'm sorry about that by the way. Did your mom want some?"

What my mother wanted hadn't crossed my mind in months. "Send them to me later." She was staring at me, smiling. I checked in my rearview mirror at my face, but there wasn't any spinach in my teeth. "What?"

"You look like Tuxedo Mask."

"Who?" But before I could even get the whole question out, her friends were at the passenger window doing that abnormally high-pitched squeal thing. We got out of the car. Hana was surrounded by her gal pals, each of them offering compliments to each other like beads during Mardi Gras.

Her friends were under-the-radar girls, ranging in the 200-300s for academics and appearance. They were the girls that resided outside of clubs and cliques. Some of them were artists, some wrote smutty fan fiction, others glued themselves to Minecraft after school. They weren't complete outcasts, but they managed to create their own happy little bubble within the school.

None of them really all that memorable though.

Their dates were even less memorable. Then again, neither was Hana without her scars.

They all knew who I was, they'd seen my face walk through the halls for years, a relentless typhoon of tenacity whirling my path. Then, the same face appeared every Monday morning for the weekly announcements, dark eyebrows in a serious line. They voted for this face for four years, but I had no idea who they were. I also didn't care.

Another round of pictures followed, the standard poses: normal, cute, silly, romantic, fierce diva who don't need no man. Even Hana held a Charlie's Angels pose and I didn't even know she was capable of engaging in a large group.

What's-Her-Face's dad honked the limo horn and the chirp squad filed in. "Hey," Hana stayed back with me, lifting her mask. "Are you okay?"

I couldn't answer immediately because no response felt quite appropriate.

"They're all really nice," she reassured. "You'll get used to them." She perked up again, thanking the driver for holding the door. She gestured for me to get in first.

The interior of the limo was dusty black, but none of the seats had tears. The bar had been cleared out, filled instead with sparkling cider and club soda. One of the girls with a short red dress and a unicorn mask opened the first bottle and topped off plastic flute glasses for everyone. As we pulled out of the driveway, the speakers bumped late 2000s pop and spontaneous karaoke started. Even louder conversations about how it would be the best night of their lives filled the crevices of the limo, consuming all of the oxygen. I wanted to kill myself.

Figuratively.

"Hey, Ricky, right?" The cologne-soaked young man next to me leaned over, his apple cider spilling over the side of his cup.

I moved my leg away from him. "Yeah, what's up?"

"Oh, it's just nice to meet you! I'm blah blah blah." He held out his free hand with a smile.

I didn't want to shake it, but he kept his palm open and welcoming in front of me. "Nice to meet you too." I shook his hand, careful not to retract too quickly. "What year are you? I feel like I've seen you around, but we don't have any classes together, right?"

"Blah blah blah." He said a lot of meaningless things that I nodded at with a smile. "But I was thinking about running for ASB president next year as a senior." He laughed. "What schools have you applied to?"

"The usual ones, what about you?"

"Well, I just took the PSAT, so based on that I was thinking I could get into blah blah blah." His nose hairs were just long enough that one or two jutted out from his nostrils, significantly darker than the peach fuzz on his upper lip. I doubted he had a chance at winning ASB president. I'd never heard of him before. The current junior class president would likely take over my position once I was gone—graduated.

His date wore a puffy yellow dress and an even puffier yellow feathered hat with a white lace mask that looked like a table doily. It was an eye sore. Actually, most of these people were eye sores with boring conversation skills.

I'd rather witness the progression of my own colon cancer.

I clued back in to wannabe-president, who had just finished talking to me, waiting for my response. I nodded, "Wow, well good luck with that." I raised my glass, the plastic hitting with a dud.

I turned away while he downed his drink. "Hana, do you see my phone over by the door? I think I might have dropped it while I was getting in."

She tilted her head, immediately searching the space between her and the door for a phone that wasn't there. "What color is it?"

"Black."

She continued searching.

"Here, can we switch spots? I'll look for it." I had already begun scooting into her spot, grabbing her sides to lift her up, over, and next to Mr NoseHair. A human shield from conversation. "Thanks," I added, reaching under the side of the seat as an excuse to rest my head against the window.

Once we arrived at the dance, a long thirty-seven minutes later, I was grateful Jensen had been able to book a larger space than our high school gym.

The decorating was adequately done. The colors were slightly off, a tall-tell sign that they were randomly bought from different stores. For a girl so interested in interior design and marketing, Katie couldn't coordinate her way out of a trash bag. The music, while relevant and up-to-date on current hits, was too choppy and switched genres far too frequently to get into a rhythm. Turnout was impressive, perhaps the only thing that was, but that would also be a negative once the dancing BO set in after a few hours.

I needed a real drink.

"Hana," I gently reaching for her hand as we walked away from the entrance. "Let's dance."

She looked up at me, almost confused, but quickly nodded and followed me further into the auditorium. I always went somewhere with an agenda in mind. It had been my general motto for surviving the routine of high school life. Tonight's plan was to ditch Hana as often as possible. Aside from her occasional habit of self-mutilation, she was horribly unstimulating.

No offense.

Plus, her insufferable friends, giggling and gossiping like squabbling ducks, were not making the event any more bearable. If I could start the night off with her early, open with a dance and the swing her off into her friend's arms, I would have enough time to have real fun and she wouldn't feel totally abandoned.

A shot or three would be enough to get me through the night.

I pulled Hana in closer, close enough to show we were together, but definitely not within grinding range. Her fingers were limp in my hand when I led her to an open spot on the dance floor. The song was a pop top 100 hit, suitable enough for my simple two-step, but Hana just stood in front of me with her eyes wide and her mouth open. I withheld the urge to close her jaw. "Don't tell me you don't know how to dance." I asked.

"I don't know how to dance."

"I don't believe you. Everyone knows how to dance." She fumbled over her next words and ultimately gave up looking for an excuse, holding her hands in front of her. Literally just standing there, her eyes darting between the people around us. I couldn't tell if she was uncomfortable dancing in public, or in front of me specifically. "Copy what I'm doing," I added, being sure to mimic warmth in my voice. It would help open her up, which was when she was actually useful to me.

She smiled nervously, looking down at my feet. I took both her hands in mine, gently guiding her to follow my lead. Tentatively, she stepped to the left, then brought her right foot in. Then stepped to the right, bringing her left foot in. "Mhm," I encouraged, nearly on the brink of snapping over the fact that I was coaching her how to step her feet together. Ridiculous. "Okay, now, uh, bounce a little." I exaggerated my movements to make a point.

"Like this?"

Exactly not like that.

"Yeah, like that." Whatever bounce she was doing, she was bobbing her head too often and too enthusiastically. Hana's eyebrows raised behind the mask. I let go of her sweaty hands. "See, you can dance." She couldn't. "Just feel the music and move to the beat."

Hana went back to looking at the ground, but at least she was moving now. It was a start.

The girl next to us bent over, touching her knees to her elbows while her partner gyrated into the back of her mini skirt.

Hana tripped over her foot.

It was a start.

There wasn't much I could work with in terms of technique, so I swayed in front of her in beat to the music. I had taken one of my mother's pills right before the dance. How long did it take them to kick in? It had been a couple days, but I still didn't feel any noticeable change. No wonder my mother didn't get better. I would take two next time.

Hana was staring at me again. I smiled, blinking away the chalky taste of antidepressants. "What's up?"

"How often do you go to dances?"

Too often. "I try to attend all of them."

"Oh, because you're ASB president, right?"

"No, I just really like to show off my skills." She laughed, but I barely managed a smile. My eyes trailed down to the sleeves of her cardigan. "Hana, you aren't hot?"

"What? Oh, no, I'm fine." She stopped dancing to pull down on her sleeves.

I didn't want to push her too far too fast, so I just let my fingers lightly trail down her arms. "Alright, as long as you're okay." She didn't pull away. By the end of the night, I was going to have that cardigan off. I started to sway, coaxing her back into comfort. "Hana," I nearly shouted so she could hear me over the bass. Instead of answering, she looked up. "What's your favorite color?"

"What?"

"Your favorite color. What is it?"

"Oh, uh, I don't know. Blue?"

"You don't know your own favorite color?" I had guessed it wouldn't be a stereotypical 'girl' color, not that any color had a gender. But Hana was an outsider, pink and purple and lavender and other variations wouldn't be high on her list.

"Well, they're all okay! Blue is the nicest I guess."

"Why blue?"

"I don't know, I never thought about a color that much." Hesitantly, she moved closer to me as we danced, leaning up to my face. "Why? What's your favorite color?"

"Red."

"Why?"

Because red was power. It was the jagged arrow on the stock market. It demanded attention and commanded obedience. It was the color of the ties in a board meeting. The soles of a woman's heels as she stood over a naked man's body, tied, gagged, and his eyes begging for another whip of her leather. It was the carpet walked on by false idols of the media, constructing the social norm with each step on its plush body.

Red, the color painted on the nails of a woman on the corner, dragging the cigarette from her lips. The same color as her fitted dress. Red was the warmth that ignited when someone finally said the three magic words. Red spread throughout the skull in ripples, hot red lines spelling love in cursive over and over. Red was euphoric. It was passion.

It was betrayal.

It was blood.

I shrugged. "I haven't really thought about it either."

"Oh okay."

She looked back down at her 8th grade graduation heels and our conversation was over. Approximately 3 seconds passed before I decided I needed to get blackout drunk to tolerate the night.

"Hana, I'll be right back." My eyes had already glazed over from the situation, fogging it from my mind. I left her staring after me, and the crowd consumed her. I needed to find Jensen and Blake, though probably in the reverse order. Cover first, then the distraction.

I waded through the sweaty bodies like the shallow end of an inner-city pool in summer.

I unfortunately found Jensen first. He didn't look much different than usual, wearing a sharp navy blue suit, dress shoes, and an actual masquerade mask. It took him half a song to realize his grinding victim had escaped and I was standing in her place instead. "Jensen, please tell me you have a flask."

His eyes rested a couple inches left of my face. "So forward, shouldn't you buy me dinner first?"

"That's the least appealing offer I've gotten all night."

He stopped bouncing side to side and simultaneously whipped out two flasks from opposite inserts of his jacket pockets. "I finished a forth already, sorry."

"I can tell." He started to say something else, but the flask was already at my lips, bottoms up. The alcohol burned on the way down, sweet like ice on a bee sting. Half a flask and two girls elbowing me later, I pocketed the flask in my jacket.

"That was a little excessive, but okay." Jensen perched an eyebrow, pocketing the other flask in his own jacket and following me through the crowd. "So, I found a guy," he shouted in my ear from right behind me.

"When's the wedding?"

"Shut up."

"Go on."

"He brought something a little harder than alcohol. Uh, I know you said you would be down so I told him yeah, but, I don't know, what do you think?"

"Sure." I held my fist to my mouth, forcing the residual taste down my throat. "Let's do it."

"I didn't even tell you what it was yet."

"That's the exciting part, right?"

"It's anthrax."

"No it's not."

"It's cocaine."

"Really?"

"Yeah." He looked around, whispering what I assumed to be, "Is that too hard?"

"We'll find out, right?" I placed a hand on his shoulder. "But first we need Blake." I looked for the nearest conga line. He was a beacon of golden blond in a human train. "Blake!" Second in line. "I need you."

He laughed, popping his shimmy to the front. "So forward, shouldn't you buy me dinner first?"

"I'd rather skip to dessert."

Jensen scoffed behind me.

Blake clapped his hands above his head. "What's up? You want in?"

God no. "I need you to keep Hana company for a while. She's with her friends now, but I don't want it to seem like I'm ditching her."

Blake tapped his chin, "But just so we're on the same page, you're ditching her?"

"Immediately."

"You make my life so difficult." He placed his hands on Emma's hips in front of him, whispering into her ear. Then he jumped out of line. "Okay, I'm going on Hana duty. Please hurry back though, and," he sniffed my breath. "Don't do anything too stupid."

Why did people want me to be bored?

Jensen led me out of the auditorium, down a dark hallway to a secluded bathroom. Our footsteps grew louder the farther away we walked from the dance floor. Jensen approached the door first, clearing his throat. "Hey, it's me, Jensen!" He knocked, but there was no answer. Jensen leaned his back against the door, addressing me. "Ricky, so you really like, actually-actually really for real actually want to do this?"

"Would you rather pretend to enjoy dancing for another three hours?"

He nodded, looking down. "You're right, yeah, you're right." Then quickly back up at me. "So, why was it funny when he said it? What was that all about?"

"What?"

The door opened and Jensen fumbled into the bathroom, almost knocking over the scrawny kid with overgrown bangs. He was a transfer student last year, mediocre grades and a general bad reputation around school. I wasn't surprised this was Jensen's connection. It was amazing he wasn't searched at the entrance. Neither was Jensen. Either of them could have walked in with a military grade weapon stashed under their jacket and the press would probably label them as misunderstood.

Privilege; noun – a special right, advantage, or immunity granted or available only to a particular person or group of people.

"I didn't know you'd bring him." He looked me up and down as if he didn't already know who I was.

"Nah, relax. Ricky's cool." Jensen punched my arm before ushering me inside. "You know Ricky, right? Ricky this is Max…I think that's his name."

The kid hooked his thumbs in his front pockets. "Anyways, yeah, here's the stuff." He guided us into the handicapped stall.

A toilet seat?

Really, how classless did it get?

The bathroom was eerily silent as Max-I-think-that's-his-name, wiggled a white powder out of his mini plastic baggie and onto his mother's engraved cutting board, balanced stably across a toilet that hadn't been properly cleaned for a few weeks.

It looked like a mound of sugar, though the color was a bit off. If I were more inclined, I would question the fact it was a little beige, but I was finding it hard to care about anything. Max took a small single-blade razor out of his pocket and my heart quickened. That was the kind of razor I needed.

"How long do you want it?" Max gestured between Jensen and I.

Jensen turned to me.

I looked at Jensen.

Jensen's eyes widened, unblinking. When I didn't hint at any indication of giving a shit, Jensen frowned, looking very hard toward the ground. I personally had never taken anything harder than my mother's prescription medication, and although Max was Jensen's contact, I doubt Jensen had either.

But what was the harm in a little cocaine?

"Just," Jensen finally spoke up, clearing his throat and taking a wobbly step closer to the toilet. "Just do whatever you usually do."

Max separated a small batch of the powder, spreading it out into a thin line the length of my pinky finger. He created a matching second line, then a slightly longer third line. "Aight, cool. Do you have a bill or something to roll?"

Jensen pulled a fifty out of his wallet and handed it to Max.

"Really?" Max commented, but rolled the bill anyway. Then, in a barely a blink of an eye, Max pinched one side of his nose and erased one of the lines with the makeshift money straw. Max tilted his head back, sniffing hard into the air, his eyes squeezed tight.

The music from the dance changed pace to a slower song. Max sniffed again, groggily getting to his feet with a wide grin on his face. "It's not bad, not bad." He repeated to us, or perhaps to himself, holding the straw out to either me or Jensen.

Jensen pretended to check his text messages.

I took the straw, moving past Max to the toilet. Snorting cocaine should be relatively self-explanatory, right? I slowly crouched to my knees, the cold of the tile seeping in through my black dress pants. I was starting to feel the alcohol take hold. As I clenched and unclenched my hand, the movements were delayed. I sat on the heels of my shoes, my left hand holding my knee.

The line looked a lot longer once it was right in front of me. I held the straw to my nostril. I sniffed for practice, like if I had a cold and I was that one annoying kid in class that just sniffed his snot back into his nose instead of blowing it out. My skin itched, pulled too tight over my muscles and bones. Blood pounded against my eardrums to the beat of John Legend playing just outside the door. Static danced on my shoulders and down my back, making the hairs on my arm stand. It felt new, exciting. This was a scratch.

I pinched my other nostril, bending down to the floral cutting board. I hovered the straw just barely above the line. Probably better to just go fast.

It went down surprisingly smooth. I instinctively swallowed to get rid of the feeling at the back of my throat. I followed Max's lead, tilting my head back and sniffing a few more times. I didn't know if I was supposed to feel anything, but it could have just been the alcohol numbing the feeling. My nose felt fine. Amazing, actually. I looked back down at the cutting board.

Only half the line was gone. "Max, pass me your razor," I instructed. This was a learning opportunity. A razor materialized on the corner of the board and I straightened up the rest of the line just as Max had done earlier. This time, I sniffed softer, like I was smelling a flower.

A paintball exploded on the inside of my skull. Not the painful impact associated with it, just the color expanding across the blank walls of my mind. The alcohol swam in the tunnels of my body, washing the paint to the tips of my fingers. I put my hand on the tile, expecting the color to spill out across the white bathroom floor.

I sniffed again, closing one nostril and rising to my feet. I expected to be bouncing off the walls by now, but it had only been 3.6 seconds. I stumbled slightly, but caught my balance quickly. I started laughing.

"Ricky, dude, are you okay?" Jensen was at my side, and though he was smiling too, his smile twitched at the corners and his hands were shaking.

"I'm drunk," I laughed, rubbing my face. It was numb, but it felt right at the same time. Numb was my favorite feeling. I gave Jensen a pat on the shoulder, handing him the straw and nudging him toward the toilet. "Sniff slow."

I left Jensen, wandering out of the stall. When I had my first kiss, I was numb. Well, technically my first kiss was in second grade, but that one didn't count. My first real kiss was in seventh grade. Her name was Aurora and her hair was the color of a pastel galaxy and felt like California dry brush.

We had PE together and it was the only time I saw her the entire school day. Forty-five short minutes. She was quiet. When the coach called her name in attendance, she wouldn't respond, staring forward with blank eyes. When we had to run the mile, she would slip through a hole in the fence and make flower crowns in the grass behind the trees. She was always absent on swim days, but only for PE.

Her home address in the directory led to a bent stop sign in the middle of a hiking trail. She was dropped off in front of the school twenty-three minutes before the first bell rang. She always got out from the back of the car, though there was never anyone in the passenger seat. For twenty-two minutes, she would sit in the far corner of the cafeteria and draw in her sketchbook. She showed me a couple times. Aurora designed a lot of plaid patterns, varying soft and hard scratches across the pages.

I had asked her to hang out after school, no pressure if she had other arrangements. She silently followed as we walked down the street from the school, an easy two mile stroll in our small suburban bubble. She was a little taller than me back then, but she took toddler steps, trailing a few feet behind. I debated whether to try striking up a conversation, but ultimately couldn't decide on a topic so I let it go.

It was chilly that night, with the sun setting earlier in the fall. I climbed on top of the monkey bars, motioning for her to join me, but she leaned against one of the poles instead. "Why don't you talk?" I finally asked.

"I don't like talking." The whisper barely escaped her lips before they closed again. Her voice was the slight sizzle of a snail being salted.

"Why?"

"I don't see the point."

I waited, but she didn't continue. I tried again. "It's a lot easier and faster than staring at people until they decipher what you mean."

"People usually hear what they want to anyway."

I must have made a face, because she quickly looked away into the darkening trees. But again, she didn't continue. "What do you mean?"

"What do you hear?"

Her lips weren't rosy or pink. They were fleshy and chapped, and they said nothing. "I have no idea." I followed her gaze to the trees. "You don't make any sense."

"It's not my fault you don't know how to listen."

"Okay, jokester, why don't you teach me how to listen then."

"I wish I knew how." Her face was emotionless, completely neutral. From her bleached eyebrows to her cleft chin. An infinite vacuousness. It was perfect.

I reached out, tapping on the bar closest to her. "What are you thinking about?"

"Huh?" She finally looked back to me with her eyebrows raised, the ghost of a smile behind her lips. "I'm not thinking at all. I'm observing. Like, those trees over there, the bark dust," she paused. "You." She put her hands in her pockets. "I'm just observing. Much easier than thinking."

"Sounds," I hesitantly settled on the word, "Repetitive." She shrugged. I tried to read if she was insulted, but I couldn't tell. If I didn't keep asking questions, she would stop talking. "Why don't you like thinking?"

Her thin lips opened, but nothing came out. A dim flash of something lit her eyes for a brief millisecond, but it could have just been a car passing on the street. "It's tiring." She finally said, then melted back into the emptiness of the park surroundings.

"Are you tired of thinking?"

She nodded to the trees, lost in a void of dark silence. Her cheekbones contoured into knives under the streetlamps.

"Neil Gaiman would probably write a book about you," I joked, but she didn't laugh. I swung my legs from the edge of the bars. "If you sit up here, you can observe a lot more things." My hands ached from cold, but if I put them in my pockets I could lose balance and face-plant in front of her. I'd rather have my hands amputated.

She slowly pulled herself up next to me. Another car passed by. Aurora's nose was red and bordering on runny. I wiped my own nose, just in case.

"Are you a good listener?" I finally said. Her shoulders barely lifted in response. I looked to the sky. "If you stay completely still, you can hear the stars." The brightest of them twinkled in the clear sky, chimes in the wind. As I took a half-scoot closer to her, I couldn't feel anything else but my heart in my throat and my thigh next to hers. Heat radiated from her jeans, her hands, her face. "What am I saying right now?"

She stared back at me, observing. "Do you want to kiss me?"

"Yes."

"I guess I'm pretty good at listening then."

"So, is it okay if I kiss you?"

"Are you a good listener?"

I squinted at her, but she revealed nothing. A foolproof lock box. I squinted harder. Not even the sizzling snail made a sound. Comprehension was never my best subject. I sighed, "I don't know. Could you please tell me?"

"It's okay if you kiss me."

Our lips touched, soft, then I pulled back. I wiped my nose, just in case. Another car passed. I watched her face, holding my breath. I was leaned into her, our faces just centimeters apart. I shifted between her two unmoving eyes, not even the stars above reflected in them.

Her eyes ticked back to the trees. Empty.

My heart moved from my throat to the soles of my feet. "Did you want to kiss me?" I took a half scoot away.

She inhaled deeply, closed her eyes, and let her breath trickle out in a cloud.

I listened and I heard the answer. "I'll walk you home, it's getting really cold." I wiped my nose again.

"That's okay." She untangled herself from her secure sitting position, carefully lowering herself down into the darkness. "I know the way from here."

"That doesn't sound very safe."

"What's the worst that could happen?" I tried to listen to her unspoken words, but she had already disappeared.

I laid back on the bars, heaviness fusing my body into the metal. Hypothermia was a suitable medicine for rejection.

Max motioned me over to the bathroom sink and I briefly glanced over myself in the mirror. My reflection had no comments, it said nothing. I slid my mask back down over my eyes, then proceeded to wash my hands. "Take a little water and snort it up your nose. It'll help later on with the drip." Max demonstrated.

"What drip?" But I did as instructed. Snorting water seemed like it would be more problematic than the cocaine, but my nose couldn't feel anything anyway. I tilted my head back again, leaning against the counter for support, sighing loudly. Jensen was taking his time with his line. "I feel great." I wiped my nose again, just in case.

"What?" Max's eyes were bloodshot.

"I feel great," I repeated, shouting. The sound echoed through my body. I could feel the strength coursing down my arms. I could break the counter if I slammed my fist down.

Jensen coughed, pulling himself to his feet. "Wow," he mumbled to himself, staggering to us.

I grabbed him by the shoulders. "Don't you feel great?"

He nodded vigorously. "I can't tell if I want to go fast or if I want to go slow."

Well, obviously the only choice in life was to go fast.

"Let's do something." I said.

Jensen looked me in the eye, though one of us was unable to hold eye contact. Probably him because I had never been so focused in my entire life before. "Like what?"

"Let's go live."

We looked at each other, me holding onto his arms and Jensen using me to stay upright. My fingers tightened around Jensen's shoulders and my smile dropped. "I'm serious. Let's live." I searched his eyes for the itch, the same itch that I had to scratch, but I couldn't tell if Jensen had it too. I needed to go somewhere. I needed to do something. How much could I live before I died?

Max took a swig from the flask.

Jensen opened his mouth as if he had something to say, but then closed it. I waited, then he opened it again. Then he closed it. Then he opened it.

"Stop that." He started laughing. "What are you doing?"

But he kept doing it. And then I was laughing. And then Max was joined in. We collapsed on the floor in laughter for a full ten minutes before we heard the loud banging on the door.

-7-

I'd never seen a group of drunk and semi-high teenage boys shut up so quickly.

I was the first to rise to my feet, pushing through the fog of booze and a little cocaine which tilted the room. I gripped the aluminum trash can for support, wiping at my nose and straightening my tie. I could compose myself just fine, but the other two would give us away. "Guys," I took a deep breath. "Get your shit together."

Jensen laughed, then gagged on his own spit.

Max snorted another line off the toilet.

Jesus Christ.

The door knocked again, this time louder. My mind ran through the possibilities. It couldn't be security or any sort of police, because they would announce themselves and come in anyway. A chaperone was a possibility, but it was most likely a student looking to use the restroom. Though, since this restroom was hidden in the back, they were either trying to hook up in the bathroom, or they were looking for someone. They shouldn't be too hard to shoo away.

I cracked the door, leaning my body against the frame to block the rest of the bathroom from sight. "May I help you?"

Samantha's disapproving frown greeted me. "Where's Jensen? I thought I saw him come back here." She didn't look her best tonight. Samantha wasted hours in front of her bedroom mirror, holding her hair straightener above her head so long her arm muscles cried. Maybe her hair looked better a few hours ago, but now it was a collection of limp frizzy Twizzlers that made her face look fatter. She liked to get ready to musicals, Wicked and Chicago and the like. I had been in Samantha's room a few times. It was neat, for the most part, just crowded with too many clothes and even more books.

Samantha pursed her lips, crossing her arms. Her shoulders were a bit too wide to be complimented by her sleeveless hot pink dress. She should know better by now.

"Jensen is peeing." I responded.

"Then why are you in there?"

"To answer doors for him. He is a very busy man."

She cracked a smile, but her arms were still crossed. "Okay, whatever, but his date is looking for him and she's the most annoying person in the world. I don't think I can take one more second of her blabbering about 'Hart of Pretty Little Vampire Gilmore Gossip Diary Girls' or whatever she melts her brain with."

"She's a solid seven though." Samantha pulled her lips in, narrowing her eyes at me. "You're usually a seven if that makes you feel better."

"Thank you." She barely hid the sarcasm.

"Not tonight though, unfortunately."

"I hate you."

I looked back into the bathroom and Jensen was finally on his feet. Max had cleaned up the toilet area and put everything back in his backpack. "Jensen, your dominatrix is here to collect you." I opened the door wider and took a step back, letting her walk in.

Samantha took one look at him before turning to me. "Seriously Ricky? He's fucking plastered."

I shrugged.

"Oh my God, how much alcohol did you guys have? And why is Max here? Ew, get lost."

Max grabbed his crotch, flipping her off. He did indeed get lost though, slinging his backpack over his shoulder and sulking out into the dark hallway. I'd ask Jensen for Max's number later.

"Samantha, this is a dry event. As president, I am here to enforce that rool."

"What?"

"Rule."

"Okay, both of you are cut off. Now." Samantha huffed, her panties bunching. She went to Jensen first, grabbing his elbows firmly. "Jensen, give it." Ignoring his loose excuse that he had no such thing, she opened his suit jacket and pulled the flask out of his pocket. Samantha opened it, tilted it back against her lips. "It's empty, really?" She held it upside down. "You guys are going to need a liver transplant before you're out of college." She turned to me, moving in slow motion. "Ricky? Or do I have to search you too?"

I threw my hands up innocently, fixated on my fingers spreading apart from each other. "There was just one. But Katie snuck in some vodka, so if you want some, you'll have to find her somewhere."

"Thanks."

"I try to be helpful." I didn't know if Katie actually had any alcohol, but it would keep Samantha away for a while. Trying to find Katie at a dance was like looking for a rock in high grass. "Is Blake still with Hana?"

"Um, yeah. That's how I noticed you were gone, actually. That and Jensen was gone. Should've guessed you two would sneak off and have fun without me."

"It's more fun when you're gone."

"I hate you so much."

I moved past her, catching a judgmental glance from the corner of her eye. "You don't like Hana, do you?"

"I really don't, no offense."

I smiled, "None taken." The itch was satisfied. "Come on, we should get back to the dance. You're slacking off, Ms. Vice President." She led me out of the bathroom, but I couldn't feel her hand wrapped around my arm. I couldn't feel anything. Nothing was exactly what I needed.

Samantha hauled me back to Blake and Hana, leaving with a look I didn't care to decipher. My own thoughts were barely audible over the music. The DJ was better than expected.

"Ricky! You're back!" Blake was the first to notice me, stopping mid-swing to wave. Hana also stopped, clamming back up upon seeing me. "What took you so long?" He continued as I walked closer. Hair clung to his forehead, sweat drops outlining the side of his face. It wasn't an afternoon jog, but dancing could be just as much of a workout. "Poor little Hana here was so worried."

"What no, what." She stuttered, shaking her hands in denial.

"Oh, you should have heard her, Ricky, really." He placed a hand on his chest, imitating what I was sure was completely made up. "Oh woe is me, my date has abandoned me, woe is me. At least I get to dance with someone sexy."

"What no, what."

"Basically exactly like that." He pulled her a little closer, ignoring her shaking hands, swaying with the music. "So. Where were you?"

"Snorting cocaine."

Blake rolled his eyes, "Well, better than crack I think."

Hana finally managed to sew together a sentence. "Yeah, Crack is wack."

"See, even Hana knows drugs are bad. Good job, Hana. Get ready for a dip." Blake slowly leaned her back, but kept his eyes on me. Concerned. Nagging. "How do you feel?" He mouthed to me.

If a hummingbird was in the room, it would be moving in slow motion.

I shrugged.

He handed Hana over to me, bowing out of the dance. "Hana, always a pleasure. I'll see you guys later, okay?" He smiled to Hana, but leaned over to my ear as he shimmied by, "Stay out of trouble."

Well, that just didn't sound like much fun.

I took both of Hana's small hands into mine, picking up where Blake left off. They felt so fragile, like if I squeezed just a little bit tighter she would fall apart. Or maybe I would. "Sorry about that, Blake didn't make you uncomfortable, did he?"

"What? Um, no, he was fun. I mean, funny. I mean, like, normal, I don't know." She looked to the side, but followed my simple dance sway. "Where'd you go?"

"I had some ASB stuff to take care of, even off the clock, we're on the clock."

"You're a really hard worker."

"Comes with the territory." Hana's cardigan, or shawl thing whatever it was called, was already halfway down her arms, the rounds of her shoulders sticking out for a fresher air. "What are you doing this weekend?" I shouted a little too loud, but she didn't seem to notice.

"Nothing. What about you?"

"Let's hang out."

"Oh, okay."

And that was it. Keeping up the conversation was painful. How could someone be so terrible at talking? "Cool, I can pick you up and we can go from there."

"Okay."

Faking was hard. I didn't know how girls did it so frequently. "You should take off your sweater thing."

"My what?"

"The thing around your sweaters—your shoulders."

She pulled it back over her shoulders, suffocating them. "I'm fine! Really, it's not even that warm." Her face mask acted as a dam for the line of sweat under her brows.

"It's giving me a heat stroke."

"Sorry." She looked away again and stopped dancing.

"Come get a drink with me. It feels like I'm overheating." It felt like a furnace, like I was swimming in lava. I turned away before she answered, paddling through burning waves of students.

I made it over to the punch area, pouring myself a cup and downing it before Hana even had time to catch up. "Ricky, are you okay? Do you want to go outside for a bit?"

"I'm just dehydrated I think." She almost reached for my arm, but dropped her hand at the last minute. I grabbed another cup. "Do you want some?"

"Uh, yeah, sure." I handed her a cup mid-sentence. "Thanks." She took small sips as I gulped mine.

"Are you having fun?" I said, pulling her further away from the dancefloor. Outside and away sounded necessary. "Is this your first dance?"

"Yeah, I guess I'm enjoying it." She stumbled behind me, her arm stretched as far as it could go while she dangled from the other end. "And this is my second dance. I'm having more fun this time, so thanks."

"Why?"

"Why what?"

"Why are you having more fun this time?"

She squinted, making some kind of face at me. "I don't know," she mumbled, "I guess because I have a date?"

I laughed, stopping momentarily to twirl her around. Hana was like a little rag doll, with droopy eyes and lifeless limps. As long as she was moving, she might as well dance. "Do you like looking dead?" The words tumbled over my lips and into the air.

"What?"

"Looking dead but feeling alive. Isn't it the best?"

She shook her head at me. "What are you saying?"

"It's too loud, forget it." I swung her around more, laughing at the way her feet fumbled to keep up with her body and her hands tensing to keep the cup from sloshing around. "You're getting better at dancing."

"I don't think this counts as dancing."

It didn't. "Sure it does." As long as we were moving, we were dancing. As long as we were dancing, we weren't dead. "Come a little closer." I pulled her in, my hand snaking around to her waist. "Just move with me."

Like a stubby palm tree in the wind, she swayed.

"Bend your knees," I instructed. The lights were distracting, moving strobes directing my attention to the flashing ceiling.

We swayed at a half-arm's length, inch by inch moving toward the exit. I could taste the freedom. Our surroundings were blurry grey silhouettes. I had lost track of everyone except Hana, who kept her eyes on my shoes, concentrating on keeping her knees bent and her body loose. Her hair tumbled over her shoulder, blocking her face from me. Since when was her hair down?

I rubbed my neck, digging my fingers into the skin behind my ear. The door was in sight, just a few bodies away. "Hey, I need some air, I'll be right back." Dropping her hands, I didn't wait for her, bee-lining to the neon green exit letters and pushing myself out of the music.

The heavy doors closed softly behind me, and I was greeted by the chilled wind across my face. I sniffed, lifting my head to the night sky.

Inhale.

It smelled like car exhaust and nearby teenage funk. Dances never went well for me, they either ended too soon, before I could find the contraband, or it dragged on hours after the contraband wore off. My fingers tingled, but no matter how much I stretched them, the itch didn't subside.

"Ricky!" Hana slinked out of the door, pulling her cardigan closer around her shoulders. "Man, you walk really fast. You basically ran."

I needed to get out.

"Did I? I hadn't noticed," I laughed, putting one hand in my pocket. She stared at me, waiting. My ribs tightened around my lungs. "You can go back inside if you want, I was just going to stretch my legs a little bit."

"I don't mind, I can wait." She smiled, but kept her distance.

My chest heaved, pulling my eyelids closed. My head pounded, off-beat to the muffled music from inside. I pocketed my other shaking hand. My stomach churned in knots. I bent at the waist from the cramp, squeezing my eyes shut tighter.

"Ricky?" She took a step forward.

The world spun. "Just stretching," I laughed, even reaching out my hands, still shaking, to touch the edge of my toes. My eyes burned from my brain pushing against my skull, a thud. She took another step. "It's healthy to stretch after so much activity, you know? Especially since my legs tend to cramp up."

"Oh, right. Yeah, that's good then. I'll stretch with you!" She bent over, fingers stopping a few inches from her feet. "This actually feels nice."

This felt terrible.

I bit my lip to stop the trembling. Exhale. Exhale. Exhale. They didn't have Lamaze classes as an elective unless you were pregnant.

"How long do we hold this?" She chirped.

Exhale.

"Count." Was the only word I could get out without choking.

"One," she started. Hana's voice was slow, calm, the low tide on a flat beach. "Seven." In my head, I counted with her, the numbers steadily becoming louder than the pins in my face. My tunnel vision widened beyond just my fingers, the ground clearing. "Nineteen." The tingling seeped away, leaving just the familiar buzz. "Thirty."

Inhale.

We both stood, Hana yawning. Staring. At me. I quickly pulled my phone out of my pocket, tapping at the black screen. "Oh, hold on," I held up a finger. "My mom's calling."

"Op, okay!"

I shot her a thumbs up, then put the phone to my ear. "I'll meet you inside," I mouthed to her. "Hey ma, yeah, I'm still at the dance. Hm, with Hana."

She nodded, and with a wave, she ducked back inside. I waited a beat, then walked to the side of the building, shaded by the trees. My feet dragged, my fingers no longer had the strength to hold my phone. I guided myself to the ground, my back against the building as I sluggishly collapsed into a seating position on the sidewalk.

I didn't regret many things in life, perhaps because I had only been alive a little over seventeen years and that wasn't a lot of time to accumulate many regrets. But perhaps it was because, no matter the outcome of a situation, it was an opportunity to learn.

I met Katie during my freshman year of high school, the same year I met Andrea. In fact, Andrea introduced us. They had been childhood best friends for most of their life, surviving everything from Katie meeting her birth father to awkward thigh-high sock tans from years of private Catholic girls' school.

The first time I met Katie, Andrea and I waited outside of Katie's house. It was in a nice enough community, next to the freeway and ungated, but there weren't any crack houses so that helped property value. Andrea was driving us to Jensen's house to hang out and thought her friend Katie would want to join. I didn't say no, or bring up the fact that she probably shouldn't cruise around a bunch of minors with just a learner's permit.

Katie's lithe frame skipped out of the front door, her hair braided into two long black pigtails low by her ears. Katie wore glasses back then, square and thick rimmed. I turned back to Andrea, "She's a lot smaller than I imagined. From your stories."

"She gets that a lot."

Katie opened the back door, climbing in. "Really? Booted to the back seat, Andrea? I'm hurt." Her voice mimicked a canary. She shut the door, then stuck her head in between the front seats. "Is this the guy?" She turned to me, reaching for my arm.

I moved out of the way. "Ricky."

"I'm Katie! I've heard so much about you."

Unfortunately, she hadn't heard so much about personal space.

Before Andrea could properly introduce us, another figure barreled out of the house, just as small as Katie, but about twenty-five years older and with already greying hair. She yanked open the door, "Katie!" she yelled, then continued completely in Vietnamese and completely ignoring the social etiquette to keep all family arguments and disagreements within the house. My family followed that rule religiously.

"Mom!" Katie shot back.

Her mom plucked at Katie's wet hair and continued yelling –or maybe talking, hard to tell—while wagging her finger at her daughter.

I looked at Andrea, "What is happening?"

She stayed on her phone, unfazed by the spectacle. "It's normal, she'll notice us in a second."

Exactly a second later, Katie's mother stopped yelling, then smiled at both of us. "Oh, hello Andrea! And who is this?"

"Ricky," I introduced myself, looking to the backseat to return the smile.

Her eyes lit up, a grin overtaking her face. "Ricky? THE Ricky?" There was a hint of an accent, but it wasn't prominent. "I've heard so much about you!"

"That seems to be today's theme."

She lightly slapped Katie on the arm. "Why didn't you tell me Ricky was in the car?"

"You didn't give me a chance to say anything!"

"I'm sorry for my daughter, Ricky."

"Mom!"

For some reason, ultimately unbeknownst to me, people assumed I was a good kid. I speculated my grades were a large driving factor for this assumption, paired with the fact my jeans hadn't been on my floor for four days and my shirts were clean of pit stains.

She gave me a once over, smiling. "Well, as long as Ricky is going, you can go, Katie."

"Thanks, Mom."

"Roll your eyes again, Katie, and –" She said something in Vietnamese, but with a smile. Her mom handed Katie a bottle of green oil, then closed the door and walked back to the house.

"I'm assuming that's your mother?" I asked. "What's the oil for?"

Andrea cut in, looking over her shoulder. "Did she say something about me? I thought I heard her mention my name?"

"Oh, yeah," Katie looked down, buckling herself into the middle seat. "She was saying she really liked your hair, she wanted me to ask what shampoo you used." When Katie looked up, I met her eyes in the rearview mirror.

"So, where are we going?" Katie asked, stripping off her baggy grey sweater to reveal a beaded green spaghetti tank top.

Andrea looked at her friend in the mirror. "We're pre-gaming at Jensen's. You know him, right? He's in your grade." Silence. "He's on ASB with Ricky." Silence.

"He threw a fit in AP World History because he lost an argument on colonialism," I chimed in. If Katie wasn't in my history class, then she must have been in Jensen's. And if she wasn't in AP World History at all, then I had no desire to know her.

"Oh! That guy! With the weird haircut." She wiggled off her frumpy sweatpants, black fish scale tights dawning her legs. "He seems like a fun time." She pulled her hair out of the pig tails, shaking it out.

"Katie," I interrupted her costume change. "What's your GPA?"

Andrea threw me a look, but Katie didn't hesitate. "Weighted? 3.8."

"Afterschool activities?"

"I don't have any, not really."

"Well, where do you want to go to college, what do you want to be?"

Andrea reached out, taking hold of my hand. "Ricky, really?"

Again, no hesitation from Katie. "Well, I honestly don't really know."

"What are your strengths?"

"I don't know."

Her honesty was effortless. "Katie, would you like to be our ASB secretary? I think you would be a really great fit." One of my only regrets was offering the position to Katie.

Andrea squeezed my arm, but Katie, again, jumped to the answer. "Oh, sure, why not. Sounds fun."

Andrea released my arm, going back to the steering wheel. "I'm glad you two are getting along."

My second regret was getting close to Katie and her third wheeling. I regretted that she was funny and smart (enough) and was always excited to try something new. Katie didn't mind skipping a class to check out the new exhibit at the planetarium or covering for me when I was too hungover to make it to class.

Andrea smiled at both of us. "You two are the most important people in my life."

I regretted that we couldn't hang out anymore without Andrea's ghost draped over our shoulders.

-8-

I was now convinced that Jensen's medicine cabinet was the Mariana Trench. Well, his parent's medicine cabinet anyway. I stepped back, taking in the waves of prescription bottles crowding the slim glass shelving.

Frankly, it was impressive that someone could have so many problems and yet still be functional. Or maybe the medicine was the only thing keeping them functional.

Their bathroom was copy and pasted from an Italian architect's dream portfolio. The walls were champagne and the large oval mirror was lined with ornate molding. The light bulbs were as warm as the heated tile and tall candles bordered the white marble sinks.

The medicine cabinet, however, wasn't simply hanging onto the wall like some sort of middle class peasant nonsense. It was in a standing display case, with a frosted glass door. The six foot case flaunted the bottles as trophies of their success, milestones on their financial journey through capitalistic America, achievements unlocked by their hard work and unwavering determination.

If they sold their mental health to the financial devil, at least they could offset some of it with prescription marijuana.

Quickly shuffling through the first few shelves, I found most of the contents were nicotine supplements and sleeping aids.

Other shelves had bottles of expired antidepressants, stimulants, and something I didn't think was legal in the country.

I grabbed a few bottles of Adderall and Ambien from various shelves, plopping them into my backpack, then washed my hands before rejoining the others downstairs at the front door. It was supposed to be just ASB and Blake, but Hana texted this morning reminding me that we were supposed to hang out. I didn't remember inviting her out, but she might as well join.

As usual, the K9 Indoor Kart Racing was busy on the weekends and the air conditioning was set too high. Not usual, this would be our last time setting foot in the building.

The entire building was themed after a giant dog park. I took a seat on the arm of a fire hydrant bench as Blake and Samantha went to the front desk to sign everyone in. Hana stayed close to me, standing next to the bench, close enough that I could feel her hips brush against my arm when she pretended to text so she wouldn't have to make eye contact with anyone else. Katie did the opposite, taking as much space as possible on the bench and gossiping loudly about some girl in her class.

"Hana," I said softly, tilting my head towards her. "Do you know any dog puns?"

"What?"

She said what a lot. "Start thinking of one."

Her body tightened and her laugh was more or less just forced exhalation. "Wait, what? Are you serious? Why?" I was surprised she didn't put up more resistance to joining the ASB crowd, forced to hanging out with people who could pronounce her name but would still spell it wrong. Maybe shy wasn't the right label for her. How would she do under pressure?

I made a show of lowering my voice even more, leaning in so I was practically talking into her elbow. "When the time comes, make the right decision."

"What?"

"The spotlight will be on you."

Hana brushed a couple strands of hair out of her face. "What are you talking about?" I brought a finger to my mouth and pointed to Blake and Samantha as they returned with a waiver form.

Samantha approached with an outstretched arm toward Hana, a paper dangling between two manicured fingers. "You've never been here before, right Hana?" The redhead didn't wait for the inevitable head shake. "That's what I thought. Here ya go, you just have to fill out this waiver and turn it in."

"Oh okay." Hana took the paper and searched for a pen in her bag.

We first started coming to this particular racing spot when Jensen had his fifteenth birthday here. He practically invited the entire freshmen class, buying out the building and reserving a live band to play. The party was catered by an amazing fusion restaurant from the city and a professional party planner attended to the finer details. Blake, Samantha, and I were the only ones who showed up.

Blake chimed in like a needlessly loud church bell on Sunday morning, reminding everyone that it wasn't too late to avoid burning in a pool of sin. "And we're all set for the next race, so as soon as these guys finish," he gestured to the gokarts currently zooming by on the track, "It'll be our turn. So bark up!"

Samantha moaned, "Please tell me we aren't doing this again."

"Doing what, dear?"

"Dog puns. Can we just do one race, please."

Jensen laughed, "Looks like someone hasn't had a bone in a while, relax Samantha."

"One, don't be a pig, Jensen," Katie started.

"I believe bitch would be a more appropriate reference."

"Interesting that you chose bitch over dog," Blake said, tapping his chin. "I'm gonna barkmark that for discussion later."

Katie rolled her eyes, continuing. "Two. Seriously, you guys do the same puns every time we come. At least make them dif-fur-ent."

Samantha moaned louder. "Not you too."

Hana leaned in, speaking into the top of my hair. "Ricky, what is happening?"

"I warned you. You should throw one out there, quick, while the laughter is still bubbling."

She stood up a little straighter, bracing one hand on the back of the bench and leaning half-committedly into the circle. "Haha!" More struggled laughs erupted from her mouth but she still sounded like she was on the other end of a hostage negotiation line. "All of these deserve."

The group stopped for the punchline.

Hana clammed up. "Um."

The young woman at the cash register stopped chewing her gum.

"Ah." She wiped her hands on the back of the bench.

The go karts pulled over to the side. The world was silent except for the bead of sweat running down the back of Hana's neck.

"Uh, they all deserve," she looked to me, trembling.

I pulled the trigger. "Apaws. They all deserve apaws," I finished, putting her out of her misery. The outside world resumed.

Jensen lost it, holding his sides. "What was that? That was the worst delivery in the history of comedy. I wish I had pup-corn for that."

"Yeah, Hana, we're going to hound you about that all day. But it's a start, good job." Katie smiled, then turned to me. "Thank you for pulling the pug on that though, it was bad."

Blake nipped at my shoulder with his fingers. "Speaking of apaws, Ricky, did you buy that song for me yet?"

Blake had always been obsessed with music. Television too for that matter, whatever provided an outlet that could block out everything around him. When we were kids, he would run all the way across town so he could watch our cable programming with a dark walnut sized bruise almost shutting one of his eyes closed. He would plop himself in front of the screen, a bag of frozen peas resting on his cheek, and laugh as little cartoon animals went on adventures with him.

Vamonos Blake, away from life's problems.

Blake also used to think he could fly. When we were still in primary school, we used to hang out in my backyard tree for no reason other than we had nowhere else to go. The clouds looked so close then, the ground so far.

"Do you think I can fly, Ricky?" Blake was missing his bottom canine for an uncomfortably long time.

"No, I don't."

"Really?" He stretched out his arms, trying to pet the sky, just out of reach. Blake was all limbs, thin twigs sticking out of his shorter trunk. "I feel like I can."

"Why? You've fallen out of this tree at least a billion and one times."

"I don't know, I just feel it." He swung his legs, threatening to topple him off the branch, but Blake and his bad bowl cut didn't seem to mind. "You know how you just feel something, so you believe it? With all your heart?"

"No, I don't."

Pssbt. He blew his lips at me. "It's like the wind. You'll know it when you feel it. You can do anything."

Even fly.

The gokart race had started and I was in second place. Samantha was barely in first, her bulky red braid sticking out from under her helmet. The front of my cart skimmed her bumper as we drifted the corner.

Katie was a few seconds behind me, her lightness making up for her lack of control, and Jensen was behind, complaining about how his steering wheel wouldn't turn and the whole race was rigged. Blake liked to take his time and cruise, like he was coasting down Highway 101 on a warm summer day. I had lost track of Hana at the starting line, but I assumed she was somewhere in between.

We turned again, and on the straight, I pressed all the way down on the gas, gaining on her cart from the outside. Samantha glanced in my direction, then did the same. We approached the last series of turns before the checkered finish line, full speed. An attendant waved a yellow flag in our direction, a warning to slow down before the curves.

We didn't.

Samantha had always been my number two. It wasn't that she wasn't the best at anything, she had perfected her craft in select areas. At water polo, alto lead in choir, and her junior debutant, she was the best. If she wasn't the best, she would strive to become the best. A force to be reckoned with, for sure, Samantha had the persistence of a pit bull's jaw. But head to head, when we competed against each other, I would always win.

She wasn't a sore sport, however, she would just work harder. It was one of her few redeeming qualities. As much as I hated the rest of her qualities, Samantha kept me on my toes, reliably one half step behind.

Samantha's success was fueled by passion. Mine was methodical.

It was only a gokart race, hardly anything of substance, but if I could win, I would. Napoleon Bonaparte didn't reform education and taxation in France by accepting second place. I let up on the gas a millisecond before her, turning into the curve early. She turned late, her kart sliding with the drift. I accelerated past her, into the next curve.

Her cart blocked me, rushing to regain the lead. Passion.

I rammed her cart into the tire wall.

The attendant waved a red flag at both of us, then turned down the speed on our carts.

"Hey!" Samantha growled at me, whirling her head side to side in an attempt to see me. She was pinned into the wall by my cart. "You fucking cheater."

I reversed, straight into Katie who had rounded the corner.

"Ricky! Get out of my way!" Katie revved her engine, so I continued reversing, pinning Katie as well.

Samantha used her hands to push her car back, so I slammed into her again. "Fuck you, Ricky!" My name roared from her throat, red curls bouncing back from the impact.

The attendant waved another red flag at us, blowing his whistle. The engine to Katie's cart sizzled to half power as well, right as Jensen smashed into both of us, effectively completing the road block at the curve.

My head jerked against the headrest, the seatbelt digging into my shoulder. The whistle was at full volume as the attendant ran over to us, waving his collection of flags all at once.

"Jensen, you moron." Katie lifted the visor of her helmet, glaring back at him.

"My bad."

"Jensen, you fuckhole assbag!" Samantha's visor also snapped up, along with her belt buckle. "I was about to win God dammit."

"Okay, relax Samantha, literally not even that big of a deal." Jensen fully took off his helmet, shooing off her anger.

The whistle attendant shouted at us, "Hey! Stay in your vehicle!"

Hana was the only one sensible enough to stop, her helmet bobbing as she waved at me. She lifted her visor, "Is everyone okay?"

Samantha ripped her helmet off, discarding it on the track. "I hate you, Ricky."

"The feeling is mutual." I unbuckled my belt as well. "I'm actually starting to think you like losing."

"Fuck you!" She huffed, turning around in her cart at me. "You know what?" She stood up, making the attendant yell for backup. She hurdled over the gokart barricade, making a dash for the finish line in her wedged sneakers.

Passion.

I paused, then climbed over the tire wall too, but cut out the curves Samantha was currently sprinting through. "Work smart, not hard," I called out to her. I started running down the straight shot towards the goal.

"Cheater!" She exclaimed, finally making it to the stretch. She kicked off her shoes, feet pounding against the ground. Heavy thuds.

It was just so easy to win.

I stopped laughing, my pace slowing. The gratification seeped out of the goal, leaving just a black and white line painted across the asphalt.

Red would look better.

Samantha caught up to me and latched onto my sleeve, pulling me back to launch herself in front of me. She even turned around to gloat a little as she jogged backwards, crossing her eyes with her finger and her thumb in shape of an L on her forehead—she collided with a much larger male attendant, chucking both of them onto the ground.

The shadow of a woman twice my size loomed over me. "Out."

I held up my hands. "Headed to the exit, Ma'am." I locked eyes with Samantha, crumpled on the ground, as I stepped over the finish line before evacuating the arena. The large male attendant picked Samantha up off the ground, leading her off the track by the elbow, in second place. The rest of the group had been escorted to the exit.

That was how we all got kicked out of K9.

Well.

Except Blake, but he pledged to never return out of solidarity, even though he really liked dogs.

Jensen picked me up later, since it was Saturday night and I needed to get blackout wasted. "She seemed pretty cool," Jensen added, turning the ignition to his car off, and looking to the others in the backseat.

"Who?" I left my usual statue posture of staring out the passenger window. I had taken half an Ambien a few minutes before Jensen picked me up.

The backseat, consisting of Katie and her new best friend Lauren, shuffled through their little clutch bags. Katie dolled up nicely, her hair slicked into a high ponytail and her body expertly stuffed inside a dress that could probably fit an American Girl Doll. Lauren wore a similar ensemble with boobs that provided shelving for her chin. Her hair fell in waterfall waves almost down to her waist. Her manicured nails fished through her clutch for our fake IDs.

Jensen continued, getting our IDs from Lauren and holding one, presumably mine, out to me. "Hana. She was cool." He studied his ID, then held it under the cabin light. "Hey, this actually kind of looks like me, who'd you get it from?"

"Remind me to give you his contact later, I have it written down in my planner," Lauren answered, then puckered her lips to reapply her lipstick.

"Yeah," I finally found my words, sitting up in my chair. It was getting harder to tune back into conversations. "She's alright I guess." I took the ID from Jensen who was still holding it out for me, bless his little helpful heart, and squinted at the face. Slightly too sharp a jawline with stubble I didn't currently have, but the eyes and nose were creepily spot on, and those was the most important feature to identify people with anyway.

"Ricky," Katie tapped on my shoulder from the backseat. "So if there are any creepy guys that won't leave me alone, do you think you could like, step between us or something? Like, if I give you a signal?"

"What kind of signal?"

"I don't know, like a," she trailed off, presumably doing some signal behind me as a demonstration.

"Sure."

Jensen leaned into the back. "I could help too." Radio silence from Katie. "Psh, whatever. What about you, Lauren? Need any help from unwanted boy attention?"

"My heels are stronger than you."

"Uncalled for." He turned to me, smiling. "Come on dude, liven up! What, are you tired or something?"

It took too long to find my words again.

He gave me a quick slap on the shoulder, "Nothing a vodka redbull can't fix, right?" I managed to raise my eyebrows and nod. "Alright, chain-gang, let's rollout."

The bouncer flipped over my I.D with scrutiny, even going as far to hold it up to the light as if it were a suspiciously crisp one hundred dollar bill. Thick clouds of cheap cigarettes hung low, fogging the already dim yellow bulb buzzing at the entrance. He could check until the next Ice Age. It was a real I.D, it just wasn't mine. Jensen shifted his weight to his other foot, alternating between sliding his hands into his pockets and running them through his hair.

The bouncer looked us over one last time. I doubted he really cared either way. He had a newborn at home that still hadn't mastered sleeping through the night, a stressed out wife with postpartum depression, and a mortgage that was more than half his paycheck. He looked past us, into the dark void of the sky, "Inside wrists of your right hand."

I held back a smirk, all of us flipping over our hands for him to stamp. Jensen waddled behind me, sliding a twenty to the coat check stand.

The club itself wasn't too extraordinary; Loud music, louder people, lots of shadows. "Jensen, how did you even hear about this place?"

He grinned, ear to ear, "I have my connections. Do you like it?"

"It's a club."

His grin fell, slightly, then he noticed the bar on the other end of the room. He pointed to it, then began the long trek to the crowded bar that would take longer than Moses out of Egypt. "Stay close, I'll get the first round."

Lauren was already gone.

The music was nothing more than pounding against my skull, but satisfying, like hammering a nail into a wall. Bodies brushed past me, on me, around me, slick with perspiration and ecstasy. The first time I had been to a club was two years ago, to a shoddy 18+ joint a few blocks away.

When Andrea gave me my first fake ID, her lips contorted to suppress a grin. "I figured this could work, right? I mean, you kind of look like my brother, right?" The car was still warm, even with the engine off. Nothing was particularly special about that night, just that it was our first Saturday of the year that didn't have some sort of book report due on Monday. And it was our something-month anniversary, or something. Nothing important.

"I feel uncomfortable that you think I look like your brother," I said, rubbing my thumb over card. He had shaggy brown hair in the photo with a deadpan expression and wide eyes. "How long is he in town anyway?"

"Tony? Probably just until Sunday, I'm surprised he came home for just a normal weekend. He's always complaining about how busy his classes are and stuff." She shrugged, "I'm going to use his girlfriend's, she's spending the weekend too."

"Does she…look like you?"

"Well, she has green eyes, but close enough, right?" She held up the girl's ID for me to see.

"Do you and your brother have a creepy attraction to each other?" She looked exactly like Andrea.

"Don't be disgusting."

It was weird. I slipped Tony's card into my wallet, watching Andrea re-bobby pin her hair in the rearview mirror. "So, how's your dancing?"

She smiled into the mirror. "Well, all I really have to do is shake my butt. You're the one that actually needs to know how to dance."

"The two step is my safety net."

"Since when do you play safe?" She glanced at me from the corner of her eye, in time to see one of the three times she said something that caught me off guard. "I'm expecting you to drop it low, Ricky."

I laughed, "Ask, and you shall receive."

"What?" Andrea gave me an unamused look, her features slowly morphing into the present day bartender, one eyebrow cocked to his hairline.

"What?" I repeated, the syllables toppling off my lips. Music flooded back into the scene, the hot wet air coming down soon after. Suffocating.

"Open or closed?" He repeated again, then signaled to someone at the other end of the bar that he was on his way. I think I had maybe forty-seven dollars left from tutoring in my bank account. "Better close it."

The bartender leaned in, squinting. His earring was distracting. "Uh, I'm going to assume you said close."

"Sure."

He left my view, or maybe I just closed my eyes. Jensen magically appeared next to me, his hand on my shoulder. "Dude, I've been looking for you for like ten minutes, you're already back?"

"I finished my drink."

"Ah, that makes sense then." We nodded at each other. "What drink did you get anyway?"

I shrugged, and on cue the bartender slide a dark shot glass towards me. Then lit it on fire. "That, I think."

"That's a good time."

I lifted the shot glass and downed it. Tasted a little like warm pumpkin pie.

Jensen pried the glass from my fingers before I dropped it. "Shit, aren't you supposed to blow that out first?" He wiped his mouth after he finished off his drink.

"What?"

"I'm going to grab you some water." But before he could make it to the self-serve water station, Katie dragged us back to the dancefloor, swaying her hips to the music. I let her nimble fingers wrap around my wrist, coaxing me into the mood with her.

She parted my legs with her knees, pulsing her chest against mine. I steadied myself on her shoulder, but she moved my hand into her hair. "Get loose, I got you." She shouted, but the words were just a whisper.

Let go.

She danced under my arms, a nymph under the lights. She had always been agile on her feet. I asked her once why she didn't try out for a sports team, like track or soccer, but she laughed off the suggestion, citing no one on the team had a sense of humor.

"What about Blake?"

"Well. Except Blake."

She didn't want to join the dance team or cheer squad either, even though she looked for any excuse to dance to whatever music played in her head. Apparently those teams were too vapid as well.

"What about Andrea?"

"Oh yeah, she's on the team. I forgot." But not an exception.

Katie snapped her fingers in front of me, and we were back in the club. "Over my shoulder, straight ahead," she repeated, then ducked out of view. People left so quickly.

I was approached by the girl Katie pointed, dressed in something closer to black plastic wrap than actual fabric. She sauntered forward like a panther. Stalking. The glitter in her cleavage caught my attention more than her face, and within a bass drop she was rolling her shoulders next to me.

"Hi," she purred, eyes dilated so only a ring of green outlined her pupils.

"Catwoman," was the smoothest line I could come up with. She put her hands on my shoulders, claws digging into the back of my neck.

She didn't bother for conversation, which was fine by me, tossing her head to the beat of the music and bringing me along with her. Dancing didn't make any logical sense, but it was therapeutic.

As long as we were dancing, we were living. As long as we were moving, we weren't dead.

I melted into her, swimming in and out of consciousness. I was light, but not weightless. Jensen kept me held down, yelling in my ear about his dance partner stepping on his expensive shoes.

One of my feet on the ground and the other in the clouds, I blended between the two like an anchored balloon in a field, brushing along the grass. "Hey," her hot breath fogged the inside of my ear, wet lips brushing my jaw line. "Follow me to the bathroom?"

Might as well.

"Maybe you need some help?" Her voice was genuine, and suddenly we were transported into the bathroom. My back against the last stall on the left, the door slightly cracked because the lock didn't slide just right and the light flickered in sync with a buzzing hum but there was no fly. My eyes rolled from the back of my head down to her, kneeled in front of me with one knee in a questionable wet spot near the base of an even more questionable toilet.

"Maybe." My voice was barely above a whisper, the tightness in my chest gripping my vocal chords.

I noticed her hair was a dirty blonde, with grown-out highlights. She wiped her red lips with the back of her hand, rolling off the condom with the other. "It's probably just the alcohol, don't worry about it," She swatted at the invisible fly, holding onto the toilet paper roll to get to her feet. "You just need a pick-me-up."

I couldn't remember a time that I didn't need a pick-me-up.

She dangled a tiny Ziplock bag in front of me, the white huddled in one of the corners. "Pick me up!" She repeated with a giggle.

"Where were you keeping that?"

She ignored my question, flipping her hair over her shoulder. "You cool?"

"Like a pickle."

"Cucumber?"

"Pepperoncini."

"What?"

"Nevermind." I fumbled with the zipper to my pants before finally giving up. "We're not going to use the toilet, are we?" A rented concert hall bathroom was one thing, but a grungy nightclub broken stall where the tampon trashcan didn't have a lid was beyond even my drunk judgement.

"The toilet? What? You're so funny!" She giggled too loudly again, hair flipping to the other shoulder. "Should be enough for both of us." She opened the bag, dipping her pinky finger into the bag, then quickly sniffing the little mound.

"Shouldn't we wash our hands or something?"

"Just don't think about it."

"Okay." I copied, dipping my pinky. Cocaine used to be medically prescribed as a pain killer.

She giggled, as I did a post-sniff, squeezing my nostrils. I pinched the bridge of my nose, squeezing my eyes shut to stop the room from spinning just a little. She was talking, but her words swirled around my head until a warm rush of euphoria shot down my throat. "What's your name again?" She pressed her hand against my chest.

I couldn't remember what my fake ID said. "Does it matter?"

She shrugged, "I guess not. But it's nice to know since you know."

"Ricky."

"Kim." I nodded. "I don't usually do this, yanno."

"Whatever you say."

"But you're cute," she dragged a nail down the side of my throat, a numb pressure. "Do you want more?" I couldn't shrug fast enough, so she finished it off, squealing and tightly closing her eyes while she bounced from one foot to the other.

"Where do you get it?" My only connection was Max, but if I could get right to the supplier, maybe they had other options. "I want to buy some."

She grinned, "Here, give me your hand." Magically, there was a pen on her hand and a scribbled number on mine.

"Is that your number?" Or was it where she got her drugs?

"Michael," was all she said. She looked up from writing, her eyes wide. "You like taking risks, right?"

Getting a blowjob in a dirty club stall with a stranger and some coke. "I guess."

"Yay! See, you'll be perfect! We'll have fun."

What was that supposed to mean? "Sure."

She wiggled her fingers into my belt loops. "Should I try again? Or, do you want to try me?"

I did feel more awake, a hot wave moving from my neck to my chest, down my arms like pulsing lightning bolts. I needed to get moving. "Dancing. Let's dance." She took my hand, leading me out of the stall and back in front of the sink.

"Here," She placed my hand under running water. "Better?"

Actually, I was. Cocaine was an impressive party trick. "Yeah, thanks." I splashed myself, dabbing my face with the bottom of my shirt, then looked up quickly in her direction. "I usually use a towel."

"Whatever you say." Giggling, she brought me back to dancing. I didn't know where we were, in relation to Jenson and the others, but we were still surrounded, the beat more electronic now. My face was level with Kim, my knees bent and her heels a solid five inches. She grabbed my face, roughly sucking on my bottom lip before shoving her tongue in my mouth. I opened, more uncaring than willing, my hands finding their way to her waist.

"So, Michael." The first thing she said once we could both breathe. I had already forgotten the context. "He's eccentric, but he doesn't mess around with his business. He'll make you do a bunch of weird blah blah blah."

I nodded along, my eyes straying past her to the sparkling lights up above. The couple besides us proclaimed their love for each other loudly, a music of their own, draped over each other like chiffon. Elated. Weightless.

"Rickyyyyyy—" Jensen's wail pulled me from the world, then shout-whispered close to my ear, "Who's your new girlfriend?"

"Kourtney?" Or something. I had to hold on to him.

"Kim," she corrected over my shoulder.

"Khloe?" Jensen laughed, his eyes rolling at his own joke.

"Kim." She reached around me to slap Jensen on the arm. "Oh my GAWD, you're so funny!" Jensen couldn't stop laughing, his thousand dollar teeth almost glowing in the dark. Three years of braces did wonders. His parents spent more time on his teeth than they did on him.

"Ricky, let's get some water now, okay?"

"Okay." I repeated, turning around to my dance partner/new cocaine associate. "Need to go, I'll see around?"

"I'll text you."

I kissed her again, more out of politeness than attraction, then I got kicked out of the club because I couldn't stand up straight.

-9-

I hadn't planned on cutting at school, it just sort of happened. The way nip slips and teenage pregnancies just sort of happened. The term was accident.

Oops.

The razorblade dragged across my forearm and I gritted my teeth as the river welled from my veins, trailing down my fingertips and dropping to the tile with inaudible satisfaction. I didn't need a hall pass. The entire school was my domain to roam. All I had to do was raise my hand and I would be dismissed to the wild barren corridors for as long as I liked. I could always forge an excuse if I chose to skip a class. No one ever bothered to follow up. My body shook, clutching the razor between my thumb and my pointer finger. It wasn't a I'm-cold-and-didn't-bring-a-jacket-to-the-movies kind of shake, more of a foggy shake, like I-hadn't-eaten-in-two-days kind of shake and I could see hallucinations approaching the edge of my bed at night.

A gasp escaped my lips, relief following the blade as I did another line. The ever reliable sting. A literal slap on the wrist for doing something I wasn't supposed to, but no one could stop me. I was the only one who could punish myself.

Why was I punishing myself?

The slice was a freeway curving down my arm, a sea of red brake lights and frustration.

The bathroom door creaked open and my heart sank into to the pit of my stomach. My breath caught itself in the back of my throat. I had ripped the razor out of my backpack so fast I didn't bother locking the stall and I didn't have time to think of an excuse. I scrambled to close the stall door just as their footsteps approached. I hopped onto the toilet, my foot slipping into the bowl.

"Is anyone in here?" One of them called out, knocking on a stall door. I debated whether or not to pull my foot out of the toilet water. "Hellooooo?" The voice rang again, knocking on another stall. My hands pressed against the walls for support, water slowly soaking higher into my jeans. I could see the footsteps stop in front of the stall next to me, a dirty pair of size 10.5 converse original. I couldn't see the other feet, but it sounded like there were at least two others. No one saw me walk into the bathroom, so it couldn't have been related.

"Knock knock." He opened the stall door next to me. Blood trailed its way down my arm and seeped into my sleeve pulled up to the elbow. My eyes darted to the stall, and the latch was just centimeters short of locked. Shit. Sloppy.

The shoes walked to my stall.

Shit.

Then they left.

"I think it's empty, man. Do you have it?"

"Yeah," another voice replied and I instantly identified him as Max. There was some shuffling, and it gave me a second to finally exhale. Just a drug deal, should be pretty fast.

"Where do you get this, anyway? Like Colombia?"

Cocaine.

"Nah, just some chick at a club nearby." There were only two clubs nearby, the 18+, hopefully out of business by now, and the club I went to with Jensen. "She knows a guy so it's really cheap." Was he also getting his supply from Michael?

"Why is there glitter on the bag?"

"Don't worry about it." Max zipped up his backpack, throwing it over his shoulder.

"Thanks, man."

"Nah, thank you."

The third voice mumbled something along the same lines. My toes were turning into raisins. The footsteps headed out, someone pressing all the hand dryers along the way.

I lifted my leg out of the bowl, dripping cold toilet water all over the tile, slowly soaking through the single-ply paper tossed at the base of the seat.

I dabbed at my arm again, but it was still bleeding. After poking my head out to ensure the coast was clear, I grabbed a few of the thicker paper towels from near the sink, pressing it firmly to my arm. I leaned my head back as far as it would go, the ceiling tiles blurring.

"Oh," someone gasped from the entrance. He stared at my arm, then up to me, frozen. "Are you okay? Do you need the nurse?"

Completely blank, that was what the cuts did to me.

He took a step forward, snapping me into action.

"No, I'm fine, it's just a cut." I shrugged a shoulder, "Don't mind me."

He shrugged back, "Okay," on his way to the urinal.

The bleeding stopped, leaving behind a stinging line. I rolled my sleeve down and left the bathroom.

The lost and found, a graveyard of forgotten clothing articles from 1872, provided short basketball shorts that I could change into. There usually weren't too many jeans lying around, probably for the best.

I made it back to math class, just in time for another unnecessary group activity. "Hey, Ricky," Blake waved me over from the front door, seated in a group with Hana and another boy ranking in the upper 200s.

Walking over, I could already feel the scratching again, my skin begging for another cut. "Hey Blake. Hana." Could Hana feel it too? Could she tell my skin ached?

"You're welcome for being saved from having a crappy group." Blake had even moved my backpack over for me.

"Mm, close, but thankfully Hana is here to prevent that." I sat down, reading the board to catch up on the activity as the others copied the problem.

"What are you doing after school?" Hana asked.

"I think I just have a tutoring session and then probably homework." Oh and a date with Kim for exchange of drugs in the middle of the day, middle of surburbia, middle of a mom-n-pop boba café.

Better judgement would advise against this, but better judgement was never any fun.

The date kept my mind off my itching skin, however, and the day passed before I could even think about sawing myself open again. I checked the text message one more time, just to be 100% sure I was actually buying drugs at a café.

I passed a table of two college looking girls, seated outside, crutches propped up against the side of the shop and a leashed white lapdog nested under their feet. One of them, probably named Jackie or Tammy or something, shifted her eyes to me as I passed.

Jackie's boyfriend was only sometimes an asshole. He remembered her birthday and other important anniversaries, but that was all he did. He only remembered. Jackie had to do all the planning, organize every date, suggest every restaurant or night out or vacation destination. His love, or rather lukewarm like, dwindled as the months went by, prompting Jackie to overcompensate to keep her dream of their happiness alive.

She would ask if there was anything wrong, anything from his end that wasn't working, but he would assure her everything was fine. Not great, but fine. A tame 40%. Maybe Jackie was clingy with separation anxiety, but her boyfriend left her unsatisfied. Not often enough for their relationship to end, but with a frequency that made her notice a high school teenager walking into a boba shop. What would her life be like to be with someone that actually cared about her? Someone that loved her.

What would it be like?

The boba shop was what I expected, too colorful. They had a frozen yogurt setup and also apparently sold crepes as well. Versatility was the key to success.

"Ricky!"

I barely avoided jumping at the sound of my name interrupting the soft Korean pop music in the background. Kim sat at a very small table in the corner, waving politely in my direction. Her hair looked a lot blonder in sober daylight. When I approached, she stood up for a quick kiss on the cheek. She also looked a lot older in sober daylight. "Do you want anything? Milk tea? Their sweet crepes are to die for."

I squinted through the bright white lights at the chalkboard menu, but nothing had sounded appealing in days. "No thank you, I just ate."

"I'll feel uncomfortable, go get something." This time, there was order in her voice as she ushered me toward the cashier, suddenly looking a lot like someone's mother.

The cashier paused her Instagram scrolling, sliding her phone under the counter and tucking a loose strand of black hair behind her ear. "Hi, what can I get for you?"

"I don't know, I'll try a boba I guess."

"Okay, what kind?"

"Uh, whichever one is best."

"Have you ever had it before?"

"No, so just whatever is best."

"Well, what kind of flavors do you like?" She smiled wider as I stared back at her. "Our flavors are listed on the board behind me."

I didn't feel like reading. "Which one do you like the best?"

"Do you want more of a tea flavor or something more fruity?"

"What do you recommend?"

"Ummm, well, do you like strawberry?"

"Sure."

"Or mango?"

"Literally anything is fine."

"So even the grossest thing would be fine? Really? What about a honeydew green apple vanilla pudding milk tea?"

"I don't care."

"But you'd actually drink it? That's gross. Is it a dare or something? I think I could make a pretty nasty combination. How gross do you want it? This one time, we had a contest to make the most disgusting drink, and this guy, Bobby, he doesn't work here anymore because he got his girlfriend pregnant or something and his parents sent him to Mississippi thinking the girl would stop contacting him, which is kind of wrong I think, but I don't know what I would do either in their situation I guess. Yeah, anyways, he threw up."

Every single one of my facial features screamed in agony. "Just make whatever is most popular. Please."

"Sure! Small or large?"

I had never wanted a meteor to crash into a small boba café before this moment. "Small." I handed her my card to swipe and she bopped away to fix whatever was the most popular. I checked over my shoulder and Kim was happily sipping her drink and staring out of the store windows. The cashier slid the drink to me, a thick purple straw balanced on top.

I joined Kim back at the table. "I'm de-lighted you decided to try something. Have you ever had it before?" She smiled, small lines forming at the corners of her mouth.

"No."

"Well, that's one thing I can give you!" She winked, and her incoming crow's feet winked back. "Thanks for inviting me out, I wasn't sure I'd hear from you again."

I wasn't either, but it turned out the number on my hand was hers and not where she got her drugs. "Oh, what, no, I had an awesome time with you."

"It's a joke, lighten up, kid." She placed her drink in front of her, a stern look settling onto her face as she interlaced her fingers on the table. Her left hand sparkled.

"You're married." Not a question. I met her eyes.

"Yes." She rubbed the inside of her palm with her thumb. "B-but." I stood up. "Wait, hear me out, sit down." I stayed standing, but I didn't leave. Not without more drugs anyway. She sighed, looking down at the table, shaking her head. "He's a fine guy, my husband. No, he's great. He's so kind and understanding. I loved him."

Past tense.

She continued. "But it's not there, the spark. He's my best friend, but that's all. It's been like that for a long time, maybe before we were married. I'm not even sure if it was ever there." I looked at the cashier, in case she was the one Kim intended to be her therapist instead of me.

The cashier laughed at her phone.

"I haven't been faithful for a long time. A-and he knows that. We've kind of talked about it. He said I should do what makes me happy."

"What makes you happy?"

"Having fun, being my own person," she smiled up at me again, reaching out her hand. "Being free."

Being free.

My head inflated with helium at the very word, air swirling images of myself laid out on my bed, too exhausted to get up, too wired to fall asleep. I rubbed my eyes with the back of my hand to clear it. "Why don't you just divorce him then?" I pocketed my hand, away from her searching fingers.

Kim chuckled at me, that bitch, patting the table. "Life isn't that simple when you're older." She picked up her milk tea, wetting her fingers with the condensation. "But the point is, I wanted to tell you so we can get off on an open and honest relationship."

"Relationship," I repeated, and even I could hear the skepticism in my voice. She was at least fifteen years older than me, but she assumed I was at least twenty-one. "I'm not sure how that would work, or what you're looking for."

"Just something casual, light, fun," she swatted at the air with a giggle. "You're so silly. Relationship. It's not that serious."

For someone so old and condescending, she sure giggled a lot. "Let me see him."

"Who?"

"Your husband. Do you have a picture of him on your phone or something?"

"Well, yes, of course, but—" As I made a move to sit down and rejoin her at the table, she quickly fetched her phone from her purse. "Why do you want to see him?"

"I just want to know who to expect when he finally gets tired of you being a strumpet."

"I'm not British." Another giggle. "You're so funny and cute." Cute didn't seem as big of a compliment from someone the same age as my teachers. "I have an album." She reached across the table to hand me the phone, taking a long sip of her drink. I watched as the black balls shot up her straw, one after another.

Her husband seemed nice enough, from what I could gather the nanosecond before I exited the picture of him playing in a pile of autumn leaves and opened her messages app. Whatever compelled him to stay with someone so—

Black balls, one after another. Kim still hadn't taken a breath, her cheeks sunken in as she sucked, uninterrupted by her seamless swallows.

—someone so giggly, was beyond the realm of my understanding.

Her messages were crowded with different numbers, a mix of men and women. A text from two days ago caught my eye, but her drink was getting low and her attention drifting back to me. "How long have you two been married?" I threw her a question, opening the conversation on her phone.

"Mm, going on," She looked up at the polka dotted ceiling. "Twelve years in June."

The conversation was with a man named Michael, the name she went on about at the club. He was having a party tonight, and more product for her to try out, but unfortunately Kim couldn't make it because already had plans. Michael texted her the address anyway.

"Do you ever want to get married, Ricky?"

I looked up, closing the message app and switching her phone back to the album of her husband. "Married?" I slid the phone to her. Andrea liked to talk about weddings a lot, hypothetically of course, batting her eyelashes as she squeezed my arm. "I've never really thought about it."

Kim nodded. "You're still young, that makes sense." She took one last sip, her straw sucking air.

"I guess."

"It's not for everyone."

"I can tell." Her eyebrow raised at me, wrinkles forming on her forehead. "So, what are you doing tonight?"

"Oh, I'm meeting with a friend, nothing extravagant," She pointed her straw towards me. "What are you doing, cutie? Studying for your exams?" I hadn't checked my emails all day. Where were my acceptance letters? I could have applied early admission, but I was following along with Blake's university prep schedule to help guide him.

Inhale.

"What makes you think I'm in school?"

"I can tell you're smart, and you seem half-way motivated," she paused, lifting a hand to cover her mouth. "Even though I met you blackout wasted."

"I wasn't blacked out."

"You kept calling me Aubrey or something." She giggled and my breath left my lungs. "You could barely keep your eyes focused on one thing."

"I need to go." I stood up, swallowing. My hands were already starting to clam up. I just needed to focus on something, anything, and it would go away. But I needed to get out first.

"What? Wait—" She halfway raised out of her seat, but I had already started for the door. "You haven't even touched your drink, wait!"

The cool of the metal door handle felt refreshing, a release. "I'll text you later, have fun tonight."

Homework was an easy distraction and necessary to keep up appearances that I actually cared about the few months left of high school. I had already finished my paper at lunch, so there was just math left. I punched the formula into my calculator with the end of my pen.

It was mindless work and my thoughts kept racing back to that feeling. My fist tightened around the pen and I forced myself to concentrate.

Blake criss-crossed his legs on my bedroom floor, shuffling his card deck in front of him. "Come play Go Fish with me."

"No."

"I'm bored."

"Play with yourself."

"Already did." Blake blew his lips out. "Come onnnnnn, it's not even due tomorrow." He threw the card box at my shoulder. I spun my chair around to look at him and he wiggled his finger at me. "It's like a brain exercise or whatever. It'll keep you young."

"You're not going to let me say no are you?"

He smiled.

I sighed, "Alright sure." As he cheered, I tossed my phone over my shoulder to my bed, joining Blake on the floor. "How was work?"

"Huh? I didn't have work today, remember?"

I was briefly taken aback, but I covered it with a laugh. "Oh, right right, that's tomorrow."

"I have practice tomorrow." Blake, co-captain of cross-country. Top 210 in academics, mostly from my tutoring and grade altering, top 20 in both personality and looks. Not so successful at keeping a girlfriend, but that was his own business.

"Right, practice, I forgot."

"You? Forgetful? Maybe you're getting old and senile." His bridge fell apart at the last minute and he took his sweet leisurely time picking the cards back up. "So."

"So?"

Blake dealt seven cards to both of us. I already had a set of tens, so I placed them down in front of me. He took a deep overly dramatic breath. "What's up with you, Ricky? You've been all distant and shit and I don't like it." His eyes stayed on the cards, but he felt my flinch. "I didn't mean to say that. It's not that I don't like your feelings, I just don't like that you're feeling that way. If that makes sense." He looked up, "Do you know what I mean?"

The skin on the underside of my arms itched. "No."

He huffed, "You're mopey, you're being all lazy and wasting the day away, you don't talk to anyone—"

"Anyone like who?"

"Like me!"

"Blake, are you feeling a little neglected?"

"Shut up, don't make this about me. But yes. And also, I just feel like, you're drifting and you're not a drifter. You're a trailblazer, but it's almost like your flame is extinguished and it worries me." He messed up the bridge again.

"That's a very inspirational speech."

"Don't belittle me, asshole." I half-rolled my eyes, leaning back on my hands as Blake shuffled through his cards. "Do you have any sevens?"

"Go fish."

Blake drew a card, slowly. "Honestly, I feel like you're drinking too much and it makes me uncomfortable."

"Drinking too much?" It hadn't crossed my mind.

"Really?" He scratched his eyebrow. "You don't think so?"

"No, I don't." My chest hurt. "Do you have any twos?"

"Go fish." He pursed his lips as though he were about to give a presidential campaign speech, dealing cards in my direction. "Well. You know the first step is admitting you have a problem."

Alcohol wasn't the problem. "Whatever."

Inhale.

I drew a card, a seven.

"Ricky, do you have a four?"

"Go fish."

"What are you doing tonight, then? Drinking?" Blake drew his card.

"No, I'm actually hanging out with Hana." I hadn't told her yet, but that was what we were going to do. "Give me your seven."

"Cute." He studied his hand, plucking out his seven for me. "Do you like her?"

"Yeah, she's nice." I backpedaled, Blake already imagining being a Best Man. "I mean, I just like talking to her, she's interesting, but I'm not into her like that. Do you have any queens?"

"Uh huh, sure." Blake handed over another card.

"Do you have any kings?

"Go fish." I drew the king I needed, then placed the matching pair down. Blake took a long time, readjusting the cards in his hand. Every passing second felt like a silent eternity, my vision tunneling on the back of his cards.

"Actually," I stood to my feet, skin burning. "I should probably get going to Hana's house if we're going to make it up the hill before it gets too late."

Blake looked up at me, a sudden jerk compared to his previous turtle pace. It was giving me motion sickness. "Up the hill? What are you doing?"

I had to use both of my hands to push myself standing, black spots twinkling in my head. "Stargazing." Was the first thing I could think of.

"Huh, right. But you're not into her like that."

"Whatever." I grabbed my phone, paused, then grabbed the top blanket from my bed. If I could get out, I could avoid the scratch.

"Wait, what about the game? You're just gonna ditch me again?"

"You can't really ditch someone that never leaves."

"You suck, I hope you have a miserable time without me." He took one last look at his hands. "Wait, did you ever get a four?"

I threw my cards at him. "Go fish."

"Go fuck yourself."

The fact that Hana was only a quick ten minute drive was a plus. I could tell her I was coming over and it would give her just enough time to get dressed and meet me at the door.

I texted her that I was outside five minutes before I actually pulled up to her apartment building, so she was already on the doorstep waiting for me in a dreary oversized sweater, black leggings, and her combat boots. Her hair was in two long braids, poking out from under a beanie. She hopped down the stairs in time to my bouncing knee, antsy from the itch.

Thud.

Thud.

Thud.

A heartbeat, just barely under my skin. I tugged at the end of my long sleeve shirt. It was a quick relief, but getting harder to hide. My arm was beginning to look like a game of tic-tac-toe.

I unlocked the door for her and she slung her backpack in first, then the rest of her. "What's up?"

When was the last time she cut? "Uh, just bored," I smiled, bringing my eyes away from her arms. "Did you have homework or something?"

She nodded, touching her backpack in case I didn't see it taking up half of her leg space. "You don't mind if I work on it, right? You said you just wanted to hang out?"

"Yeah, just hang out," I repeated, then backed out and started driving. "What time do you need to be back?"

"My mom is working overtime tonight, so she won't be back until the morning. So, whenever I guess."

"Whenever it is then."

She was mostly quiet for the drive, focused on her sheet of paper but her pencil never moved. She tapped the end of her pencil against her notebook. "Do you like stars?" I finally asked.

"Stars? Like, in the sky?"

"They're typically in the sky, yes."

She continued to tap her pencil.

Thud.

Thud.

She let out a breath. "Yeah, I mean I guess they're pretty cool. Do you?"

"I do." When I was seven, my father helped me paint the walls of my bedroom black and we put glow-in-the-dark constellations on the ceiling. That was the last thing we did together that I actually cared about.

My walls were white now.

"Are we going to look at stars tonight?" She asked, tilting her head out the window, the sun slowly setting behind the mountains.

"If that's okay with you."

"That sounds fun, sure!"

"Great." She finished up her homework as my truck climbed the mountain. I was relieved, finding there was no one else parked in my usual spot. The mountain was hushed, only the rustling of nature quietly alive and just out of sight. She stayed in the cabin with the overhead light on as I covered the bed of the truck with the blanket I packed and the one I always kept in the back of the cabin. "Hey, it's all ready," I knocked on the back window.

"It looks so cozy!"

Cozy wasn't exactly the right word. It looked like the time Blake climbed up to my window one night, at least seven or eight winters ago. I wasn't busy at the time, just reading some odd book, my back pressed against the wall of my bed and my legs tucked under the blanket.

I was mildly concerned about when I would get a growth spurt, most of the girls in my grade were already inching their way taller than me, but we had a puberty seminar that explained boys grew later so I wasn't too worried. I just didn't like being slower.

A rapping came from my frosted window and I immediately looked to see the culprit. Maybe it would be something exciting like a talking raccoon, though those weren't real. Blake's tiny hand tip tapped to me, then a frantic wave after he saw my attention was on him.

Blake used to resemble a scarecrow, drowning in size S clothes that threatened to swallow him whole. He balanced on the branch outside my window, smiling.

I dog-eared the book, setting it down on the corner of my desk before I sauntered over to him. His busted lip from the week before was mostly faded, and there wasn't anything new from what I could tell. I lifted my window and the pre-Thanksgiving chill swept in.

"Hey Ricky!"

"Are you staying the night?" I moved aside so he could climb in.

He hummed, sliding through the open window. "I haven't decided yet."

"So. That's a yes. Have you eaten dinner yet?"

"I'm actually not really hungry right now."

"I'll go grab some leftovers from dinner, it was average."

I brought back a plate of carved ham and rosemary mashed potatoes, a practice run of the actual Thanksgiving menu for next week when the entire family joined in. My mother didn't want any more shit from her sister-in-law this year for a poorly glazed ham.

Blake sat in the middle of my floor, scooping the mashed potatoes onto a cube of cornbread. He was blabbering about something, probably turkey pardoning or Pilgrims and Native Americans, but I was watching his lips move, wondering why I was incapable of hearing the words coming out.

"Blake," I interrupted his miming, "Was it cloudy outside?"

"Cloudy?" His voice rang back in tune. "Uh, yup, it was pretty cloudy I guess. You couldn't even see the moon." He trailed off, forgetting to paste his smile back on.

"Hm." I pulled all the blankets off of my bed, tugging them over to Blake. "That's okay, I can make the stars appear." As Blake slurped up the last of his green beans, I flipped off the lamp.

Plastic stars illuminated the dark, almost lighting up my own eyes. Almost. I plopped down on my blankets, patting the space next to me. It wasn't much, but it was enough. When I was older, I would invest in fluffier blankets.

"I don't want to spill the gravy."

"You worry too much."

He joined me, leaning back. "When do you think he'll stop?" I hadn't noticed Blake holding his side before.

"He probably won't." In the corner of my room was Orion. It was a lot more brilliant in the real sky, but I chose the darkest corner for those stars. I liked Orion because it looked like a virus. "People are kind of like viruses."

"What's a virus?"

"You know, like. The organism that gives you the flu."

"Oh, you mean like a bacteria germ?"

"Sure."

"Oh," he paused. "So you're saying people make other people sick?"

"In some cases, probably." Viruses require a host to survive. Without a host, they die. But once they get to the host, once they achieve their goal, what was the point? Then what?

"Do I ever make you sick, Ricky?"

"No, I don't think so." I rolled my head to look at him. "Do I make you sick?"

"No, you make me feel better!"

Some people didn't know they were sick until the virus had already taken over their body.

I wouldn't have described that room as cozy, lying on a mound of blankets messily thrown together so we would have somewhere to be –anywhere that wasn't there. Cozy was warm and welcoming. Cozy was an invitation to stay, to enjoy the now. It wasn't cozy, but back then, it was something.

Hana wiggled her eyebrows, "I said it looks cozy!" She spoke a little louder, as if I simply hadn't heard her instead of stopped listening.

"Oh. Right. Yeah, cozy." I usually tried to pack at least four or five blankets, pillows, snacks, and a thermos, but this was a rush job. "Let me help you up." I held my hand out to her, but it was shaking.

She didn't notice. "Thanks!" She grunted, climbing into the back. "So, how does this work?"

"You've never been stargazing before?" She fumbled over an excuse. I sighed, shaking my head. "That explains a lot."

She swatted in my direction, half-heartedly. "Seriously though, do we just look up?" Hana's neck cracked as she lifted her face 90 degrees to the night sky.

"Scoot over here," I instructed, even though I scooted toward her. I stretched out my legs, lying down and patting the space next to me. "A lot easier on your neck if you lie down." Hesitantly, she nestled into the crook under my arm, her warm body resting against me. Lavender floated from her hair. "Easier?" She nodded, stiff.

Our eyes adjusted in silence. "Which one is the north star?" She asked.

"In the north." She nudged me. "Do you know what the big dipper looks like?"

"What's a dipper?"

I side glanced at the top of her head, but she was serious. "Kind of like a ladle." I pointed at the end of the big dipper handle, following the outline with my finger. "Do you see it?"

"Oh, that thing? That's the famous one, right?"

"Sure. Now, if you follow the point of the big dipper," I moved my finger across the sky. "It will lead you to the north star."

"That one?" She pointed at blackness. I moved her hand to point at the actual star. "Ohhh, I see it now." She paused a beat. "I thought it was supposed to be the brightest or something."

"It's not. But it's basically the center of the northern sky, if that's at all impressive to you." I began tracing again. "It's also the end of the little dipper."

"How many dippers are there?"

"Depends on what you consider a dipper."

She nodded. "What else is there?"

"An entire universe." I pulled her closer, for warmth, burying the side of my face in her hair. It wasn't too cold outside, but it felt like my entire body was shaking. How did she not notice?

People were made of stars. We were the universe. Hana's voice was a mosquito buzz behind the loud ringing in my ears. She was saying something, but I couldn't hear her under the water. I was so heavy, sinking, the stars swallowing me.

"Ricky," She turned the top of her body to face me. "Are you asleep?"

"Hm?"

"I said this is really nice."

"It is."

"I like hanging out with you."

"You're surprisingly okay to hang out with too."

"Surprisingly?"

I nudged her back. "We'll have to do it more often then, yeah?"

"Deal." Hana tucked her head back into my chest and I

drifted back to the peaceful underwater. Not exactly cozy, but it was something. I could've stayed there forever, underwater, asleep.

-10-

She was making me soft.

I closed my eyes, desperately trying to power through the nauseating affect Samantha generally had on me. She actually liked me, so I almost felt bad about leading her on.

By leading her on, I meant sleeping with her.

Or was she sleeping with me?

Samantha was the one who should've felt bad taking advantage of drunk little ol' me. Standard house party, but I didn't know the host, not that it mattered at a house party. The host was a sophomore at the community college nearby.

Jensen knew him from their bible camp days. It was the host's birthday party, but he passed out in the downstairs bathroom thirty minutes in.

I decided to mingle. "Tell me again how the theory of relativity works," I prompted some dude in the dining room. He had been going on and on about being a physics major, but couldn't even tell the difference between special theory and the general theory.

"It's all relative," he answered, leaning against the wall, lapping up the rest of his drink. "You'll get it in a couple years."

I lubricated my mouth with more jungle juice. "A couple of years huh? Then how long will it take you?"

Samantha pulled on my arm, "I've been looking for you." My drink sploshed down my arm. "Okay Sloppy, that's enough for you." Her fingers moved lightning fast, snatching my drink away. I could see every detail of her hand, from her translucent arm hair to the individual cells on her skin. The music was so loud music notes throbbed in the air.

"Samantha wait," I reached back for my cup. She tightened her grip between my fingers, leading me away and shoving a glass of vodka in my face. Or water. One of those. We ran into an end table, knocking over a glass vase that shattered when it hit the floor.

Samantha pushed herself against the wall, pulling me into her by the front of my shirt. Everything was too hot. Her fingers around my neck, her breath on my chin, the pit in my chest.

She had cornered me in the back hallway, too drunk to tell the wicked witches from the good ones. Samantha shoved her tongue down my throat and her hand down my pants and then we were in a room with a bed and my clothes already half stripped away.

"Wait," I croaked out, clutching onto my long sleeve shirt.

Samantha halted, "What?"

If I did nothing, the pit would take over. But what was I supposed to do? What did it want? Questions shot out of my mind but I didn't have any answers.

Samantha shook her head at my jumbled words. "What are you saying?"

I didn't know. I wasn't good at listening. Did it even matter? Doing something, anything, was better than nothing. I swallowed the frog in my throat. "Fuck it, alright." I took the condom from her.

If I was completely honest, Samantha wasn't even all that bad, aesthetically. But I couldn't stay aroused. She might as well had been my grandmother. She wasn't even all that bad personality-wise either. Just not my type.

"Are you okay?" She asked, yet she kept moving her hips back and forth against me like she was riding one of those 50 cent merry-go-rounds outside the grocery store.

"Never better."

Please make her stop.

She ran her fake nails through my hair again, tugging softly as she exaggerated her moans.

I was slipping out.

Fuck.

"Samantha," I tried, but either I mumbled too softly or her fake orgasm noises were too loud. The room was spinning. She threw her head back, sending matted red curls flying over her freckled shoulders, exposing her lacy black bra.

I was going to throw up.

Samantha bit her lip while she writhed her body with one last loud exhale. "Wow," She was breathy from her performance, climbing off.

The ceiling was a white cheddar popcorn texture. We laid on the bed, facing opposite directions. Minutes ticked by, but there was no clock. Only music notes sweeping in under the bedroom door. "Samantha."

"You don't have to say anything, um." She flipped over, grabbing a piece of whatever she was wearing from the floor where it had been hastily discarded. I let her dress alone but I couldn't close my eyes without the room spinning. She watched me watch the ceiling. "Do you need help?"

Probably. "Getting dressed?"

"Yeah." She continued gathering clothes from the floor.

"Did we have sex?"

"What?"

I spoke louder and focused on sounding out each word, the individual letters curving into the air after I spoke. "Sex? That's what we were doing, right?"

"Well, if that's what you want to call it."

"There's the sass I know and tolerate."

She huffed, throwing my pants at me. I still hadn't moved.

"Ricky, seriously, what was that?!"

"You're going to have to be more specific." I was so tired, but my mind was too occupied, unable to let me rest. Instead, it morphed the ceiling texture into little popcorn faces, staring down at me.

Samantha just huffed more, making gestures I couldn't make out in my peripheral vision. "Is it me? Am I ugly or something?"

"About a 7."

"That's not funny anymore!" Her voice rose louder. The popcorn faces widened their eyes. "You know I like you! Okay? I said it, I like you and I know you already knew that but you just like to mess with people and play games. I'm really fucking tired of it!"

The popcorn face with the beard shook his head. "She has a point, Ricky. You're being a fuckboy." The one with only half a face agreed with him.

Fuckboy, fuckboy, fuckboy, they chanted.

I rolled my head towards Samantha. Her arms were crossed and all three of her eyes had eyeliner trails down her cheeks, frizzy curls weighted to one side of her heavy head. A very sad clown in a bodycon dress. I sighed, the exhale shutting up the ceiling audience. "Do you want to know the truth, Samantha?"

She didn't reply, but took a step forward, desperate for something I couldn't give her.

The truth would be too easy.

"This is too fast for me. I'm way too drunk right now and," With a little struggle, I managed to prop myself up on my elbow. "Sex is supposed to be…" I saw a rom-com once, what was that phrase they used? "Special. Not like this. I'm sorry, I should have probably said something, but I got caught up and well, you know the rest."

"Really?"

I had to think really hard to read the intonation in her voice. "Samantha, you're so smart and dedicated. And you're beautiful."

"Ricky."

"Okay, maybe like a 7."

"Shut the fuck up." She threw my socks and shoes to me, but she was smiling, teeth slightly stained yellow from her three thermoses of coffee she downed every day during school. "So, what do you want to do?"

That was a good question, Samantha.

The faces on the ceiling didn't know the answer either. "Could you get me some water? And," I closed my eyes, feeling the burn behind my lids. "Maybe a trashcan too. Please." I heard the door shut behind her and I reached over to my pants, dragging the denim over to my mouth. I fished out an antidepressant and swallowed, falling back onto the bed.

Sometime later, I wasn't keeping track, she came back in the room. Her makeup was cleaned up and her hair thrown into her homework ponytail. She placed the trashcan at the side of the bed and the water on the wood nightstand. "What's wrong?" Samantha asked, but I was lost in the ceiling, miles away.

She climbed over me and onto the bed. The bed welcomed her with a light moan from the mattress, the down comforter plush. Too soft. No support, or at least, never the right amount. Samantha wrapped her arms around me, rolling me on my side to face her.

We looked at each other for a long time, which could have been eternity or only four minutes. She ran her hands through my hair, scratching my scalp with her nails, massaging the thoughts back to my subconscious. "You have sad eyes, Ricky."

I blinked, narrowing them. "What's that supposed to mean?"

"I don't know. They just look a little blank."

"Maybe there's something wrong with your eyes."

"You know what I mean." She looked down, towards the base of my neck. Her hair still smelled like cucumber. Or maybe it was pepperoncini.

"Scoot closer to me." I rested my chin on her head as she nuzzled into my chest. "Why do you like me?"

"What?"

"Is there something wrong with your ears too?"

"You're an asshole."

"Why do you like me?"

I could feel her breath against my skin, too hot. "Because you're incredible." Her eyelashes brushed against me, but only one set because the other one had fallen off earlier. "You can do anything, Ricky. You have so much going for you. It's inspiring. You're so smart, and cute, and you're funny but in a weird rude jerk way so it's kind of hot."

"Go on."

"Shut up." But she laughed. "I just like you, okay? I don't know why and I wish I didn't because you don't like me back."

"Should I lie to make you feel better?"

"I hate you so fucking much."

"Have I always had sad eyes?"

"Huh?" She pulled her head away to look at me again. "Um, I think so? Sorry, I didn't mean like, crying-sad, just kind of like. Nothingness. Wait, that sounds bad too. Just forget I said that, okay? It's the dark and mysterious look." She opened her eyes really wide. "What do mine look like?"

Desperation. "Um. Brown?"

"Well, duh. Look deeper."

Still just desperate. "Bright, I guess."

"Really?" She smiled. "Like, youthful and stuff?"

"Sure."

She paused a beat. "Do you only like girls with sad-mysterious eyes?"

"I haven't noticed." The pit opened again behind my lungs.

"Hana is kind of mysterious like that."

"Hana is just a friend." I sat up, taking a sip from the luke-warm water on the table. "Why are you so jealous of her?"

She ignored the question. "What's wrong then?"

I made myself puke for half an hour straight.

Last year, I took the SATs a total of six times and the ACT three. I was ambitious, but mostly bored. I didn't necessarily desire to go to an Ivy League, but it would be fun to test my eligibility. My entire life I spent endless nights setting myself up for success, constructing thirty and forty year life goals. College was only the beginning.

My first time taking the SATs, I sat in the front of the classroom, finishing each section almost twenty minutes early and tapping my #2 pencil against the desk at all the people behind me that couldn't keep up. I had started studying freshmen year of high school so the questions were just remnants of all the practice tests I had clobbered through in my reviews.

I hadn't faltered on a math question since first grade and I could write Federalist Paper-grade essays in my sleep, but reading had always been my least favorite activity. Reading was too slow, too ambiguous. I consistently missed one or two questions in the reading section of the practice tests because I would get bored halfway through the passage and just assume the rest.

There was a saying about assuming things.

The new SAT, different from my practice tests, only had two sections, and most students (and the one random adult trying to go back to school) opted out of the optional essay portion since it wouldn't directly affect their hard score, which was now out of 1600. Since I was neither most students nor a random adult, I stayed seated and frankly set a new standard for SAT essays.

I got a perfect score.

My second time taking the SATs, I was curious if I could do it again. Results were useless if they couldn't be replicated. Blake sat in front of me, absentmindedly biting the nail on his left ring finger as he skipped every other math question. And then every other reading question. And then basically gave up entirely towards the end, drawing giraffes in the test pamphlet to pass the time.

I had already gotten my score, but could I get away with doing the same for someone else? Before the thought was finished, I had already erased my name and bubbled in Blake Harper on the front while he attempted to go back to answer half of the test that he skipped. I even changed a few of my answers, just to make things more believable.

When they announced the end of the test, the test takers harmoniously packed their belongings silently, rose to their feet, and walked to the front of the classroom to turn in their tests. Blake whispered shit, shit, shit under his breath, aimlessly bubbling in the rest of his answers.

I waited until the millisecond before he stood up to do the exact same, slamming into him and knocking both our tests on the floor.

"Sorry," I quickly apologized, snatching his test from the ground.

"No blood no foul," he brushed it off with a tired smile and picked up my test, briefly glancing at the front to make sure it was his. Easier than I expected, but thrilling none the less.

The other four tests I had taken were for people who I roughly resembled enough that there wouldn't be any questions when I took the test at four very different locations. One, for Jensen, who literally paid me two thousand dollars. After that, I was a freelance test taker.

If I believed in gap years, I had already saved up enough money to backpack through South America.

Samantha was docked points in the math section. She retook the test twice and received the same near-perfect score. When I looked at her now, lying in bed next to me with her hands still in my hair and recounting about some bitch on the swim team trying to get out of practice, I only saw second place.

Four cups of water, two multivitamin gummy bears, and a turkey avocado sandwich later, Samantha's near perfect math worked well enough to numb the fire in my chest. I scooted to the edge of the bed, placing my feet on the carpet. "Do you mind taking me somewhere?"

"Only if you finish the sandwich." She found my shoes and slid them onto my feet. She looped my arm over her shoulder, counting to three as she helped me to my feet. Samantha led me into the hallway, music overtaking my ears. "Do you need to use the restroom?" She swept my hair away from my face. "Maybe freshen up a bit?"

"I get the hint."

I stumbled into the bathroom, but at least I had half the mind to lock the door behind me. I turned on the sink faucet, letting it run, leaning over the cabinet.

And I started bawling.

I don't know why, or how, but as soon as the first sob erupted, my entire chest was writhing. The sounds coming out of my mouth were unrecognizable, they weren't me, and they weren't stopping. I clutched onto the counter for support, letting the tears and snot and whatever else drain down my face.

Splitting aches shot across my skull, a tart whisper snaking through my mind. I pulled at my hair, still convulsing with tears. Why did this keep happening?

For the past month and a half, especially the last two weeks, I couldn't stop crying. Most of the time, it was random. The events were seemingly unrelated: sitting at my desk, in the shower, driving basically anywhere at any time. I would be minding my own business, staring straight ahead, and a wave would sweep over me for the shadows of my mind.

The one thing they had in common was that I was alone. Always alone. The bathroom ceiling was lined with stars, but whenever I looked to them, they faded, dissolving into the plain cream paint.

I flung open the medicine cabinet, knocking a few bottles off the shelf. I lifted a little cup out of the cabinet, blinking through tears.

A little orange disposable razor.

And tweezers.

There were a lot of reasons to extract the blade from a disposable razor, I reasoned to myself. For example, a razor blade could be useful for scraping algae off aquarium tank glass. I didn't particularly like fish though.

Reason was calming.

I jammed one tip of the tweezers under the front case, twisting the tweezers until the case popped off, exposing the blade.

Also, a razor blade could be used to remove dried paint from clothing. Lots of people painted. Millions of artists around the world painted their feelings and memories and their own truths, a token of themselves in each piece. People sometimes painted nurseries. That didn't always work out though.

My breathing had slowed, only hiccups now slipping out. My hands were deliberate, prying the blade from the plastic.

Razors could also be used to remove pills from sweaters.

I held the blade in one hand, staring at it, while the other yanked the sleeve of my shirt up to my armpit.

In cold weather, a razor blade could be used as an emergency ice scraper. I scraped the razor across my bicep, slow, dragging it through my icy skin.

Careful not to press to hard, or the glass could shatter.

It was only one cut, enough to quiet the cries and cover the hole, nothing too drastic. I wadded up a handful of toilet paper, pressing it against the wound and exhaling, but the pain was deeper this time.

I pulled the paper back and more blood seeped forward. I wasn't careful enough.

Shit.

Down on my knees, I rolled up nearly half the toilet paper roll but red still soaked through. It wasn't the bleeding I was concerned about, I couldn't care less actually, but it was the fact that I needed to be somewhere in an hour. I was not an unintentionally late kind of person.

I leaned my arm against the counter, elevated above my head. If the bleeding stopped after twenty minutes, then I could wrap it up and call it a night. If the bleeding didn't stop, I would have another issue.

"Ricky?" Samantha knocked on the other end of the door. "I brought some water for you. Open." I didn't answer. "Open, or I'm not dropping you off."

Another issue. "I'm throwing up, give me a second." The doorknob rattled, but the lock was secure. I picked myself up. My eyes were red and my face blotchy, but I was calm. There was no way I would be able to keep her outside with one injured arm and the other applying pressure.

"Open the fucking door." She was banging now.

I rolled down my sleeve over the wad of paper and unlocked the door, keeping my foot at the base so it wouldn't open more than a few inches. Samantha shoved her head in the crack. I extended my hand out to her instead, taking the glass. "Thank you."

"Let me come in."

"Can I just throw up in peace, please?"

"No."

"Why are you always so annoying?"

"Why are you always such a drunk mess?"

I didn't know.

She backed off, eyes wide. "Fine, I'll stay out here. But promise me you'll drink the water, okay?"

I lifted the glass to my lips, my cut bicep screaming in protest. "Happy?"

"Slightly."

"Marginally."

"Shut up."

I closed the door.

I pressed my back against the door, sliding into a sit. "Just give me ten minutes, okay?" I heard her slide down the other side. For twenty minutes, we sat. On the other side, she pulled flashcards out of her purse, shuffling through physics equations. On the other side, I cried in silence.

Cold air had an annoying habit of sobering me up. Samantha's car was a small coup that looked more expensive than its actual price.

Cars usually had the personality of their owners.

As she closed the door on her side and started the engine, the middle light faded off, casting us both in the shadows. It only reminded me of the pathetic sex act attempted only two hours ago. "How are you feeling?" Samantha asked, angling her body towards me.

"I think the three gallons of coffee you waterboarded me with is working."

"Good, can't have you trashed wherever you're going." She checked her blindspot, then pulled off. "Where are you going again?"

"A house party."

All the streetlights in this neighborhood were sterling white, systematically placed together so that no sidewalk step went unlit. No risk of enlightenment, no opportunity for mischief. The cool glass fogged from the heat of my breath and I rested my eyes, letting the pounding of my head block out the white noise.

She parked, but spoke into the steering wheel instead of at me. "Ricky, are you sure you're okay?"

"I will be." I unbuckled myself, opening the door. "Thanks for the ride, Samantha."

"Which one?"

We made eye contact and a smile spread across her lips. I wish I had the energy to smile back. I closed the door, stepping out onto the curb. The house was a small one story detached unit, with an ill-kept yard and trash on the sidewalk.

I walked up to the front door, almost expecting some sort of bouncer or guest list check person, but there was no one outside except two cats humping in a bush. I placed my hand on the door handle, but I couldn't tighten my fingers around the knob. My hands were shaking. I looked back to Samantha's car, in case she was waiting and needed me to give her confirmation that she was free to go home and I would be just fine and wasn't about to die in a stranger's house.

Samantha had already left.

I pushed open the door and was immediately greeted by the smell of warm musk and cheap perfume.

Music invaded my eardrums once again, my fingers fumbling to slip my phone out of my pocket as I was swallowed into a humid crowd.

"Hey man, what's up and where's your drink?"

A red cup was shoved into my chest. Then another drink found its way to my lips. Then a shot. Then a line. And another shot.

Moderation was not my strong suit.

I was stumbling, pushed forward by dancing bodies, floating just a few inches off the ground. The house was a lot bigger when sobriety was thrown out of the window. Each room was a new room, each face a new face, each drink a new drink. Someone pulled me into a group picture and, with the flash of a camera, I was outside of a different room with different faces and a different drink.

This new different room was closed though, hidden behind a steel door. It was unusual to have an industrial door inside a residential home, but maybe warehouse was the new chic. I tugged on the knob, but it still didn't open. A man twice my size and half my clothes approached me. "Are you looking for a good time?"

"Excuse me?" In one push, I was against the wall, his hands against me and his mouth to my ear. "Wah-wait—" Sputtered out of my mouth and I resisted, though his chest was a lot more solid than his black mesh crop top led me to assume.

"Body check." He breathed in my ear, his nose running up the side of my face to my temple. It was then I noticed his hands were patting me down, pinning my hands above my head to check for knives, using one of his legs to push mine apart and dropping to his knees in front of me to find any weapons that may be hidden in my sock. I felt my arm threaten to bleed again under my makeshift toilet paper and tape bandage.

The pat down all happened in less than 33 seconds. "All clear," he announced over his shoulder, and a large boulder moved from out of an impossibly darker corner.

"Follow me," the boulder said. I couldn't think of a reason not to. He produced a small key that looked like it would snap in two under the weight of his fingers. He turned to unlock the steel door, dead bolted. Beyond the door was a hallway leading to another door.

I gave my blind trust that the boulder would escort me to the final destination, given I had no idea where I was going and all, but instead I received a sturdy push in the back and the steel door shut behind me.

So much for the follow me thing.

I walked down the narrow corridor before me, the dingy light barely highlighting the path. I kept my hands outstretched to keep myself from walking into the wall. Toward the end of the hallway, voices. I rubbed my hands together, then against my jeans. My heart was racing, but the itch was gone, replaced instead by curiosity.

Hadn't felt that in a long time.

I opened the last door and stepped in.

-11-

I didn't know what I expected. Perhaps a bunch of thuggish burly men who barely spoke English – Russian, East African, Yazuka, Colombian, the usual stereotypes portrayed in the media – punching each other in the face with brass knuckles while their pit bulls tore out each other's throats.

Or maybe just a single bald pinhead sitting at a sturdy desk, surrounded by skyscrapers of money and a few beautiful escorts that liked to call themselves Instagram models. Anything from a raunchy BDSM fantasy to a grungy basement filled with rats and asbestos. The one thing I wasn't expecting, however, was a decently normal looking room with decently normal looking people.

I took a quick glance around the room, unsure of which details were relevant. Directly in the center was a circular poker table from a budget craft store. The floor was linoleum, splotched with a dark rusted color, like if someone mixed red and grey Play-Doh. The walls were covered by uneven grey paint with a few abstract pieces of art hanging from the wall, all the same rusted red art motifs against a stark white canvas. The lighting was unfortunately dim and held the tint of yellow often found in the bathrooms of possessed houses. There was a nice little antique lamp in the corner.

How quaint.

"Looks like we have a sixth."

There were five people sitting around the poker table, all but one turned their head to watch me as I entered.

The closest to me, on the left, was an older man. Not old, just older. If I had to take a guess, he was in his late forties and he took care of himself well. His hair was mostly black, cut short. He was shaven, but a shadow was starting to show. The top button of his white collared shirt was unbuttoned, crease-pressed and wrinkle free.

On the far left of the table was another man, a few years older. I could spot his beer belly from the other side of the room. He filled out his oversized t-shirt very thoroughly.

Across from the midlife reject was a young woman, mid-twenties, but black didn't crack so possibly older. She quickly looked away from me, staring at her folded hands in her lap. She was a walking Forever 21 mannequin.

Closest to me on the right was another man, sickly thin and difficult to guess his age by all the meth sores on his face. Or maybe it was heroin. But who was I to talk, only God and hiring managers could judge him.

The man at the 'head' of the round table, the point at the top of the star, smiled at me. He was the one who had spoken before and he ushered me closer. His blond hair was buzzed, steel grey eyes piercing under hooded eyelids. His face held no expression as he stared at me, observing. He wore a casual button-down, light blue, long-sleeves. *"I was expecting Kim."*

He watched for a reaction.

I did the same.

"Please, sit."

I let a pause hang in the air before carefully pulling out the metal chair. It scraped across the floor like a nail against chalkboard, making the girl flinch and the white collar man turn his nose up at me as he repositioned himself at the table.

One by one, they lost interest in me and turned to the Head of the Table. He barely blinked, slowly picking apart my details. His eyes lingered before snapping back to greet me. Then everyone else.

"What brings you to the Back?" He asked me.

I cleared my throat, ears ringing from the absence of party music. "A door, mainly."

Someone stifled a laugh, but the Head of the Table made no expression. *"Well, the more the merrier. Call me Michael."* The atmosphere was cold, dangling above everyone as Michael reached in a large bag at the foot of his chair and pulled out oxygen masks.

"Are we doing puffers again?" The Mannequin asked, shifting her weight and leaning in to get a better look.

"Something like that." His blinks were slow and deliberate. Michael placed a small tank in the center of the table and then a stack of notepads. *"I have a new blend and I would appreciate your feedback before distribution."* He passed the notepads to the right as he continued to talk. White paper, clean. Fresh. Untainted.

I turned the notepad over in my hand, automatically reaching for my backpack that wasn't there and a pen that didn't exist.

White Collar leaned back in his chair, folding his arms. "So we're just breathing? Last time you had the best coke I ever had in my life. We can't sell air." Is this where Kim got her product? Some experimental drug group? "What's in it for us?"

"Who says you can't sell it?" Michael passed around the oxygen masks. *"Sell by the tank, sell by puff, fill balloons with it, distribute it however you like, I don't care."* The masks were made of clear plastic. *"But I am not going to sell you something without first knowing the effects."* He glanced up at White Collar, *"Feel free to leave. No one is forcing you to stay."*

White Collar rolled his eyes, but otherwise shut up.

Michael continued, "*As always, I'll go over today's rules. If you decide not to play, this is your chance to back out. No questions, no losses. Well, except the loss of an opportunity.*" He stared at White Collar for an uncomfortable amount of time. *"Whoever the tank points will take a hit. Sound good?"*

"So, it's spin the bottle?" I asked.

"Is that a problem?" He slow blinked at me.

I shrugged, "Just wondering, your house your rules."

"Who goes first?" Methy broke the staring contest, dragging Michael's attention back to the rest of the table.

"I'll go first, then we will move counter clockwise." He picked up a mask, pulling the strap as he slid it over his head. *"After your first hit, please write down how you feel. Then I will remind you when to write your next entry."* His hand lingered over the air tank. Then, with a flick of his wrist, Michael spun the tank.

It spun too fast and in slow motion all at once. Huffers didn't sound too dramatic. Most of the kids I had known to sniff paint and glue said it usually made them feel light and giggly, sometimes it knocked them out. The tank finally stopped.

It was self-absorbed of me to assume I would be first.

I should stop assuming.

Methy practically clapped as the tank slowed to a stop in front of him. He wiggled his mask over his head as Michael helped connect his tube to the tank. After a quick twist of the knob, the tank hissed and the air flowed to Methy, his eyes rolling to the back of his head. After about three seconds, Michael twisted the air off.

"Write down how you initially feel."

While Methy was writing, Michael spun the tank again. It was also self-absorbed to think I would be second. Mannequin, Beer Belly, and Methy again were all chosen before the tank finally landed on me. I looked down at the canister, then my eyes rose to meet Michael.

"Put your mask on, Kid."

I floundered with the head strap and it snapped the back of my head loud enough for everyone to hear, but the mask fit snug over my nose and mouth. I took the end of my tube and attached it to the flow nozzle, as I had seen the others do before. He leaned over to twist the knob.

Inhale.

My mother had always been insufferable.

Even before she was a brain-dead washed out zombified version of a human, she was a vacant waste of space.

As a child, her parents simply labeled her a day dreamer. Noticing she didn't eat bugs or pick her nose like most children, they incorrectly thought she was a shy quiet kid. They felt lucky. She was the perfectly little angel, with large brown eyes, chocolate ringlet curls, and a light sprinkle of freckles across her cheeks. There was nothing wrong with being a perfect little angel. While piles of dolls and tacky kid's makeup palettes lay untouched in the corners of her room, she would crawl into her bed and nap after school, surrounded by all of her unnamed stuffed animals.

Thirteen was a big year for my mother. Along with the fun of puberty and moving to a nicer neighborhood, my grandparents bought her a trampoline. Nothing too fancy, and it was only big enough for one or two kids to jump on at a time. My mother's childhood dream was to be a cheerleader (spoiler, she never made the team) and my grandparents were excited for her to finally take an interest in something other than staring off into thin air like a pet that could see ghosts.

However, instead of bouncing around the trampoline like a rabid animal, she used all of the energy in her body to hoist herself up on the trampoline then collapse onto the black jumping mat, her body rolling to the center of the trampoline.

She spent hours there, sunken in the mesh fabric.

She probably would have developed skin cancer by now if she had grown up anywhere other than Caribou, Maine.

My mother's teenage boyfriend was named Andrew. She occasionally told stories about him whenever she had too much wine and her friends were complaining about their husbands.

She met Andrew at fifteen, when he decided to finally introduce himself. He lived in the house directly behind her, his bedroom window overlooking her backyard. My mother, despite what everyone assumed, was not shy. Andrew was.

Every day when he got home from school, he would peek out of his window and gaze at her uninhabited body, brown curls encircling her still face like a halo. She looked like Bambi. Occasionally, whenever Andrew peeked up from his homework to check, she would have rolled over or shifted an arm so he at least knew she was alive, even if that was all he knew about her.

Until one day she didn't move.

It was late fall and snow had already blanketed her backyard with white. The first time Andrew had seen my mother do anything besides climbing on and off the trampoline was when she cleared her trampoline of snow. It was almost erotic. But now she hadn't moved at all, bundled up in her knee length down jacket and bright pink mittens. If he squinted, it looked like her eyes were closed.

Andrew waited until half an hour went by, probably not the wisest decision for a first responder. His forehead was pressed against the window and his thin lips fogged the glass as he whispered for my mother to make a movement, any movement, something to assure him she was alive.

She didn't move.

"Ah, shoot," he violently cursed, clenching both his fists. He grabbed his beanie with the fleece ear flaps and tumbled down the stairs, a knight on the trek to save his princess. But first, "MOM!" He shouted, "Where did you put my snow boots?"

Another ten minutes, he was knocking on the front door of her house. Another-another ten minutes, after no one answered the door, he scampered into her backyard. "Hey! Hey!" He shouted, scrambling up and onto the trampoline. "Hey!" He continued, the only word left in his flustered vocabulary. He crawled to the center, reaching out to shake her shoulder.

She snapped her head toward him, jerking away from his hand. "Who are you?"

"I—" His eyes darted between her two questioning eyes as he retracted his hand. "I'm Andrew."

"Why are you in my backyard?" She propped herself up on her elbows, looking him over. "*Andrew*."

"Well I." He crossed his legs under him. The millions of times he had prepared this very conversation immediately evaporated from his mind. "I thought you were dead."

"*Dead*? Why?"

He shrugged. "Because you weren't moving."

She laid back down. "Huh." My mother nodded to herself, resting her hands behind her head. "I could see that, yeah." She glanced at him. "You *can* join me if you want, Andrew."

And join her he did. Andrew dated my mother for almost two years before he too grew tired of her. He grew tired of the way she only thought about herself, withdrawing into the comfort of her trampoline rather than his arms. He grew tired of how she would sit in silence for hours, eyes glazed over while he asked her what was wrong again and again.

He grew tired of the way she laid there like a corpse the one and a half times they had sex. Andrew didn't know exactly what to expect, sex was probably going to be weird and awkward and uncoordinated, maybe even embarrassing, but it wasn't supposed to be like that.

Love wasn't supposed to make him feel so worthless.

Week after week, month after month. He was tired of how she would just shut down, sometimes in the middle of a sentence, like a laptop forcing itself to sleep, unsaved documents be damned. He did everything for her, waited on her hand and foot, gave her every ounce of his emotional and physical support whenever she didn't ask for it.

My mother gave him nothing in return. Andrew was a shy kid, but he had enough dignity to know when he was being a doormat.

They broke up, not that it made a difference to her. After high school my mother moved down to Boston because her parents had connections to the Dean of Admissions at BU, but not even that did much help because she couldn't find the motivation to get out of bed the entire first semester. She dropped out in time for finals.

My mother got a job at a bowling alley downtown. It somehow worked out because if she didn't show up, her boss was usually so stoned he couldn't tell my mother apart from the broom leaned up against the bathroom wall.

My mother would laugh about the story now, a polite laugh, as she swirled her near empty wine glass in front of her face. Her friends would join in on the laugh, asking how big was Andrew's dick. My mother shushed them and they huddled closer holding up estimates on the young man's genitals. They were laughing in the present, but my mother's eyes were still looking up from the trampoline.

Michael tapped on the table, grabbing my attention. He had already shut the valve. *"Write down how you feel."* He disconnected my tube, throwing it in my direction so he could continue to spin the tank.

I didn't have words. I tried finding myself, lost between a Boston bowling alley and a basement on the west coast. My brain pressed against the inside of my skull. I squeezed my eyes shut, waiting for the little red and yellow spots to disappear. When they didn't, I stared down at the pen in front of me.

"You alright, Kid?"

Someone else at the table chuckled as the bottle began its next spin. My fingers closed around the pen. I was inflated, elated.

I thought I was happy.

My father attended Harvard at the time my mother lived in Boston and one of his hobbies was bowling, something I still didn't understand to this day because he was absolutely terrible at bowling. Robert would stare at her from across the dark room, ignoring the teasing taunts of his classmates when he threw another gutterball. Those first few weeks, he liked to imagine my mother was staring back at him, equally lost in lust.

In reality, she was staring at nothing, adrift in herself.

What Robert was most known for, as well as anyone who had attempted to date my mother, was determination. After about a month or so of relentless wondering, he straightened his pre-law student tie, walked right up to her, and asked her out. Three and a half years later, she became Mrs. Schenk. After another four-ish years, her name officially changed to my mother.

Might as well have been the bowling alley broom.

The air tank landed on me again, for the third time. Some of the others were talking, mostly nonsense. Others were silent, making chicken scratches on their notepads. I thought I heard myself laugh, but it wasn't clear.

"What do you think?" Mannequin asked.

"I remember when I was just starting out," White Collar nodded along to her. Mannequin worked an office job, at least that was the implication. They didn't speak in complete thoughts.

Then the air was flowing again.

Inhale.

My cheeks burned, the first feeling I could recognize in the last—whatever amount of time had passed. I needed the table to stand, "I think I'm going to head out if that's okay."

Michael looked in my direction, detailing my appearance from across the table. *"How do you feel?"*

My head rolled back to the ceiling from the weight of thinking. "I feel like nothing."

He paused, taking a second to collect my notepad before leading me out. *"Good."*

That was exactly how I was supposed to feel.

I wobbled outside the house, the party still continuing behind me. Without me. I lifted my arms to the sky. My body, from my ears to the tips of my toenails, was shaking, exhilarated. Exhausted. It was like ejaculating for the first time, less messy, but just as confusing. All I knew was that it felt amazing.

I threw up in the bushes and passed out on the ground.

I spent thirty minutes lying on the sidewalk.

My body pulled itself up from the cold ground, a puppet on strings. I wasn't sure where the energy came from. Maybe it was determination. Maybe it was muscle memory. I had always found a way to get it done, but what did I need to get done this time? One foot in front of the other, the puppeteer dragged my feet in a random direction, arms dead at my side. I'd never been pummeled by a speeding circus bus on fire, but I was about 80% there.

My body limped along, hunched and swimming through syrup, but steady. My fingers glided along the walls of the buildings I passed, the only thing holding me down to Earth. I was still elated—empty—from the hiss of the air tank filling my mask, which was why I didn't notice the homeless man sleeping against the side of the building. Which was why my foot caught on his leg and I slammed face first into the cement. Again.

"Hey, asshole, try looking where you're going." He grumbled, throwing my legs off him. He didn't have a tent, but his sleeping bag looked well-worn. Next to him was a blue backpack with a broken zipper. He looked how I felt, with blood dried around his nose and soulless eyes. "Some of us are trying to sleep."

I rolled my head to look at him, "Hey asshole, try looking where you're sleeping, some of us are trying to go." But go where? My puppet strings placed my scraped up palms on the sidewalk, pushing my body to a sitting position. The puppeteer knew the way.

The hobo sucker punched me in the face before I could get all the way up. I laid there, disoriented, staring up at the sky. Lifeless, but not dead. Somewhere inside, the drugs kept a part of me dancing, dancing on strings. The clouds covered the stars. My eye watered, but it didn't hurt. Puppets couldn't get hurt. "Do you know how to find the North Star?" I croaked.

"Get the fuck outta here, this is my corner."

It wasn't the brightest in the sky.

-13-

"Knock, knock."

Somehow, I ended up at her house. "Ricky," her tone dripped with worry. But instead of rolling my eyes, I smiled as Hana hurried over to me, checking over her shoulder at her front door. Everyone worried too much. Or not enough. Never the right amount though. "What happened?" She clutched her phone in her left hand, my text for her to open the door still visible on the screen.

I shrugged, covering my sucker punched eye. "Running into a doorknob is a lot more common than you would think." It throbbed, but didn't hurt. Just felt inflated, a dull pressure against my skull.

A thud.

"How did you run into a doorknob? Your whole eye is swollen!" She hesitated to reach up, but her fingers crawled back into fists as she lowered them down to chest level.

"It was dark."

She checked back over her shoulder again, crossing her arms over her navy blue PE shirt. She wasn't wearing a bra. Food stains splattered her pinstriped bottoms that stopped two inches above her ankle. She leaned in, a loud whisper. "Why did you come here?"

"Are you going to let me in?"

"Um," Her eyebrows came together and she looked over her shoulder a third time. "It's really late." Then why was she still awake?

I tilted my head to the side, testing her. "Late is relative."

"It's late for my mom."

"Is she around?"

"She's sleeping."

"What's the problem then?"

"Wait, you didn't even answer why you came here. Or why blah blah blah blah." I leaned in while she was talking about whatever, supporting my shoulder against her door frame. She took a step back, maintaining her previous distance from me. "Why are you here?"

"To hang out." My jaw was starting to swell.

"What do you mean hang out? Like, talk? Do homework?"

"I don't know, maybe some Netflix maybe some chill."

"Do you know how late it is?" I did not. "TV would wake my mom up."

"Chilling probably isn't much quieter."

"What?" Hana wasn't budging. Any of my other friends would have just let me in without questioning my motives. I had forgotten what that felt like, but thankfully not how to deal with it. Feigned honesty.

"Okay, look Hana." I lowered my eyes to the floor, "I was jumped. They took everything. It's too far of a walk to my place and you were the closest friend I could trust right now." I looked up at her, slight head tilt, lips turned down in a minimal frown. "I'm sorry to put you in this situation, but I don't have anywhere else to go."

"Do you want me to call the police? That sounds pretty serious."

"No, it was just my phone, it's insured."

"I meant for the whole eye punch part."

"It'll heal." She frowned. "I really just want to sleep it off for now, I can deal with it in the morning. Is that okay?"

Checking over her shoulder one more time, she bit her bottom lip with a silent nod. "Well, just." She opened the door a little wider, stepping to the side. "Just don't say anything."

Easy.

A quick smile and I glided past her. The apartment smelled faintly of Tandoori chicken. "Should I take my shoes off?"

"Um, whatever. It's fine." She checked the apartment hallway, then locked the front door, setting both the chains and dead bolt. The living room was minimal: a simple plaid love seat placed across the television sitting on the floor. Next to the TV, they had an old generation video game console with a small pile of games. The coffee table was stacked high with bills, a calculator, and multiple pens for scratching down minimum payments in a tattered budgeting notebook.

The dining room shared the same aesthetic. A square table, painted to look like wood, with a vase of flowers in the middle. A few school awards decorated the walls, awards that meant nothing on a transcript: perfect attendance, 8th grade graduation certificate, best Halloween costume, perfect attendance, ribbons from various summer camps, hall monitor, perfect attendance.

Her SAT scores were also pinned to the wall and I took the liberty of nonjudgmentally taking a peek.

1020.

Hana led me into their compact kitchen, which, in my humble opinion, was a train wreck. Bad oil-paintings cluttered every wall and mix-matched bakeware crowded the counter space.

"Do you want something to eat? Like a banana or bread or something?" Bread would probably help for the morning, but I shrugged. She grabbed two bananas, turned off the light, and led me down the pitch black hallway. "The bathroom is on the right." I couldn't see anything. "My mom's room is to the left and mine is all the way at the end." She whispered, pausing at her room, "Um, also, it's super messy because I wasn't planning on visitors. Yeah, so. Keep that in mind."

Girls always over-exaggerated their super messy. It was fine. Certainly not spotless, but at least the clothes on the floor weren't worn for two weeks and covering discarded Doritos Cool Ranch bags and jizz tissue. I'd seen worse.

"Here, banana?" She handed it to me before retreating to her bed right next to the window, white comforter with blue polka dots.

"Thanks." I took the banana, peeling it automatically. Her room had a very plain theme about it, no real purpose into the décor. A small picture collage hung above a cheap desk with random small knick-knacks on every hard surface. "How long have you lived here?"

"About a year? We move around a lot."

"Why?"

"I think my mom likes moving, as weird as that sounds." She laughed, looking at the ground. "Maybe she's restless."

Restless was a good word for it. "May I sit on your bed?"

"Um, yeah, go ahead, sure." She waved her arms around like a duck flapping in a pond, gesturing me to help myself to wherever.

Her bed felt like a wrestling mat, but the comforter helped. I mechanically ate the banana, but the taste didn't touch my tongue. Hana's half-opened closet revealed unpacked boxes above her clothes. "Do you like moving around?"

"Not really, it's a hassle." She hovered around the other edge of the bed, but eventually planted herself on the floor. "But it's kind of fun having a brand new clean place."

"Kind of like starting over?"

"Yeah, kind of."

"That does sound pretty nice." I slid off my shoes, scooting further onto her bed. "What about your dad?"

"What?"

"Your dad? Father? Prominent man figure in your life?" I paused, "Or do you have two moms?" Hana stared back at me, a solid ten seconds without saying anything. Prey scared easily. "Oh, sorry, you don't have to answer if you don't want to, I didn't mean to pry or anything." I smiled, biting into the banana. I could only taste the stale chunks of vomit still lodged between my molars.

"My parents are divorced."

I waited, trying to judge her expression, imagining her small hands covering her ears as a screaming match over custody proceeded in the next room. Waiting outside of school, quietly sitting on the brick wall by the cafeteria, two hours late because it was his weekend to pick her up. The smile fading from her cheeks when she opened a three-month belated birthday card with no money falling out. And then eventually no belated birthday cards at all. "Good divorce or bad divorce?" I asked.

"I've never heard of a good divorce before."

"Point taken."

She laughed, lightly, resting her head on the side of the bed. "They're fine now, I guess. I see him every two weeks or so. He's doing great, I'm glad he's happy. He remarried last year. I was in the wedding and everything, she's really nice."

Boring. "How quaint."

"Mhm, yeah." She began peeling her banana.

"What about your mom?"

"What?" She looked up at me, pausing again. "Oh, yeah, she's okay too. She's not married or anything, but she seems happier."

"And you?"

"What about me?"

"Are you happier?"

She squinted, biting into her banana. "Um. That's a weird question." I moved around mushy banana in my mouth. "I mean, I used to be really mad. I was mad that they didn't put their differences aside for me."

"Very selfish."

She laughed, "I was nine. And an only child. Of course I was selfish." She took another bite. "But somewhere along the line, I guess I was just grateful they weren't fighting anymore."

"Do you have a big family?"

Her shoulders rose a little. "What do you mean?"

"Your extended family?"

"I guess, isn't everyone's?"

I shrugged, dropping the subject. We finished our bananas in relative silence, my mind a warm buzz. "Ricky, do you randomly pop into everyone's houses like this?" She concentrated on drawing the carpet circles with her ring finger.

"Only my friends' houses." I waited for her to look up at me. Eye contact was key. "That's what friends are for, right? To hang out? You've never had a sleepover before?"

"But you're a guy."

"Is that weird? I could leave." I feigned making an effort to get off the bed, but she quickly shook her head.

"No, no, it's fine. Just. Nothing, it's fine."

"Are you sure? I could go, it's not a problem."

"No really! It's kind of nice having you over." She looked to her bedroom door, then lowered her voice another notch. "I'm just worried." She pointed at the door.

"Doesn't it make it more exciting though?"

"Yeah, I guess it does." She withheld a smile, standing up to throw away her banana peel. I handed her mine, and she put them both in a plastic bag before leaving the room.

I stretched out on her bed, laying my head on her pillow that smelled like a lavender field. The euphoria of the night had faded, leaving only a dull ache behind. A thud. I closed my eyes, flinching at the pain.

If I could feel, I was alive.

She came back, taking two and a half minutes to quietly shut the door. "So, what now?"

"Come sit on the bed, I can't hear you."

She tiptoed over, climbing onto the center of her mattress. I peeked my uninjured eye open at her as she studied me like a mushroom in a wild field. Was I one of the safe ones? Or was I poison?

A good question.

"Can we sleep?" I asked, scooting down into a laying position. My chest was heavy, coming down from the sky, sinking my body into the sheets.

"Oh, yeah, sure. It's pretty late," she lisped from behind her night retainers. "Is it okay if I turn the light off now?"

I grunted, the last of my strength for the night. She reached over to the wall, flicking the switch, then wiggled back to the bed. Hana was facing me, mouth open and eyes wide. Her words were caught in her throat, teetering on the edge. She wiggled from under her blanket.

"Goodnight Hana," I helped her out, since she had been so generous to take me in.

"Goodnight Ricky," she finally let out. "Um, how do we." She shifted again.

"What?" I had to peer through my mind's fog to speak and I didn't know why she couldn't just close her eyes and let me drown myself to sleep.

"Is this okay for you? Um, do you need more space?"

She was nervous. I took a pillow from the top of her bed and put it between us, pulling the blanket up to my nose. "Does that work?"

I felt her head nod against her pillowcase, then nothing.

"Hana?"

No response. It had only been eighteen seconds.

"Hana? Really? You're sleeping?"

Nothing.

Must be nice.

I turned away from her, closing my eyes and waited for the nothingness to overtake me as well. How could she sleep with my head thudding against the bed so violently?

Her soft snores reminded me of a puppy, slightly drooling with an occasional leg twitch. I rolled over to face her, watching her chest rise and fall every three seconds. Her arms, exposed. I reached out, gauging her face for any signs of consciousness. My fingers traced the raised scars along her arm, just a few lines spread out from her elbow to just below her shoulder. Around those scars, her skin was butter soft as I trailed the railroad planks back down to her wrists.

Her hair was braided to the side, a thick black rope that would probably suffocate me if I ever managed to fall asleep.

The same hair that fell over her shoulder as she pulled out a razor blade. Did she sit at her desk and cut, glancing out the window that pointed to the wall of another complex? What emotion was in her eyes? I had once thought it might be sadness, the most obvious emotion, but maybe it was anger. Maybe it was restlessness.

Maybe it was boredom.

Or maybe that was just me.

Did she feel the stinging too? Not only after the cut, but in her eyes, right before. Did she feel the tremble in her jaw? The pit in her rib cage. The labored breathing. The heaving. The panic. Did her vision tunnel and her lungs quake?

It was happening, right now. I backed away from her, pressing myself against the wall. My hands were shaking and even closing them into fists wouldn't stop it. A gasp escaped my lips, too fast for my hands to cover.

Hana shifted, moaning something.

More were coming out. I grabbed her pillow, resting it on my bent knees, and buried my face into the thin fabric, catching sobs. They flowed like the blood from my arms, a river streaming down my face. I hugged my legs, trying to control the shaking.

My chest burned, a corset tightening around my lungs. I was falling down a hole, my skull hitting every rock on the way down. I struggled for breath, eyes scorching and pressure closing my throat.

It never lasted too long, maybe five minutes or so. Just long enough for it to wipe my mind of everything, using all of my body's resources to take back control. Inhale. It usually didn't happen around other people though. Exhale. Maybe I was dying of alcohol poisoning. Inhale. These hurt so much. They were exhausting and embarrassing and they just kept happening. Exhale. The pain was only temporary. Inhale. But I would do anything to stop it right now. Exhale.

Inhale.

I woke up next to her, my knees still pulled into my chest and my hands latched across my legs. The sun beamed in from behind her window curtains. Hana stirred, giving me enough notice to wipe my face before she rolled over, propping herself up on her elbows. "Oh my God, Ricky." Her eyes stretched all the way open, two perfectly round dark circles.

Could she tell?

I frowned, scooting back from her, shielding my eyes from the sun filtering in, but mostly from her. "What's up?"

"I completely forgot you were there." She laughed, then quickly covered her mouth. "I thought I was going to be murdered." She turned over, away from me. We both checked our phones at the same time.

"We're going to be late." She was out of bed before I finished blinking. "Ricky, we're going to be late." Hana scurried to her closet, snatching the first items to fall off the hanger. "Come on, get up!" Then she was gone, closing the door behind her.

I stretched, then laid back down.

"We're going to be late!"

Ten minutes had passed and she was already dressed and drumming at her imaginary watch. I stretched again. "Late for what?"

"School!" Her fingers swiftly tied knots in her shoe laces.

Oh yeah.

I rolled over. "Want to help me find my car instead?"

"Your car?" Her hair brush slowed, but only slightly.

"My car. I left it somewhere last night. Do you want to help me find it?"

"You're not going to school?"

"There's nothing even remotely important happening today."

"Don't the teachers mark you as absent?" Miss Perfect Attendance.

"I can write you an excuse, don't worry about it. Come on, let's dance."

"Dance?"

"Ditch."

Hana put down her brush, her brows pulling together. "You want me to ditch school with you?" She whispered, as if I had just confessed to murder and asked her to help hide the body. She couldn't picture herself being even a second late to the ever important philosophy of sketching with Crayola or iPhone photography or whatever she did in her irrelevant elective class.

"That's exactly what I'm asking, yes." I slid to the edge of her bed, running a hand through my hair. Half of my face throbbed. "On a scale of one to ten, how bad is my eye?"

She scrunched her nose.

"That bad?" Hana scrunched her nose more. "Where's your bathroom?"

My eye looked a lot worse than it felt, but luckily not as bad as I thought. I gently patted the blue and yellow bruise surrounding my eye, while using my other finger as a toothbrush. Her toothpaste was the disgusting bubblegum flavor.

I rummaged through her sink drawers out of habit. Multiple bottles of Asprin, a pack of pink disposable razors, and random makeup pencils. I came across a box of JUMBO tampons, so I stopped snooping and spit out the pink toothpaste that probably did more harm than help.

Back in her room I asked, "Do you have any deodorant?" She was facing the window, but looking at the clock. I picked up the baby blue deodorant stick from the top of her dresser.

"Do you usually skip class?" She watched me at first, though her eyes diverted when I lifted my shirt to swipe on deodorant that made me smell like a field of tulips in Amsterdam.

"Not usually."

It was less considered skipping and more so considered prioritizing, most of the time anyway. After crawling out of my bathtub in the morning, still holding a bottle of cough syrup, I needed to sleep in zero period. I skipped first period to finish homework for second period in my car, worked on third period homework during second period, caught up on second period during third, then visited first period during lunch to turn in homework and a forged late slip. I napped during elective, skipped the next period with a fake ASB excuse, did fifth period's classwork during the period after and got a copy of the homework for sixth period during passing period.

I also took a seventh period to get a jumpstart on any college statements/summer internship applications/volunteer and leadership opportunities.

The usual.

It was surprisingly simple once the schedule was implemented and homework assignments were delegated and regulations set in place. It was my legacy and it worked.

Hana bit her bottom lip in a frown, her backpack still secured too high on her back. "I don't know, I think we still might get in trouble."

"Trust me, it'll be fine. No one will ever know and you can actually say you've lived a little during high school."

"I live plenty."

"Uh huh, like what?"

Her eyes widened again as she looked at the floor. "I met new friends."

"Mhm, yes, that deserves a medal."

"I went to a dance!"

"Right, with me."

"I had a boy sneak in and spend the night!"

"Right, with me."

She was grasping at air. "I'm in a school club!"

"Oh wait, really?"

"Yeah!"

"I'm impressed! Do you also turn in homework and walk yourself to class? Have you ever answered when the teacher took attendance?" Hana looked away so I reeled in the sarcasm. "Come on, it'll be fun. It'll be an experience. These are the best days of our life—" A cold pressure dropped in my stomach, chilling my entire body. "Best days of your life," I repeated. "What are you going to do when they're gone?"

"Um, get married and move to Texas?"

"Why Texas?"

"I don't know, property value?" She never really gave a second thought to her childhood dream before. "What are you going to do?"

"Go find my car. Are you going to come with me?"

"Why do you want me to go so badly?"

"Because you're so wild and adventurous." She laughed. I moved in closer. "What's the worst that could happen?"

"My mom could find out."

"You can wear a hat."

"I'll be marked absent."

"The road to truancy and expulsion." I moved closer to her. "How about, you were being interviewed by the school newspaper. For that club you're in."

"Key Club?"

"Yeah, that one."

"Aren't you in it too?"

Was I?

We were so efficient at falsifying volunteer hours, for lack of better words that wouldn't degrade our characters, that I hadn't done anything concerning Key Club for almost three months. "Sure," I agreed with a smile.

"But I wasn't being interviewed."

"I have a connection that will say you were. In fact, we'll do a real interview after school later to make up for it, so you won't exactly be lying. Have you ever been in the newspaper?" She shook her head. "Well, congrats Superstar. Now, turn around." Hana turned around. I looped my fingers under the straps of her backpack and I felt her shoulders shudder. "We have a mission and we have an alibi, what are you waiting for?"

"A reason?"

"Asking how is more productive than why." I slipped the backpack off and it plopped to the floor.

"Are you peer pressuring me?"

"Yes." She turned around to meet me. "Live a little. With me." I offered her a hand and a way out of her mundane routine. If she didn't get out now, she would be stuck with the usual forever. And possibly in Texas.

She sighed, but didn't look me in the eye. "Okay, okay, I guess."

"That's the spirit, hesitant acceptance."

"Now what?"

"We're going out the window."

"What? Why?"

I already opened the window and poked my head out. "What did I say about asking why?" I grabbed her comforter and sheet off the bed.

Another hesitant sigh of acceptance from Hana. "Okay, how?"

Unfortunately, there wasn't a nifty tree outside her window, but it was only the third story, maybe thirty feet. I tied the end of the comforter to the bedpost. It would probably hold. "You've rock climbed or rappelled before, right?"

"Uh, no."

The ground was only barely swaying when I looked down. I tied the sheet to the end of the comforter. "Super easy, all you're going to do is walk down the side of the building." She watched my hands tie knots down the sheet, her mouth wide open. "No worries, I've done this before." I took the end of the sheet in my hand then swung my leg out the window. "Super easy, just don't fall."

But what fun would that be.

The climb was a welcome distraction. The excitement covered up the hole in my chest, tucking it neatly behind everything else. The blankets stopped two thirds of the way down. If I extended myself, I was only a few feet off the ground, so the only logical solution was to drop the rest of the way.

Falling.

Flying.

My bent knees embraced the impact.

I had never been a sound sleeper. Even as a baby, my parents told me I didn't sleep through the night until I was two. I wailed from my crib, thrashing my tiny fists at the dark ceiling. The problem wasn't falling asleep, but rather I could never return to sleep once I woke up. My eternal alarm clock was set with no option to hit snooze.

Once my eyes opened, I had full energy at the crack of dawn, as if my spirit animal was an obnoxious rooster. Even on the weekends, I woke up earlier than my parents, completing my chores for the day before the news channel had a chance to switch to their daytime anchors. I poured my own cereal, swinging my legs as I finished up whatever book I had started the night before. If I was feeling particularly helpful, I would start the morning coffee pot, then retreat back to my room to play with blocks or trucks or whatever happened to peak my interest that day.

By fifth grade, I used that time to get ahead in school subjects, study for tests, and research colleges and career paths. Being an astronaut sounded cool. When that was finished, I would shake Blake awake from the blanket fort on the floor and help him catch up on his classwork. We didn't go to the same school back then, but his homework covered lessons that my school taught the grade before. I started learning how to code and asked my parents for my own laptop to practice.

By seventh grade, I used that time to plump my resume with extracurricular activities. Miraculously, I was voted class president even though I didn't have too many friends. I mostly credited my victory to the friendly and likeable Blake, whom my parents had helped transfer to my school district that year. I began to implement my seven year plan to university, creating excel sheets of influential members of the community for networking. Like any child, I assumed it was normal until someone pointed out to me that it wasn't.

Blake had dragged me along to spend the night at the house of one of his new friends. My mother dropped us off, her eyes searching as the car pulled to a stop in front of the house. "Are there going to be *girls*?"

Blake shook his head no.

"Maybe," I said with a shrug.

"He's joking," Blake quickly covered and my mother's brow relaxed. "It's not that big of group, but I know that there weren't any girls invited."

And there weren't. We walked up to the house, easily twice the size of my own, with a callbox instead of a doorbell. "Blake? Is that you?" A voice answered us from the speaker. The door opened and eighth grade Jensen grinned from the crack. He had his growth spurt early, parading the same combed back haircut. "Hey! You're Ricky, right? Nice to meet you! Come in, we were just about to play a game!"

We all slept in the second entertainment room, but I woke up around 4am, my mouth dry but my eyes watery. I wandered around in the dark, the hardwood fresh against my socks. I ended up in the theater room and crawled into a plush leather recliner, my gaze locked on the blank white wall. Time evaporated.

"Ricky?" Jensen rounded the corner, rubbing his eyes. "How'd you get in here? Did you get lost?"

"No."

"Oh," he scratched his head, plopping down in the chair next to me. "What are you doing up?"

"I woke up." Jensen looked at me like I had swallowed an ostrich egg. "What are you doing up?"

"I heard you walking around, so I investigated." He grinned. "We should sleep, Fernanda will make us breakfast in the morning." He hopped up, but paused when I didn't move. "What's wrong?"

"Nothing."

"Is it me?"

"No, I'm not tired anymore. I'll probably just start our English essay. You have Ms. Trainor, right?" I nudged my backpack with my foot.

"Oh yeah. Wait, she assigned that yesterday. Is it due on Monday or something?"

"No. But might as well do it now, right?"

Jensen laughed, "That's so weird." He snapped his fingers, a lightbulb illuminating the back of his eyes. "Ohhh." He walked backwards out of the room. "If you wanted to jerk off, you could've just said that. There's a box of tissues somewhere around here. Goodnight Ricky." He closed the door on his way out.

By my freshman year of high school, I was averaging five hours a night. I had successfully begun to build my academic empire and I had landed my first internship as a mobile app tester. It was easy money, too easy, so I also volunteered the rest of my summer hours away.

By sophomore year I was down to four, but they were intermittent. It was perhaps the most productive year of my life. I lost ten pounds and assembled the perfect ASB cabinet, with addition of Katie a few months later. I completed my college fund goal, with a little saved away for Spring Breaks.

By junior year, I could piece together three hours, but only if I had time. The worst part was falling asleep, because I knew I would wake up a few hours later. Alcohol helped. I started working out occasionally and regained ten pounds. I broke up with Andrea.

This year, when I would wake up in the middle of the night, I couldn't get up. My feet kicked at empty bottles collected throughout the week. Every goal checked off my list felt like a star disappearing from the sky.

During the day, I concentrated on the list. During the day, my job was to get it done and I got it done well. The longer I kept busy, the less time I had to spend awake at night, waiting for sleep.

I wasn't sure what I would do when all of my goals were checked off. When there was nothing left.

It was outer space without the stars.

We didn't die climbing out of Hana's bedroom window, a feat in itself. "So where exactly did you go last night?" Hana dragged her feet, kicking up small pebbles in the dirt with her boots. We had wandered off the sidewalk, strolling along the train tracks. She pulled on the edges of her sweater.

"I was at a friend's house." Kind of true, for the earlier part of the night anyway. "For a cram session."

"Cram session?"

"Why do you ask?"

She kicked another pebble. "I was just wondering. I don't know, I thought you smelled a little, hmm." She beat around the bush.

"Weird?"

"Bad."

"Oh." I forgot about the vomit breath. "Sorry."

"It's okay."

I cleared my throat, "What do you like to do in your spare time?"

She kept her eyes down as she dragged her feet, dust clouds following behind like a loyal dog. "Um. I mean, I don't really do anything."

"What do you do when you get home?"

"Depends, usually homework and eat a snack or something."

"And then?"

Hana would drag her backpack to her room, eyes blank. There was no one home, as usual. She did, however, close her bedroom door. It made her feel safe, the only place she still had control.

Hana would let her backpack slump to the floor as her body propelled her forward. She kept a razor taped under her desk, it was the only place her mother wouldn't think to check.

I waited for Hana to tell me how it felt to slice open her own skin, how it would silence the sound of her mother working another double shift or her father rescheduling their dinner date, again. Instead, she said, "Uh, I watch TV I guess."

"And then?"

She looked up at me, "Nothing. I go to sleep."

How unproductive. "Oh, cool." I smiled at her.

"What about you?" She smiled too, picking up her pace a little.

I peeked at my phone, notifications already filling the screen. "Same, I don't do much either." I slipped it back in my pocket. "It's healthy to relax."

Relaxing was a waste of time.

The ground started to rumble, low. We both looked back at the same time.

"Oh geez, the train is coming." She brushed past me, scuttling six feet away. I took a good long look at that train. It was maybe twenty seconds away, black and rust orange paint. The train blew its whistle.

The force of a thirty-car freight train hitting a sedan was equivalent to the force of a car crushing an aluminum soda can. How did a human body compare to aluminum?

My favorite soda was Pepsi One.

I inhaled, then resumed looking forward. "Ricky!" Hana tugged on my sleeve, as if that would be enough to save me from anything. The train zoomed past us on the right, deafening whatever else she was saying.

"What?" I repeated, once the ringing had subsided in my ear.

"It's dangerous to stand this close."

It wasn't like I was standing on the tracks. Worrying was boring and not useful. "Hey, but you know what's more dangerous?" I said.

Her face retreated into her neck at what I might say next.

I began to jog.

"Wait," she called after me. "Why?"

"Not why, Hana. How." I turned away from her, picking up my speed. Most of the car doors on the train were closed, but there was a cart behind us with a door wide open.

My legs pounded against the dirt, arms pumping in stride. The door was coming up. Hana wailed behind me as her clunky boots tried to keep up. I reached out for the open car as it caught up to us, grasping at the side handle just barely out of reach.

My fingers grazed the railing, but it slipped out of range, zooming ahead. I looked behind and Hana was still screaming after me, but there was another opportunity. I held both arms out, ready to clench onto the side ladder at the cart connector.

My feet beating against the ground echoed all thoughts away, leaving only my heavy breathing and searing muscles. I understood Blake's obsession with running.

I had half a second to grab the ladder.

I pumped harder, swerving closer to the train. I reached out for the metal rungs.

And missed. My body lurched forward from the failed attempt. The ladder shot out of sight. I slowed, but only slightly, looking for my next chance.

"Ricky wait!"

Four seconds before the next one was out of reach.

I ran with everything I had left. Four The next handle swept pass and I lunged for it. My right hand snatched the rung. With three big steps, I hoisted myself up. Three.

I hopped onto the platform, shouting down at Hana, still sprinting alongside the train. "Hana!" I leaned over the railing, wind slapping at my face. Two.

I thrust my arm out to her and she clutched my forearm with her hand, our arms locking. She was tripping over her own feet, running out of steam. "I can't!" She was falling behind and if she held on her shoulder would be ripped off.

One.

"Jump!"

I pulled, my other arm pushing back against the ladder for support. Hana yelped, flinging her body toward me. There was a moment where she was suspended in the air, on the inhale. She floated, weightless, and time stood still. Her hair wafted in zero gravity. She was an astronaut looking out of the shuttle's window for the first time, an entire galaxy looming around her. In her eyes she held the sun and the moon and the planets. There wasn't a word in any language that could describe the feeling.

Her eyes saw the stars, but in their reflection I could only see an abyss.

The clock of time ticked and Hana collided into me, both of us falling backwards onto the grated platform and the air escaped my lungs from the impact.

"Oh my God!" Hana exclaimed, then laughed, hitting my thigh with her fist.

"What? Why are you hitting me," I pulled my legs away, but I was also laughing. Her smile filled both her face and she sat up, looking around like a child's first trip to Disneyland.

"Ricky!"

"What?" I coughed.

"Oh my God, we jumped on a train. Ricky!" She hit my thigh again.

"Ouch, what?"

"We jumped on a train!"

"Yes, we did," I sat up, propping myself on my elbow. The underbellies of the train carts laughed with us. Her hands were balled into fists, shaking against her legs. "How does it feel?"

She smiled back, "I've never felt so." Hana looked down, searching for the word on the tip of her tongue, the same word that she used to cut out of herself.

Or maybe that was just me.

"Alive?" I offered.

"Yes!" She smacked me again at the exclamation point.

"Ow, Hana, do you lift or something?"

"Oh, I'm so sorry, I was just," Hana looked down at her legs, still straddling me. "Ah! Sorry, I didn't," She flailed, climbing up.

"You didn't have to get off."

"What? Wait, no, I—"

"I'm just messing with you," I waved off her frantic stuttering. We watched the dirt and the trees rush by in silence for a few minutes before Hana cleared her throat.

"So," she started, crossing her legs in front of her.

"So?"

"Where are we going exactly?"

"Does it matter?"

"Well, I personally would prefer going to school tomorrow."

How long could I disappear before someone sounded an alarm? "It's probably just going into the city. We could always jump on a train back. Or I know a few people who could pick us up."

She mhm'd under her breath with a nod, turning back to the changing scenery. She smelled like soft purple. I laid back down. We would have to get off eventually. I needed to start compiling study packets for AP testing in a few months. I built up a client base from selling them last year. Hana needed to get back for, well, just to show up for class tomorrow.

But for now, we could live.

The sky was hazy and yellow, with sparkling lights falling like dandelions. I didn't remember the last time my cheeks hurt from laughing. It was supposedly the best medicine, but you couldn't laugh forever.

Nothing lasted forever.

"It's dangerous to stand this close." Hana repeated, and the sky was stripped of the gentle glow. We were back on the ground, four and a half minutes in the past, the train zooming by us.

I blinked, my head swirling.

The train had picked up speed and was moving far too fast for anyone to casually hop on. There was no adrenaline, no laughing, no relaxing.

No living.

"Oh," I pinched my eyes shut, holding my head by the bridge of my nose, a migraine brewing between my temples. "I'll get us a ride real quick hold on."

"Wait, what about your car?"

"What?" I looked at her, my phone already to my ear. "Oh, forget it, I'll have someone pick it up later for me."

"Pick it up? What, do you have henchmen?"

"Something like that."

Blake picked up the phone, and I let him do his usual greetings before I interrupted and instructed him to leave class immediately, that I didn't care if he was in the middle of a test because why would he pick up his phone anyway, and to give me a ride.

"Huh. Well if you put it that way then sure, I'll be there," he lowered his voice and I could hear the teacher shushing in the background. "Text me your location."

Click.

Another shot thrown away.

-13-

Same table, different people.

Well, mostly different people anyway. White Collar and Michael were there, but the other three faces were new. There was only one girl again. Standing hearty and tall, she had dark brown hair tied back into a slick military bun and adult acne. Sweat stained the pits of her light grey shirt.

The man across from her was a ginger middle aged man with glasses and curly hair. He was someone that never grew out getting shoved in a middle school locker.

The last participant was very forgettable. No distinguishing features. Basic white cis male, height between 5'10" and 5'11". Average weight and build. Somewhere around the general age of 28-33. His name was Chris.

This time the table was gone and the room was completely bare, save for a few rusty stains on the floor.

I had another college packet arrive today, probably an acceptance judging the weight and size. I also had two essays to write for some juniors and Samantha was going to forward me this week's math homework in exchange for my AP Economics study packet. I had a light week, but every time I sat at my desk and opened my laptop, my fingers froze. I couldn't stop staring at my hands, which led to staring at my wrists, which led to either slicing them open or reaching for an Ambien.

Coming to the Back seemed more productive.

"What's your name again?" I asked White Collar, even though he hadn't offered a name the last time we were in this room together.

"You sobered up." He paused, "Slightly sober anyway."

My immediate reaction was either offended or defensive, the two were difficult to distinguish at the moment. "We were all pretty fucked up by the end of it, I would say."

"You were fucked at the beginning."

I shrugged, "Yeah, maybe." He scoffed, his arms still crossed over his freshly pressed shirt. "What's got you in such a shit mood?"

"Talking to you, for one."

Asshole.

He turned to look at me, his face scrunched in a look. "And I think it's a pretty barbaric way to get drugs around here. Inhumane. But it's cheap."

If life was cheap, then sure. "I think it's fun."

"Then there's something wrong with you."

Offended; adjective – resentful or annoyed, typically as a result of a perceived insult.

Defensive; adjective – excessively concerned with guarding against the real or imagined threat of criticism, injury to one's ego, or exposure of one's shortcomings.

After a minute, he glanced at me from the corner of his eye, looking me up and down. "Shouldn't you be studying for a test or something?"

"Don't you have some sort of boring desk job to get ready for in the morning?"

Defensive.

But he chuckled, nodding to himself. "Yeah, maybe."

Back to silence.

The Woman, decided to break the stale air. "Can we get started? I have things to do."

"Sure, let's get started." Michael unzipped his brown leather satchel. He pulled out a Ziploc bag, heavy with colorful tablets, cut into tiny quarter-circles. *"Take one, pass it on."* He tossed the bag to the Ginger.

"What is it?" He turned the bag over in his hands, carefully.

"Does it matter?" Michael stared him down until Ginger fished out a small blue tablet and placed it on his tongue.

"Do I at least get some water to wash it down with?" After another few seconds of staring, Ginger decided to swallow it dry.

The bag passed to me.

I took a pill and passed the bag along to White Collar. And so the circle proceeded, silently swallowing the pills like candy and passing the bag along, shiftily glancing around to see if anything was starting to happen to the others.

I didn't know the pill was affecting me until it was already affecting me.

It made everything dark and disoriented, like if minute by minute someone had gradually dimmed the lights. When I looked down, my hands had disappeared but the toe of my shoes were above me. We were still standing in a circle, but their bodies were invisible, outlined in white chalk and their movements were choppy animation. Michael's outline was the thickest and brightest, a constellation in the sky.

His outline walked over to Chris who was only a dim twinkle in comparison, and punched him square in the jaw. No buildup, no warning, no tension. Just spontaneous combustion against the lower quarter of Chris' face with a crack of thunder.

Needless to say, Chris wasn't expecting it.

Chris' outline flung backwards from the impact, hands flailing as he crashed into the wall.

"Michael, what the fuck?" White Collar yelled in Chris' defense. His words came out in fragments, like a teacher scrawling each letter across the chalkboard. The Woman cackled, holding her sides.

I had previously lost track of the bag, but out of the corner of my eye, Ginger scooped a few more of the pills into his mouth. The outline of a giant eating a bag of colorful planets.

Michael advanced towards Chris again, but this time, Chris squared his shoulders and charged, swinging his entire arm back for the throw. Michael ducked under, undercutting the guy in his rib.

The woman cheered, then pushed Ginger over, the bag spilling a rainbow over the universe. White Collar hesitated, then launched himself at the pills, growling when Chris stumbled towards him. There was a lot of yelling, and soon everyone was fighting.

The first rule of the Back was that it was unexpected.

I hugged the wall, my mind swimming. "*How do you feel?*" The voice echoed in the air. I looked in a direction, but it was just the wall. Or the floor. Or the ceiling.

"I feel suspended." I answered.

"In what?"

Life.

My lips struggled to put a sentence together, syllables falling in the cracks between my chattering teeth. I changed the subject and the words flowed again. "What is this?"

"Does it matter?"

"Good point."

The voice swam along with me, the view still ashy grey. *"Why are you here?"*

"It's where all the exciting stuff happens."

The corner of Michael's face blurred in front of me. "*Excitement?*"

"Isn't that why everyone is here?"

For the first time, his eyebrow tweaked up in an expression. *"Not much of a fighter, are you?"*

"What makes you say that?"

"You aren't fighting."

Astute. I shrugged and my vision expanded. I could now see that Michael's outline was standing directly in front of me and the Woman was holding her sides in laughter. "Why did you punch him anyway?"

"To see what would happen." He crossed his arms, *"My initial trials pointed toward the pills mimicking hallucinogenic mushrooms."* He answered before I had even gotten the first word of the question out.

"Who were your initial trial subjects?"

"Myself."

The room expanded a little more. White Collar and Chris were slouched against the wall, chatting casually as if they hadn't just been bashing each other's face in. "Why would you test it on yourself?" Chris dripped blood from his nose.

"To see what would happen," He paused, *"That's the real exciting part. The other stuff,"* The drug front, the games, the money, the danger. *"Merely a sidenote."*

"What are you going to call it? The pills?"

"What do you suggest?"

The magic continued to fade. We came out of the heavens, out of the stars, back to the house party, back down to reality. "Call it Fiction."

"Sure, why not." He stepped closer to me. "*So if you aren't a fighter, or a laugher, or overdoer,*" Ginger sharpened into view, every so often woo'ing and popping another quarter pill in his mouth. "*Then what kind of hallucinating druggy are you?*" He stepped closer to me and I backed into the wall.

"What kind are you?"

Michael had the haunting eyes of a snow leopard. *"How old are you?"*

"Does it matter?"

For a second, I expected to hear *Good Point* back, but real life was rarely that well written. His eyebrow dropped. *"Hm. You're more passive than I thought. Well, it looks like you'll be around this time for the excitement."* He stepped back from me and I let out a breath I didn't know I had been holding. *"Everyone, take another pill—"* He glanced at Ginger. *"Or so. Let's start with the second half of the evening."*

With that, he left, and the room was grey again. Somber.

"What does he mean by second half?" I asked aloud as the others began to regroup, passing around the bag.

White Collar grabbed a handful, dropping most of them into his pocket. "The part that we all hate. You'll want to be high for this."

The group fell silent again before the Woman spoke up. "How do you not know?" I hadn't noticed her accent before.

"It's usually past his bedtime," White Collar scoffed, and the others joined in chopped half-chuckles.

Michael sauntered back in, silent, carrying a card table under his right armpit and three folding chairs with the other. The group watched him, like rabbits cornered. I didn't know what I was waiting for, but I also popped another pill, then another. Michael brought in three more chairs and began setting up the table in the center of the room again. He looked at us, "*What is everyone waiting for?*"

On command, we joined him at the table.

"Same rules today, Michael?" The Woman asked, plopping into a chair.

The air began to wave once again. "Wait, what rules—" Did it matter? I didn't finish my question, grabbing the seat across from Michael.

Still, his eyes met mine and he answered anyway. With a thud, he tossed a gun in the center of the table. "Russian roulette."

-14-

We passed the bag around again.

"Yes, we are playing by the usual rules." Michael cracked his knuckles one at a time. *"There's one bullet, three pulls. After the third pull, or gunfire, the round is over. When the revolver gets to you, you can either pull or pass. If you pass, you forfeit a quarter of your share."* He caught my unsaid question again. *"The pot is the product you just tried. We split the pot among the survivors after the third pull."* He placed a single bullet in the revolver, spun the barrel, then snapped it closed with a slight of his wrist.

17% starting chance I would die.

"Any questions?"

"What's the market value on these?" White Collar asked, leaning back in his chair, though his fist was balled at his side.

"Probably close to $65 a pill."

The Ginger whistled. White Collar didn't have any more questions.

Michael gave everyone one more look down, before clearing his throat. *"I'll start. We go clockwise. Whoever is holding at the end of the round will start the next round."* In one swift motion, holding eye contact with The Woman, he lifted the gun to his head.

Click.

It was higher pitched than I would have expected, unthreatening.

It was just a game after all. My hands were cemented to the edge of the table.

Michael handed The Woman the gun, without ever looking away. *"Pass or Play?"*

The gun dropped into her open palm, her hand almost hitting the table from the sudden weight. As she lifted the gun to her head, her eyes never left her lap. Her finger inched around the trigger. We watched from the edge of our seats, except Michael. He glanced over her shoulder, disinterested, to the two men who had entered and protected the door. But were they stopping people from coming in, or going out? The Woman pulled the trigger.

Click.

She gasped, then began laughing again. She put the gun down slowly on the table. "Oh my God," she breathed out. "Fuck, this shit is great."

Two pulls. No bullet. 25% chance I would die.

I sat back in my chair, forcing myself to unclench both my jaw and my knees. Michael shifted his gaze briefly to me, then rested on White Collar.

The Woman pushed the gun across the table to Chris. He moved a lot quicker than she did, lifting the gun straight to his head. He hesitated, opening his eyes and shaking his head down to his shoulders. He said, "I'm going to pass." Then placed the gun on the table beside me, "Pass or play, Kid?"

I put the gun to my head, resting the end behind my temple. It was cold. It didn't seem real, the gun, this situation, any of it. My thoughts were muted, underwater. What was my percentage? My breathing was the only thing I could hear. I flinched, pulling the trigger.

Click.

A loud exhale escaped my lips, a heaviness slouching my shoulders forward. Michael surveyed me, hiding his thoughts. Then he looked to the table, nodding. *"That's three pulls, end of round one."* Their claps were noiseless, a silent applause to the drumline behind my ears. My hand stiffened around the gun, unable to move.

White Collar tapped me on the shoulder, jumping me out of the trance. "Hey, it'll get easier, Kid."

The side glance was a reflex. "Doesn't seem that hard to begin with."

Offended or defensive?

White Collar's eyebrows raised, an amused frown developing. "Right. You seem pretty relaxed."

I dropped the gun, the metal thudding against the scratched table.

"Who's in for Round 2?" Michael looked directly at me, the hint of a smirk on his lips.

My father wasn't a complete basket case like my mother, but he had his dense moments. When I was younger, I pretended he was a tough lover. I pretended he showed affection through pushing me to work harder, be brighter, and make something of myself. I pretended that he cared deep down, but outward expressions were a sign of weakness. I could understand that.

Sometimes I pretended he just didn't care at all. No matter my accomplishments –or failures for that matter– he didn't give a shit either way. That would explain why he never attended any parent-teacher conferences, or asked about my career plans, or happened to wonder where I was if I wasn't at home. I could understand that too. At least we could relate on that level.

Neither, as it turned out, was the truth.

It took a little over a decade for me to figure it out, the longest any puzzle had ever taken me. Childish naïveté. My twelfth birthday was absurdly unexciting. My mother cooked grilled cheese for lunch because Blake asked for it and I didn't care. The cheese was tasty though, something artisanal from Trader Joes.

Twelve was the last year I received a gift for my birthday. I pulled out the board game Clue from a shiny blue gift bag with green stuffing paper. My eyes flickering up to my mother.

"You like mysteries, right?" Her smile faltered, waiting for validation that I didn't give.

Blake eased the game away from me, "Oh, Clue! This is a great game! We always play it at camp, remember Ricky?" He nudged me, already tearing into the box.

"Yeah, sure." I settled in because they were going to force me to play anyway. I was wearing a light red sweater, my mother's hobby back then was knitting. It was an early birthday present. Blake was still in his pajamas.

The key to winning at Clue was a combination of information gathering and simultaneously withholding information. Blake always lost because he gave away too much of his hand. I could read him within the first few moves. My mother never gathered enough information, making wild guesses out of the thin air.

It was almost sad how I repeatedly wiped the floor with them. It was like tic tac toe, once I knew the strategy, I could win every time. But if they were having fun, it would be selfish to stop on my own account.

"I didn't know you had the revolver!" My mother gave me another point on the white board for winning, then gathered up the cards again. "I could have sworn it was in the library."

"You were barking up the wrong tree the whole time."

"Or," She looked at me, a smile in her eyes. "You're just good at bluffing."

My father bumbled downstairs, ending his phone call with a curt goodbye when he saw all of us kneeled at the living room coffee table. It was a Saturday, but he was wearing a suit as if were headed to the office anyway. He always started his day in a suit. "What's going on here?"

"We're playing Clue!" Blake chimed.

"Oh fun, I love a good strategy game." We waited, and my mother even scooched over on the floor for him, but he didn't join. Finally he said, "Well, have fun. I think it's a great day for a walk." And with a nod to himself, or maybe to us, he walked out the front door.

After all the years wondering, it finally clicked. "Is he autistic?"

"*Ricky!*"

"What?"

Blake leaned forward, "What's autistic?"

My mother sighed. She scratched the back of her head as she craned her head up to the ceiling, but our walls were smooth, no popcorn faces with the answers. "Autism is," She took another breath, pulling tidbits stored away from television commercials and pamphlets handed out at PTA meetings. "Autism is a condition."

Blake nodded along, "So like, shampoo, got it."

My mother winced, "No no." She rubbed her hands together, trying again. This wasn't The Talk that her monthly parenting magazine prepared her to give. "Autism is a neurological condition. People with autism have a harder time communicating with people and receiving information from their surroundings."

Blake erased what he previously nodded along to, then nodded along. "Oh, gotcha. But why?"

"I don't know, brains do weird, unexplainable things sometimes." She leaned her head to me. "But no, your father does not have autism." And with that, she picked up her character piece for the game.

"There's nothing wrong with autism." I tapped my chin, "Or, maybe he has Asperger's."

My mother vehemently denied it, somehow forgetting their entire relationship. She didn't know how to even begin to weave a mental condition into the world she had knitted. Her world had to look perfect from the outside, otherwise people might start to look in. "See," she said a few hours later when he returned from his walk with a birthday cake and piles of more gifts. "He has intuitive people skills!"

But I had also seen her text him to bring all of it home.

Round two.

"As always, I'll go over the rules. If you decide not to play, this is your chance to back out. No questions, no losses." He scanned over us, stopping briefly at the Woman sitting to his right, then sat the revolver on the table. *"Second round. One bullet. Three pulls."*

We took a quick intermission between rounds. We were released to mingle with the party, refreshing our drinks and deciding if we wanted to bolt. We all returned. I sat in the same spot, across from Michael. I was the halfway point. I was the determining factor.

"If you pass, you forfeit a quarter of your share. So, pass wisely." Michael passed the first shot, sliding the revolver to Ginger.

Ginger picked up the gun, the end shaking until finally resting against the side of his temple. His eyes were wide, looking between the bodies at the table. With a click, his turn was over.

Chris also passed, so it was my turn. The gun was lighter this time around, but just as cold. I lifted it to my head, tapping it twice to hide that I couldn't hold my hands steady.

Another click.

"You're good at bluffing." I couldn't tell if he meant it as a compliment or a sarcastic critique.

White Collar passed, and for the first time I noticed he was left handed.

The Woman also clicked.

She let out a sigh, setting the gun down. "Wow, that is such a rush," she said between gulps of air.

It was like we were at a Be the Best YOU! Workshop, where awkward unemployable losers tried to better themselves through pep talks and tips on exuding confidence.

There were three clicks and no deaths. The Ginger clapped, resembling one of those annoying people in the back of the plane when it finally touched down. We took another quick break, a few of the others stood up to stretch their legs and shake the nerves out of their fingertips. I stayed sitting, alternating between scratching the underside of the table and watching Michael watch everyone else.

How many times had Michael played?

The third round started with the Michael passing, again. I couldn't tell if he was a coward, or being strategic. White Collar cleared his throat as the revolver was passed around.

Click. Even with sweat dripping down the side of his face, the Ginger nodded to himself as he lifted his finger from the trigger.

Chris passed and the gun was in my hand again.

I swung the gun up to my head, barely giving my heart the chance to skip a beat before firing.

Click.

I closed my eyes, exhaling through my nose. It was only a game. I handed the gun over without opening my eyes. I was stuck deciding whether to play by the individual statistics or the entire game. One made it easier to play, the other made it more fun.

"What did I tell ya, Kid?" White Collar lifted the gun from my palm. "It gets easier." His voice was a mouse whisper compared to the loud blast that followed.

-15-

I was frozen. The Ginger was the one who screamed. Warm blood clung to the side of my face, but my body was chilled. White Collar slumped out of the chair, toward me. The Woman grimaced, looking away and faking a cough into her sleeve. White Collar slid down the leg of my chair, pooling at the floor, the gun still loosely wrapped in his left hand. Blood reached out to my shoes, but I couldn't move them from the path. My eyes didn't leave his face until the bodyguards hoisted White Collar's body away from me.

"*Do you need a handkerchief?*" With a hand signal he gestured toward a table in the corner.

Robotically I stood, my face hot but my body freezing. The gunshot kept replaying in my mind, the sound jolting me in an endless loop. I picked up the cotton towel, folded next to a bowl of clean-looking water. I dipped a corner of the towel in the water, then wiped my face.

I'd never considered myself any sort of fighter, not by any means. It was important to recognize personal strengths and weaknesses. I had quite a few strengths, but from a young age, I had always known fighting was not one of them. Physically, anyway.

Still, I somehow managed to get pulled into a literal back alley brawl the end of my sophomore year. We were walking in the city, Blake, Andrea, Jensen, and I, wasting the rest of our spring days before summer started and we needed to crack down on PSAT practice exams. I had already aced my PSAT sophomore year, but it was a fool's mistake to rest on laurels.

There was something calm about that chilly spring afternoon, the way the clouds covered the sky but the concrete still sparkled with leftover glitter from last night's Drag Queen Crawl.

At the time, Andrea's arm was snaked around my waist, and mine rested over her bare shoulders. For the life of me, I couldn't remember what we were talking about, but maybe I hadn't been listening in the first place.

Four guys rounded the corner, the leader storming toward us like a mom at a Macy's Black Friday sale. "You piece of shit!" He yelled, pointing at our group. He had a heavy New York accent, with black hair slicked into a low ponytail.

It was natural to assume he was talking to Jensen.

Jensen immediately skipped forward, closing the distance with his hands raised in peace. "Wait, hold on guys, let's calm down and talk about it." Jensen's voice switched to negotiator.

"Who the fuck are you?" He moved Jensen out of the way and continued for the rest of us.

I put Andrea behind me, "What's the problem here?" If their target wasn't Jensen, I was the next logical source of their aggression.

But he ignored me as well and snatched Blake by the front of his shirt. "Stay the fuck away from my girlfriend, you hear me?" He didn't go to our school, none of them did.

We all looked at Blake.

"I promise I haven't. Well," He shifted his eyes. "Who's your girlfriend?"

"Sakiko!"

Blake looked up. "Hm."

"You—"

"No, no!" Blake held up his hands, "I mean I haven't done anything with Saki, I barely know her, actually. Real nice girl though, she seems swell."

Andrea whispered, "Who's Sakiko? Does she go to our school?"

The aggressor tightened his grip on Blake's shirt, "You call her Saki?"

Blake flinched from the yelling and I lunged forward, pushing the aggressor off Blake with both of my hands "Get off of him!"

Blake fell to the sidewalk like a crumpled newspaper and I barely had time to blink before a crack in my nose sent me flying into the brick wall of the building behind me.

Then I tasted blood.

It filled my mouth, a sudden stream of hot iron. My hand shot up to touch my stinging lip and it pulled away with blood. Bright and red and I couldn't stop staring at it.

Jensen tried stepping in but one of the friends kneed Jensen in the stomach and he fell faster than Blackberry usage in 2009. I wiped away more blood from my nose, blinking away the ringing in my ears. Andrea screamed, Blake was crying, Jensen threatened to call his family's attorney. And I couldn't stop looking at my own blood. It was fascinating. And so real. I wasn't a masochist, but it felt right, in a way. As if getting punched somehow put the world back in perspective. I could taste again, and hear, and feel. I saw passion, not in myself, but on the bloody knuckles of the one who punched me.

I wasn't a fighter, but I wished I was.

I took my time cleaning White Collar's blood off my face. I returned to the table, slowly pulling my chair out. Red splatters decorated the left side of the seat. *"Are you ready, Kid?"* Michael's eyes flickered up to me.

I didn't have a comeback, so I just sat down.

The Woman laughed, slapping the table. "Was that your first dead body, Kid?" She sat up straighter in her chair, shifting to get comfortable. "That cherry popped all over the side of your face, huh?"

The other two men were silent. Slowly, the loud electronic music from the other room crept back into my ears. "How many rounds has he played?" My voice, quiet.

"Maybe about four or five times. He was cocky." He locked eyes with me. *"But the best of them are."*

I wasn't sure what to make of that.

"What he was, was a grump," the Woman laughed. "He has more of a personality now than he ever had before." She rubbed her hands together, scooting away from the table. "Can we get on to splitting the pot now, so I can go?"

A few days ago, during zero period ASB, I was called into the principal's office. I knocked on the frosted glass of his door.

"Ricky, come in."

The school bathroom scene played over in my head, the kid walking in, seeing the paper towel on my arm. Or maybe someone had witnessed me walking home from the trap house one night, crying, dizzy, and vomiting alcohol and party drugs. Maybe someone noticed I missed half a week to recover. Maybe they noticed the canyons carved into my skin.

But instead of an intervention, two of someone else's parents sat in the room. "Oh, hello," I quickly bared my teeth in what I hoped was a smile.

The parents, giddy with energy, bounced their knees and tapped jeweled fingers and wrists against the thick chair arms. The principal had his fingers crossed in front of him, planted atop his desk. The interior was plain, light brown furniture, a few degrees on the walls and a mostly bare bookcase.

"Ricky, this is Mr. and Mrs. Edison," the Principal introduced us. "This is Ricky." We grimace-smiled at each other. "Ricky, Mr. and Mrs. Edison are facing the ever confounding question of whether they should take their freshman son out of private school and transfer to a public school."

"Why would they do that?"

Mr. Edison cleared his throat, leaning forward. "We just want what's best for him."

"What did Google tell you?"

"Google?" He looked to his wife, who shook her head. "We didn't look that up."

The Principal caught my expression and interjected. "They were hoping for a personal experience and I thought you would be a great insight, since you're one of our top students."

The top. To be exact.

I took an empty seat. This was nothing related to me, I could relax. "Mr. and Mrs. Edison, may I be frank?" They nodded. "How are his grades?"

They discussed under their breath before Mrs. Edison took the microphone. "Decent, he's about average."

"Is he going to college?"

"Well, yes, of course."

"IVY? Private?"

They looked at each other, "We're not sure."

"Then it probably doesn't matter that much. It's more of a parental preference. If you don't mind paying, then keep him in private school. If he needs a competitive advantage and connections to get into a school, keep him in." My words came out in a flurry, spilling into the room. I forced myself to breathe. "His GPA might rise in public school, but his testing scores would also probably drop."

Which happened to Jensen, back in middle school. Even though his state testing scores dipped a little, his overall performance increased because the bar was set lower. Jensen was equally as responsible with his homework, joined the same amount of clubs as he would have in private school, and drank just as much when his parents left town regardless if he was wearing a uniform or not.

My parents almost sent me to private school, back in elementary school, but I rejected the idea. I couldn't leave Blake alone. However, if they had known I played Russian Roulette for drugs that I sold back to Max, they might have insisted.

Still wouldn't have made a difference.

I stumbled out of the Principal's office in my head and I was in the Back, sitting at the card table. Memories melded with reality, but if I shook my head hard enough and knives dug into the back of my eyeballs, then I knew it was real.

I tucked my share of the drugs in the bottom of my backpack, blinking away the fog. With our business for the night concluded, we were thrown back into the party, the door shut solidly behind us. The music swallowed me, catching my body as I fell forward.

"Hey man, you alright?"

"Just tripped," I said to the music. Or maybe I was tripping. Hard to tell. "Where's the alcohol?"

The music grabbed my hand, helping me to my feet and leading me into the sea, occasionally looking back to make sure I was still following. It was amazing that my feet could move. "What do you drink?"

"Do you have any NyQuil?"

"Dewie Hand Kill?" His eyebrows knitted together. He was drunk. "I haven't heard of that one. What about a Long Island?"

"New York is beautiful in the spring."

"What's your name?"

"Ricky."

"Here's your drink, Nicky." A lukewarm drink was placed in my hand. In my other hand, a corner of a brownie. I had lost track of everything shooting through my veins already. My limbs were working on autopilot and the only one of my senses I had left was sight, though it was shakier than the Blair Witch Project. I wiped my nose, just in case.

Everything else was numb, with the exception of my chest, and even that was starting to fade. I was in a good place, but any more might be an overdose. But it was also Friday night so.

Fuck it.

He cheered with a woo, clumsily knocked his cup against mine, slapping my shoulder and aggressively bopping his head to the beat.

The night progressed as if I were watching it through a View Master. One scene played out before me, dancing with my new stranger friend, before the scene quickly switched to another image on the reel.

We finished our Long Islands. He started making out with someone. I liked the music.

The View Master flipped to the next image.

There was a wet spot on my shirt. He made himself another drink. We shared a quick bump with an outfit-coordinated couple in the pantry. There was a lot of canned green beans.

The View Master flipped to the next image.

A fight broke out in the living room. The coffee table was smashed. A blur jumped in the middle, holding the fight clouds apart. I slipped a Xanax under my tongue.

The View Master flipped to the next image.

I was sitting on the couch. It felt like my body had melted into the cushions. A girl sat on my lap, but she didn't notice I was under her. She had short black hair and ruby red lipstick. She continued her conversation with the blur perched on the arm of the couch.

The View Master flipped to the next image.

I was curled over the trashcan in the kitchen. My hands clasped the plastic while my chin shivered against the inner rim. Someone patted my back and out flew the vomit. Out of my mouth, out of my nose, an Icelandic waterfall of puke spewing from my face. I was crying. I wished I was dead.

The View Master flipped to the next image.

I was dancing.

I wasn't sure what my drink was, but it didn't matter as long as I wasn't able to feel my hand closing around the cup or the condensation pooling between my fingers or the burn of bottom shelf vodka running down my throat. As long as I wasn't able to feel the phantom gun in my hand. The ache against my temple. As long as I was numb.

Then I didn't care.

The house spun around me, orbiting, faces and bodies fusing together while I hovered off the floor. I felt so light, almost free.

But in the back of my mind, I knew I would never fly. Not without finding my ledge to jump off. I didn't understand how everyone else seemed to be so content with sinking to the bottom, or even worse, plateauing.

My feet returned to the pulsing floor and they started running. In search of space, was what my mind called it. In search of an itch, was what my body called it. My heart, however, was eerily silent on the discussion.

I barricaded myself in the bathroom, slamming my foot at the bottom of the door until I finally fiddled the thing locked. I flung the drawers of the cabinet open, looking for a razor.

Apparently it wasn't common to keep unguarded razors lying around in the guest bathroom of a trap house. Who would've guessed?

Fuck.

My veins ached. I needed to see blood, to see life. I needed to feel real. I balled up my fist, slamming it into the olive leaf wallpaper.

Again and again, I threw my fist at the wall, pounding away at my skin. I only played catch three times in my life, and they were never with my parents. Andrea's dad had a good arm though. My inflated head wobbled, twisting lefty loosey off my neck from all the spinning.

Finally, I saw it. Bright and red. I dropped my hands, and they swung by my side like anvils on a pendulum. Torn away from the wallpaper, small indents in the popcorn plaster.

"Why are you punching the wall, Ricky?" A popcorn face with half a nose asked, my blood staining his right cheek. "It won't change anything."

"It makes him feel better, can't you see that," the other face answered.

"Seems like a waste of energy, don't you have a rally to organize?"

"Stop talking about me like I'm not here!" I snapped, and the faces vanished. I was in a stranger's bathroom, alone, yelling at a hole. I pressed my empty head against the wall, and closed my eyes.

Inhale.

-16-

I hadn't slept in two days.

"Jesus Christ, Ricky, you look like shit."

"Thank you, Blake." I ducked away from his prodding fingers. My tongue felt like sandpaper.

"Honestly," Jensen said, plopping his stack of mail in the center of his dining room table. We had gathered here today for one of the most life changing momentous decisions in our young adult lives. "I feel like opening our acceptance letters together is kind of lame."

Samantha neatly placed her stack in front of her. "That's because yours probably aren't acceptances." Her hair was pulled back into a ponytail with a pink hair clip.

"What-the fuck-ever, Samantha." He rolled his eyes, setting a bowl of tortilla chips on the table as well. Jensen had a decent shot at great universities. Jensen Mayhew, ranked 110-ish in looks, 111-ish in academics, 112-ish in personality. A slightly above average candidate except for the fact he was hands down the most well connected high schooler on the west coast, which was the top quality in any field.

Perfect grades would only go so far.

I hadn't taken my packets out of my backpack yet, letting the bag slug down the legs of my chair instead. At the beginning of the application season, we had agreed to open our letters together. Not that it was a competition, but it was a little bit of a competition. Jensen, Samantha, and I each applied to The Ivys: Yale, Harvard, University of Pennsylvania, Princeton, Columbia, Dartmouth, and Brown. If it wasn't founded before the Civil War, it didn't count.

Katie also applied to Harvard but didn't want to drain her mother's wallet by joining the Ivy pact. She didn't care for the Ivy title anyway, Harvard just so happened to be tied for the best political science curriculum in the country. For the same reason, Katie also applied to Stanford.

Although interior design was Katie's passion, Samanatha convinced Katie to pursue a field where success was less subjunctive. Especially after looking over Katie's inspiration board. Katie had a few safety schools in the running as well, just in case her steady 3.8 GPA and 1520 SAT score failed to impress after the hiccup she had during interviews.

"Man, it felt like forever waiting on these things," Katie laughed, flipping through her unopened packets.

"It's only been a few days," Samantha said, staring at our piles.

Jensen was banking on Columbia, since eight generations of Mayhew's donated generously to their alma mater, but his pool also included the universities of Oxford and Cambridge. If he didn't get into an Ivy, he would abandon the USA in search of British accents, giant clocks, and enough beer to forget the fact he would never see the sun again.

Samantha applied to MIT, UC Berkeley, Cal Tech, and Carnegie for BioEngineering and Nuclear Science. She didn't tell us until a few months ago, but they were solid options for her interests and career goals.

Blake plopped himself down on the chair next to me, quickly pulling a few of his own packets from his backpack. "Well, I'm not in on the Ivy challenge, but I'm pretty excited. It's the moment we all start planning the rest of our lives, right?"

I would have to spend the rest of my life like this.

Samantha rolled her eyes. "Start planning? If you don't have a roadmap for the next six and a half years, backups and detour routes included, then you're already at least two years behind. Right, Ricky?"

"Sure." Moving the corresponding levers in my brain to respond took so much energy. I shook my head, trying to spread myself back into the crevices of my fingers and toes. "Right, okay, let's just do it."

"Direct. I like it," Samantha smiled at me.

I couldn't find the muscle fiber needed to smile back. Was it the switch on the left or the one on the right?

Jensen grabbed his first letter. "Let's do Ivy first to get it out the way."

Katie shoved a handful of tortilla chips into her mouth, crumbs falling onto the table. "Ricky, you move like you're ninety."

I felt like I was ninety.

Blake hurried to grab my packets from my backpack, plopping them in front of me. Heavy.

"Dude," Jensen whistled at my stack. "How many did you apply to anyway?"

Blake laughed, answering for me while the words swirled around my head. "Well, I made him apply to colleges I could get into so of course, none of those overlapped."

Samantha clapped her hands together. "Okay, Ivy, everyone open!"

Letters were furiously torn, either by hand or with Jensen's silver letter opener. Aside from me, only Samantha got into Harvard and Yale, but she was also the only that was rejected from the UPenn.

Her mother got into a fender bender during their UPenn campus tour. She then proceeded to cuss out the security guard for assuming the accident was her fault and not the fault of the other vehicle with the elitist dad who jeered that her rental car was 'dinged anyway' and his piece of shit son in the passenger seat that laughed as Samantha's family was escorted off campus. But that surely had nothing to do with the decision.

Jensen managed to snag a yes from Columbia with the rest of us, as well as Princeton and Brown. Both Samantha and Jensen were waitlisted for Dartmouth, though I had predicted that from their lackluster personal statement.

"You got into all of them, Ricky?" Katie wiped her hands on her Harvard rejection letter, "That's amazing!"

I followed the recipe.

Samantha neatly divided her stacks, waitlist was sorted in the no pile. "UPenn sucks anyway."

Jensen's stacks were sorted by Columbia and not-Columbia. "Sounds like you're just a hater."

"Sounds like your family paid for your acceptances."

"What's the point of money if you can't use it to get ahead in life?" Jensen didn't bother opening the rest of his letters. "What about your other fancy schools, Samantha? Will you stay on the West Coast or venture to cold and miserable New England?"

"It's not cold all the time. Only in the winter."

"Keep telling yourself that."

Samantha got accepted into all of her Tech schools, which was for the best in my opinion. They were more suited and focused to her career rather than just being a brand.

Katie pushed the chip bowl to me as she opened the rest of her letters. I took a chip, but it could have been Styrofoam and I wouldn't have known the difference.

Katie was waitlisted for Stanford. She reread the letter again, as if it would change the outcome. Samantha leaned over to rub her shoulder, "It's alright Katie, you got into your safety schools."

"I'll see if my dad knows anyone at Stanford," Jensen offered, "I'm sure he can help out somehow."

"Thanks, guys," Katie tucked her papers back into her backpack, to cry over later. "Uh, well, that sucked. Blake? What about you?"

Blake only applied to state schools for potential scholarship purposes. He knew where to aim, with strong suggestions from me, and he got into all three of them. State schools were all the same academically speaking, it just boiled down to which of the locations was preferred and the merit of their sports team, if that was a priority.

We agreed to keep in touch with our final decisions so we could come up with a college list for the graduating class. I let Blake drive me home, but he wouldn't stop talking about things that didn't matter to me anymore. Like, "Which school are you going to pick?"

"Whichever one you pick."

"What?" He glanced in my direction, then returned his eyes to the road. "Are you serious? No, you gotta choose one of the big wigs!"

"I just applied for the game. Undergrad doesn't matter nearly as much as grad school."

"But it could help you get into a better grad school."

If I lived that long.

Blake kept talking, "Is it because you'll miss me too much? You should sleep on it, it's a big decision. You shouldn't make any rash choices."

A few hours later I played another round of Russian Roulette.

Ending the school week at the Back basement had become my new pickup. It was social hour without the talking, it was peaceful relaxation without the idle wastefulness, it was an exciting adventure without the energy strain, and it was a scratch without the cut.

It was productive.

It was my third time making it through a roulette game, and the third time was always the charm. Someone had lit up a cigar, fake Cuban, leaving the room in a light smokey haze. The gun rested in front of Michael, wiped clean from blood. I had witnessed two more deaths in total, but none of them haunted me like White Collar's, his dead eyes etched into the back of my eyelids.

The bodyguards hauled away the most recent body, across the table from me. It marked the end of the night for everyone.

The pot was divided between the survivors and we stood to leave.

"If anyone wants to stay for another round, it's completely up to you." It was how he concluded all of the games, with a dismissive glance as we simultaneously agreed to quit while we were ahead, content to live another day.

But where was the fun in that?

"I'll take you up on that," I said, silencing the noise of everyone else walking out. I stayed seated. The others paused for one last look, accepting that they wouldn't see me again. Shaking their heads without a second glance, they resumed toward the safety exit.

Michael didn't seem at all surprised, but he also didn't have that expression in his repertoire of emotions. *"Alright, Kid, I had a feeling you would man up sooner or later."*

"Whatever."

He smirked, gesturing me toward the seat sitting across from him.

"It's not polite to ask your guests to move." Then I gestured to the seat across from me. Michael checked over his shoulder at the bodyguards.

"I suppose it isn't, but I've never been one for manners anyway. Here, let's sit at the smaller table." He stood and pointed to the table the guards usually occupied.

Even as high as I was, I knew this was not a smart decision. I should have left with everyone else. I had an essay to write for someone and it was my turn to do the math problems due next Monday. But I didn't come here to be smart. "Should we flip for it?"

"If that will make you feel better." I let the comment slide, watching as he pulled a coin from the wallet in his jacket pocket. *"Heads or tails?"*

"Tails."

My eyes flickered up as the coin flipped in the air, but his stayed on me. He caught it and flipped it onto the back of his hand. *"Heads."* He studied my face as we took our seats. *"You have the first pull."*

I reached forward, grabbing the revolver in my hand. It felt heavier this time. Final.

The barrel of the gun rested against my temple. What did they do with the bodies? Did they throw them in a back alley to be identified by police or did the bodies disappear without a trace? I pulled, but it was just a click.

We exhaled at the same time. I sat the gun back in the center of the table. *"Have I ever told you where I got my paintings?"* He said, studying the gun.

I looked to the walls, stark white canvases dirtied with rust splotches. "A janky swap meet?"

Something that might have been a laugh caught itself in his throat. *"No, no,"* he paused, tapping a finger on the table. *"No. It's what's left of everyone who has played the last round with me."* He reached on the side of the table, revealing two more blank canvases.

"Their blood?" Artistic, though questionably unhygienic.

"Prop it against the wall and lean forward, for the best display." He pulled out a cigarette pack from his pocket. *"You want one?"*

"No thank you, smoking will kill you."

His eyes flicked to me.

I took the canvas from the side of the table, leaning it against the wall as he did. What shape would my brain make on this canvas?

Every year at Shollman Primary School, we had to take an arts elective. An hour each day, we were collected from our classes and taken to choir or gardening or recorder or ceramics. In fifth grade, we had water painting.

In fifth grade, I met Samantha.

She hoisted herself up on the stool next to me, her red hair just a short curly bob back then, like a poodle with a bad perm. The canvas was practically the same size as her, but she picked up the paintbrush, took one last look at the examples posted in the front, and dipped her brush.

She held herself like an eagle, poised and focused. I hadn't realized I was staring until she huffed, put her brush down, and looked straight at me. "Would you like to take a picture? Maybe that would be a more reliable reference for you." She smiled, but it was acidic. Her nose was so small I couldn't believe it was used for breathing.

I frowned, putting down my own brush. "I don't think a picture would be able to capture your terrible demeanor."

"What's a demeanor?"

"Your mannerism."

"My presence," she countered with a synonym.

"Attitude."

"Huh." She pulled a little notebook from the pink pocket purse slung across her chest. "Demeanor," she repeated. "D-E-M-E-N—"

"You missed the A." I spelled it out. "D-E-M-E-A-N-O-R."

She corrected herself, then stashed the notebook. She picked up her paintbrush again. "Thank you, rude man. Now, if you would please keep your eyes on your own work, I'd appreciate that."

She exaggeratedly turned away from me and put her brush to the canvas, sweeping pink paint across the white, but I continued watching. "You keep a list of vocabulary words," I said. I had never seen someone collect words outside of school vocabulary lists. She was giving herself homework. "Why?"

"What's it to you?"

"Why don't you just remember them in your head?"

"Maybe my head isn't as big as yours."

I laughed, caught off guard. No one had ever called my head big before. "Is that an insult or a compliment?"

"In what world is having a big head a compliment?"

"You could have meant I was smart."

"Then I would have complimented your brain." Another pink sweep. "But." She sat up straighter. "I didn't."

"You should structure your sentences better than."

Another sweep. "Or maybe you should get better at comprehension." No one had ever critiqued me before either.

"So," I prompted when she continued to ignore me. "What are you painting?"

"Tulips." Her answer was curt, but her eyes softened.

"Pink tulips."

She was wearing a soft pink shirt, with ruffles at the shoulders, and pink jelly sandals. "They're my favorite."

"Pink doesn't look good with your hair."

She gripped her paintbrush so hard I could hear the plastic handle buckle. "And what exactly are you painting over there, Einstein?"

"Picasso," I corrected, which made her clinch the paintbrush harder. I swiveled on my stool, returning to my canvas. "I'm painting the sky."

"It's all black."

"Navy blue mixed with black, actually." I dipped my wet brush into the white paint, flicking spots onto the night sky.

"Stars?"

"They're my favorite." I submerged my brush in the water, swirling white into the dark water. I climbed down from the stool, finished. Ahead of everyone else, as usual.

"Stars are boring. Plus, you're not even really painting. You're already done."

I shrugged. "Not my fault you're slow."

"I think I hate you."

"I think I hate you too."

The blank canvas stared back at me, warm from the yellow light of the lamp but cold against the concrete walls. In painting class, they taught us how to mix colors to create a flexible palate. The color of blood was easy enough, a lot of red and a little bit of a brown, or black in a pinch.

Dried blood, however, was harder. Start with a red warmed brown and add orange to age the dusty mixture. I wasn't a natural at painting, but I could follow a recipe.

I rested my elbows on the table. "Why didn't you bring out the arts and crafts before I pulled?"

Michael pushed a cigarette out of the box. Did he need something to steady his hands? *"Honestly, I didn't think you would."* He leaned forward, scooping up the gun.

"What if that one had the bullet?"

"I guess I'd be out a painting, huh?" He positioned himself closer to the canvas as he pressed the gun to his head.

Click.

He returned the gun to the center, pulling out his lighter.

I looked at the gun, then up at his face. "Pass."

"Are you trying to be strategic or are you just scared?"

"You'll have to find out."

He took a long drag before taking the gun again, not breaking eye contact.

Click.

He returned the gun to the center.

33% I would die.

"How are you liking your odds?"

"How are you liking yours?" My fingers wrapped over the gun, bringing it back to me. "I mean, if I don't die, you only have a 50/50 shot."

"If you don't die."

He sounded like the echoes of a trampoline bounce. "I'll give you one last chance," I said, my voice calm. I could feel the heat under my skin, but at least my voice showed nothing. The Xanax helped. My tone was completely void. Almost perfect. My mind was clear, misaligned with what my body wanted. Half of me was free.

Michael searched my face for a hint. Maybe he found one, maybe he didn't. The key to winning was to not give away any information, and if possible, mislead the opponent. "Going once," I said.

I couldn't remember where Blake was tonight. Was he at work? I never forgot his schedule before.

"Going twice." My finger was dry as it slide effortlessly into position on the trigger, even though I was sweating everywhere else. Michael didn't budge. He was my mirror.

"Last chance."

I'm afraid I'm going to have to pass on the offer." He cleared his throat. His voice was in my head, daring me to die.

I shrugged, bringing the gun to my temple. Michael broke eye contact, momentarily, barely the split of a second, but it was enough to give away his tell.

He surveyed me cautiously, as if I were a cornered rabid animal. Either that, or an idiot. I answered his thought aloud, "I prefer the term high functioning."

"Then what are you waiting for?"

I pulled the trigger.

-17-

Even after all this time, even after having someone's brain splattered in my eyelashes, I wasn't expecting the bang.

No one ever was.

The second before, I saw his eyes widen. A million thoughts raced through his mind, through mine, but one in particular stood out among the rest. I had won.

Until I heard the bang.

It was over.

Michael immediately stood to his feet, looking over the top of my head and slamming his hands on the table. "What is it?" He called toward the doorway.

"Cops, noise complaint."

Michael's fingers tip tapped in thought. Quickly, he stepped from around the table, pacing to the other side of the room. The bodyguard at the door spoke in a hushed but urgent tone. They began shuffling bags in silence. The music from the rest of the house was off. A glitch in the matrix.

The gun was still to my head.

"Hey, Kid, get up, we need to get out of here," Michael tossed the order over his shoulder, strapping a gun to the holster inside his jacket.

I couldn't move. My chest seethed, making my breaths sharp and sporadic. The table in front of me tunneled, the edges of my vision blurring like a cheesy Instagram filter.

The other man grabbed me by the back of my collar, hauling me out of my chair. "You deaf? Get up, come on!"

"Give him a break, he was a second away from giving me a new painting." Michael smirked in my direction, then turned back to stuffing kilos of his new cocaine blend and stacks of money into duffel bags.

He was wrong though. I had pulled the trigger.

And I had won.

"We don't have time for breaks," the other huffed again, but relinquished my shirt. I stumbled backwards, vomit catching in the back of my throat. I held the base of my neck with my right hand, but my airway continued to close.

Michael shoved one of the duffel bags into my chest as I was herded out of the back door, gasping for breath. *"You can keep the bag if you want. You earned it, Kid."*

Thrust into the dark alley, I followed them to a dry storm drain, my feet tripping over each other in the dark. A small dog barked at us through a wire fence, but other than that, the night was dead. Soothing. I inhaled to the rhythm of rustling grass.

My jello legs struggled to keep up with their hustle. I fell farther and farther behind, but they either didn't notice or didn't care. "Should we be more concerned about the police?" I checked over my shoulder for the nth time, but the heavy boots chasing after us weren't there.

Even Michael and the guard in front of me seemed to be ghostly mist, evaporating before my eyes.

That could've just been the sleep deprevation though.

"Police?" Michael just barely slowed his pace, looking up into the starless night. *"Oh, it's mostly a precaution. If it was a real problem, we wouldn't have gotten this far."*

"Remember that time last year when the house got surrounded by cars?" There was a HOA meeting in our neighborhood about that incident, it made the local papers.

The bodyguard rubbed his side as he laughed about the memory, "This is nothing, Kid."

"Ricky," I corrected.

They ignored me.

My duffle bag grew heavier with each step. Then they stopped. They waited as I slugged toward them, black silhouettes under the moon. "*Alright, well, I'll see you around somewhere, I'm sure.*" He smiled, but I saw the emptiness behind it. A mirror. "*Unless one of us dies before then.*"

"It wouldn't be surprising."

"*This was fun.*"

"That's one word for it."

"*You'll either get better or you'll get worse, but it'll always be there.*"

"What?"

The guard grunted, "Alright Chuck and Rufus," He pointed to his watch, although the hands didn't move. "We need to go."

And like that, we separated, and that was the end. It was the end because I didn't do it, I didn't die. I didn't, or I couldn't. Hard to tell. Maybe I was too passive, maybe I should have pushed for it. Couldv'e would've should've. Part of me wanted to look back, but it wouldn't change that I was alone. If Michael turned around, I would never know. It was as if it never happened. I blinked, and they were gone.

I dragged the bag of cash behind me, moving but going nowhere, mindless. All the buildup to the climax and then nothing, blue balls of the soul. Because I didn't die.

It was nearing 4am so maybe that was why, when I ended up at Hana's apartment, she hadn't answered her phone. I didn't remember the puppeteer bringing me up the stairs, but there I was, scraping my fingernails down the wood of her front door.

I was outside of my body, listening to someone else's pathetic voice emerge from my mouth. I didn't know what I was doing. Tears ran down my face, uncontrollably. I couldn't rationalize this. I was still holding the gun. It was still pointed to my head. It terrified me to watch myself, but I couldn't look away.

My fingers shook as I texted her again with one hand. Maybe she would respond to something other than 'open your door' in the middle of the night. Something that would make her pay attention, even minimally.

"Would you like to go to prom with me?"

I had asked Andrea to prom, last school year, sometime vaguely around Christmas. December 19th. She liked to do stupidly themed things like drink eggnog and walk around brightly lit houses while dressed as Santa's little helpers. The night was incredibly forgettable, a chilling 45 degrees but no wind and clear skies. Plenty of stars, but critiquing Christmas lights was just as enjoyable, I told myself.

Our fingertips were warmed by our disgusting holiday drinks we picked up from the new drivethru on the corner of Seventh and Hartfeld. The cashier woman said we made a 'cute pair' as she handed my card back.

Andrea took her costume quite seriously, ignoring the cold in a red velvet top and shorts set, long white socks, and black combat boots I had given her as a Christmas present. Andrea had been eyeing them for a while, keeping the internet window to her Nordstrom cart permanently minimized on her laptop. She missed the email about the Black Friday sale and they went out of stock within hours.

I never missed an email.

"Ricky, you aren't wearing your ears!" She poked me in the chest, her ponytail swinging behind her.

"Weird, they must have fallen off in the car." She loaned me a red and black sweater for the night, a sweater that was still in the back of my closet. Andrea was going to visit her grandparents for Christmas, so this was our last evening together for two weeks. I took a deep breath, "Hey, Andrea, do you want to go to prom?"

"Of course!" Her eyelashes fluttered. "Who do you think will be Prom Queen?"

"I don't know many girls from your class that would be in the running. Probably Kacey."

"Seriously?" She pouted, "Probably. You're right."

"You're captain now though, so you could go for it if you really want to." I cleared my throat. "But back to the point, I was asking because I would like to go to prom with you, since you would of course want to go."

"Oh, well, yeah." Her fucking eyelashes fluttered again. "I would love to go to prom with you!" Her voice hit a bad high note and she looped her arm in mine as we continued to stroll down the sidewalk.

We never made it to prom, however, because Andrea moved.

I pressed the call button. Hana would at least have a razor blade. Or spray paint. Or nail polish remover. Hair spray wasn't chloroform, but it could do the trick. "Pick up, pick up, pick up," I chanted, hiccupped. "Please pick up." If I could talk to her, it would go away. I wouldn't be alone with it clawing at my chest. I needed her. She just had to pick up.

It went to voicemail.

The duffel bag slid from my sloped shoulders, dropping to the worn straw doormat. I clutched my phone harder, digging it into my forehead. Then scraping it against my forehead. Then ramming it into my forehead. I threw it somewhere, but I didn't hear where it landed over the sound of my brain yelling at itself. I dragged my face down the door, my body following and convulsing with sobs. I didn't have a pick me up, and there was no one else that could do it for me, so I slept on the doorstep until I was numb enough to move again. Hana never answered the door that night.

I was numb until two days later when we took school pictures. The numbness felt like a heavy blanket. Wool or fleece or some Egyptian cotton blend that had lost its softness. The blanket wasn't too hot or too cold, but it was heavy. It covered my entire body, wrapping me in a nest. It silenced the world around me, turning honking cars into a quaint mime show. The blanket blurred the stares people gave when they looked at me.

Most importantly though, it muted myself. With the blanket, I was a hibernating insect within a cocoon. Vacant. The only way I could move was when my mind was gone, pushed far away, tucked in the cocoon. It was the only way I could drive myself to school and sit for eight hours without screaming. It enabled me to eat and shower and talk. The blanket was the only reason I could open my eyes in the morning and do it all over again.

The easiest way to keep the blanket over me was to drink. It was quick, simple, and not many people questioned the contents of a water bottle. I wasn't getting trashed, that would be too noticeable. Just above a buzz was the sweet spot, when the blanket covered me. That was when I could function.

The school pictures took place in the gym, a photoshoot with only a simple black stool and a white backdrop. Seniors had the first week of yearbook pictures, then the following week the juniors, and so on. Pictures took place during the last period of the day, alphabetical order spread throughout the week. My scheduled day was Thursday, but that was also Hana's day, so I skipped and went on Friday.

Samantha sighed from behind me, resting her chin on my shoulder. "This is boring." She combed my hair into place with the back of her hand.

We were in the photo line, waiting. I held onto my blue water bottle while the blanket formed my lips into words. "Agreed." Today's drink was a splash of soda, a handful of Jolly Ranchers, and cough syrup.

Samantha wore her hair curly for the picture and her eyelashes at least ten times darker and longer than usual. For the senior class, the school provided the black shawl for girls and a tuxedo from the waist up for boys. After the pictures were taken, the clothing items were deposited in bins to be reused for the next day. Samantha adjusted her shawl so the point of the V aligned with the center of her chest. "At least it's going by pretty fast."

"Quickly."

"Promptly."

"Expeditiously."

"Tout de suite."

I turned to look back at her. "That was a good one."

"Thanks."

The camera flashed and the lined moved forward.

Next.

Andrea loved taking photos, especially anything having to do with a photo booth. Her face lit up with every new flash, changing expressions in time for the next shot. She was a master at angles and no stranger to acting.

When we scrambled out of the photo booth, she would playfully punch me in the arm, complaining that I never changed my face.

"What? I totally did," I argued back, pointing out that I had smiled in one frame and frowned in another.

"Why do they look the same then?"

The camera guy looked at me after a few seconds, lifting his head from behind the camera when I didn't step forward. He waited, but I was trapped in the flash of a photo booth stuck on replay. Caught between two worlds. "Next." He repeated, looking into my eyes.

That was when I realized the blanket was gone.

"Ricky?" Samantha prompted, but her hand felt like fire on my shoulder. I felt too much, all at once. The blanket was gone and the sounds all rushed back, everyone's eyes were now on me.

My hands were shaking as they twisted off the top of my water bottle, but it was empty. "Ricky?" They all repeated in unison, a stadium of voices. I stumbled backwards, out of line, out of the gym, out of the situation.

I ran into the nearest door to escape, which turned out to be a janitor's closet. My chest heaved, but not even that could bring the blanket back.

If I couldn't get alcohol for the day, the alternative was to punch myself in the face until that went numb. It wasn't as easy or long lasting, but it worked in a pinch, pounding away until the hits were hollow thuds against my cheekbone.

I could finally get a breath in. I closed my eyes between gasps of air and leaned my head against the cement wall, wiping at the stray tears clinging to the bottom of my chin.

"Ricky!"

I squeezed my eyes tighter, willing the blanket to fall faster. I rubbed my hands against my chest, counting until I couldn't hear the numbers anymore.

The doorknob wiggled, then light flooded in. "Ricky," she announced before popping her head in. "What happened? What's wrong?"

I stood back from the wall, still hanging my head. "Sorry, I was—"

"What was that?"

That was me.

She opened the door all the way. Zero hesitation, a trait I sought out in my ASB staff. I kept my head down, my eyes low. Samantha wouldn't understand the blanket. I needed something she would understand. "I was stressed. It's stress," I finally finished.

"Stress?" She squinted. "You're stressed?"

In all the years we had been in the same class and shoved our grades in each other's faces, Samantha had never heard me complain about my workload. While she had breakdowns about balancing swim and ASB or her SAT prep class after already piling on volunteering and laboratory shadowing, I never said a word of grievance. Not once. In fact, I excelled.

"Bullshit," she called.

I stared back at her.

Samantha took a closer look at me, at the reds in my eyes. At me. "Well, shit. I'm sorry. You look." She averted her eyes. "I'm sorry." I was naked without my blanket, completely vulnerable in this little closet wasn't big enough to spread my arms. Samantha sucked her bottom lip for a second. "Have you tried yoga?"

I stared back at her.

"Yoga does wonders for the mind. Getting outside really helps too. I do it regularly now. It's Earth's medicine for that kind of thing." She smiled, then looked down at her hand, an afterthought. "Oh, here, you dropped your water bottle."

"Thanks."

"Gracias."

I didn't say anything back.

"Merci," she tried again, in vain. Samantha put her arms around me, pulling me in. I flinched, anticipating a hot sting, but it never came. The blanket had returned. "You'll be okay, you'll be fine." She hummed a bit, rubbing her hands on my back. The blanket filtered her words and padded her touch. "Come on, let's wash your face so you can get your picture taken, yeah?"

My body sunk into the cocoon. "Yeah."

If people were looking at me when we returned, I couldn't see them. "ASB emergency," Samantha's voice was static.

When it was my turn, I sat down on the stool and looked into the camera's void.

"Smile!" The camera man instructed.

The blanket was so so heavy.

Next.

After, Samantha wouldn't stop texting me. Between her and Blake, I couldn't get a moment to myself. I thought the mess at the gym was the end of it, but Friday night she invited me to Jensen's game night which turned into a sleepover which turned into Saturday morning and they all dragged me to the fucking zoo.

"You know," the Samantha poked at me. "There's a reason they ask people not to feed the animals."

"Oh yeah?" I had a quarter bottle of wine swimming in my veins. "And why is that?" I kept my fingers between the gaps in the fence, dangling the beef jerky into the exhibit.

"Because you could mess up their diet. Giraffes don't even eat beef jerky."

"How do you know? Has anyone ever tried to feed them beef jerky? Maybe it's the one thing that's missing from their sad restricted little life."

"Stop! What if it gets sick?" She tried snatching the jerky away from me, but I kept her at arms distance.

"Samantha, stop molesting Ricky." Blake swooped in behind her to pull her off me.

"He was trying to feed the giraffes."

Jensen rounded the corner with his prom date, Catlynn, and some random guy from our class. Forgot his name, but he was planning to go to a nearby community college and then transfer to university after a year. It was the best plan for him since his parents made too much money to qualify for decent financial aid, yet not enough for them to pay for his school. At least he wouldn't be buried in loans for a bunch of GenEd classes.

"Samantha," Jensen interlaced his fingers in Catlynn's, though he was standing too far away from her to look at ease. "You should know better than to feed the trolls."

"It's a giraffe!"

"Shh, ignore them, Samantha, they're teasing you," Blake cooed in her ear, to which Samantha promptly wiggled out of his arms.

"No, stop trying to shut me down!" She was once again trapped in Blake's hug. "Okay, fine. But if the giraffe dies, I'm throwing all of you assholes under the bus."

It was a cute scene, in theory, a bunch of friends meandering through the zoo and making fun of animals trapped in routine.

Inhale.

"So prom." Jensen started, pulling Catlynn and their third wheel over to us. "Do we have everything set up for that? I didn't read the last couple email chains."

"Yes," Samantha said, fully embracing Blake's hug and letting him sway her side to side. "Everything is ready to go. Tickets are completely sold out. Katie finally did her job and everything is filed and organized in the cabinet. It's all in the email."

"You're going to make me read the email, aren't you?"

"I'm assuming you can read, Columbia." Samantha looked over Blake's shoulder at me. "Who are you going to take to prom, Ricky?"

What was today? Instead I asked, "When's prom?"

"Next Saturday."

I had to wake up seven more times to get there. I took a bite of the beef jerky, but the meat was too tough to chew. "Hana."

"Hana?" Samantha's eyebrow arched into a perfect triangle. "I thought you weren't. When did that? How did you? Ask?"

"We're going as friends."

Hana replied back to my prom text later that day, after I had already hauled myself off and away from her doorstep. My feet wandered that early morning, just one foot in front of the other, my brain logged into repair until further notice. Almost three hours later, I felt the vibration in my front pocket. Another hour later, I found the strength to pull it out.

"Sorry I was sleeping! Did you want to come over?" Another text.

"Sure! To Pron!"

Another text.

"Prom**"

I was exhausted that night/morning/whatever. Not physically tired, but mentally checked out. I ended up back at my house and I didn't bother using the tree to climb in. I walked right through the front door, the heavy duffel bag dragging behind me. Not even the hanging aloe vera plants in the living room batted an eye.

My thoughts swam back to the present after a few blinks. They were all waiting on me. "Hopefully she'll be a better dancer this time," I said.

Samantha ducked back into Blake's arms. "Oh, well, that will be. Pleasant." Her tone suggested I go fuck myself. "Blake will take me to prom, right Blake?"

"Sure Babe, whatever you want. I'll give you the world." He nestled his chin into her hair. "As long as you're okay being a tag-along. I'm already going with someone else."

Samantha rolled her eyes, brushing off Blake's arms.

Instead of beef jerky, I felt the gun in my mouth and the taste of acrylic red-brown paint. I had been so close to having this feeling gone, so close that I could still taste it. Freedom. The punch in my chest, deep down, under all of my bones and flesh. It was a black hole of overwhelming nothingness. Life would continue as is, the hole sometimes fading, but ultimately still there. It might subjectively get better, momentarily for pockets of time, but it wasn't going anywhere.

I couldn't keep up the routine, or at least, I knew it would be futile to attempt. Humans could outlast a lot of predators, but not themselves.

I wasn't in cross country like Blake, I couldn't keep running.

I didn't want to.

And I didn't have to.

-18-

It would be considerate to leave a note. If anything, it would help keep investigations organized. I put the cap back on the pen, gently tapping it against my chin as I read over my letter.

To whom it may concern,

Pretty standard stuff. It wasn't technically a legal will, but I left everything I owned to Blake. I told Mr. and Mrs. Schenk to take care of him, which they already did, and my car keys would be in a potted plant in the hotel lobby. There was always a potted plant in a hotel lobby.

In one short paragraph, I summed up my preferred funeral arrangements: Cremation. No wake. No reception. No attendance. Give Blake my ashes.

I doubted they would follow even the simplest of instructions, but I figured I would write it anyway. Just in case. I left the note unfolded and clearly visible on my desk. The stark white paper was blinding against the dark wood.

I had to hold onto the chair as I stood up, the alcohol from earlier kicking in: a glass of wine with a very balanced diet of grilled chicken and my last morphine pill.

I snatched my keys from my desk and headed downstairs. The house was quiet, like a forest trail before the rain. My footsteps had no audience. I wouldn't have to explain why I was dressed in a tuxedo even though I wasn't going to tonight's prom. Blake agreed to cover me at the dance. I had to have looked convincing, because he didn't argue.

My father was in his study, eyes glazed over from the glare of his computer screen, fingers itching for nicotine but pulling at his hair instead.

My mother sat lifeless in the lounge chair in their room, bundled up in the baby blanket and pretending to read the mystery novel in her hands. The curtains were drawn, but still she glanced toward the window every so often.

The usual.

I stepped outside the house, closing my eyes and letting the waves wash over me. I had been treading water for so long, caught in the rip current. Every day the shore grew farther and farther away, but exhaustion dominated me.

The hotel I chose had no particular importance, though I had visited once before for Andrea's sixteenth birthday. Completely coincidental. I only chose it because the hotel didn't pay too much attention to IDs as long as the room was paid. It was a forty-five minute drive, but worth it for the view.

I parked, letting the hum from the engine linger in my ears until the car grew cold. The door handle slipped between my fingers as I struggled to carry out a bundle of balloons, three dozen roses, and a bottle of champagne. I had spent most of the morning gathering the ingredients for my cover. I didn't tell anyone I was ditching prom until three hours ago, and only Blake.

"What do you mean you're not going to prom?" He nearly spit out his Vitamin Water while he buttoned his cufflinks in my bedroom mirror.

"I don't feel well." I was lying under my covers, only the top of my head poking out.

"And?" He snapped his head around. "It's prom. Get up."

"No."

"What's wrong? Do you have a pimple on your forehead?"

"No." Actually, my face was a wreck. I had more zits on my face now than my entire acne history combined. "I just feel," I struggled to catch a gulp of air. "Not well."

"What can I say to convince you to go?"

"Nothing."

"Okay. Nothing." He laughed at himself. "No reaction? Really? I thought it was funny."

"Can you tell Hana for me?"

"You haven't even told Hana?"

I ducked deeper into my bed.

Blake sighed. "Fine, I'll tell Hana. She can come with me."

"Thanks."

"What's wrong?"

Why did everyone keep asking me as if I knew. "I think it's the flu."

"Which end is it coming out of?"

"You look good, Blake."

Dressed in all red from head to toe, he looked over his shoulder at me in the mirror, grinning ear to ear. "You think so?"

"Borderline five-dollar pimp."

"That's what I was going for." He walked over to me and I buried myself under the blankets until only one eye peeked from a cave opening. "Will you promise to at least come at the end? I really want you there."

"Sure."

"You want me to take the prom balloons from your car? For Hana?"

"No," I stammered, then quickly recessed again. "I'll keep them. Give them to her after."

He gave me a pat and I almost spilled everything right there. But I was in the rip current, and the ocean pulled the words to the bottom of the sea floor.

Blake winked and shot me with the point of his finger. "Try not to throw up everywhere."

I lingered outside the hotel, but I wasn't stalling. I was enjoying my last euphoria. The weeds along the garden's edge cheered me along. I walked around the hotel building two or three or maybe even four times, I had stopped counting. I walked on clouds. The sidewalk welcomed me. I never thought asphalt could be so soft. Maybe it was bouncy, like a trampoline.

My phone vibrated, refocusing me back to the experiment at hand. If all went well, my boredom would be cured. This feeling would be gone. I checked my phone, but didn't bother to fully read through the messages.

Blake: prom isn't as fun without you, but Hana seems to be enjoying…

Hana: its not too late to make it!

Jensen: I'm getting lucky tonight

Katie: The tablecloths are all wrong, but at least the DJ was worth…

Samantha: what hotel are you staying at? ;)

I was tempted to respond to Samantha. I had a soft spot for irony.

Before walking in, I pulled eye-drops from my backpack, smoothed down my hair, and straightened my tie. No need to be completely disheveled for the coroner.

The glass doors slid open with a faint whistle. "Good evening, sir," the front desk attendant greeted me, one eye on my face and the lazy one on what I held in my hand. The dark circles under both eyes said it was the end of her twelve hour shift. Perfect.

"Thank you, good evening yourself," I looked to her moving nametag. "Lindsey." Her smile was polite, but not genuine. "I have a reservation under Schenk. Robert Schenk." She nodded, typing it into her computer. "It's my anniversary," I interrupted, waiting for her to look up before continuing. I needed her completely invested in my story. "Yeah, three years. I can't believe it's been that long, you know?"

I took a slow breath, concentrating on the bridge of her nose, the spot right between her eyes. "I'm surprising her tonight with, well, all this, and then I'm going to propose." I forced a lighthearted laugh.

"That sounds so cute." She smiled, then went back to her computer. "So I see you have one night booked, the Panoramic City-View Suite in the Terrace Tower."

"And the Terrace Tower had the attached patio, correct?"

"Yes."

"Great," I nodded, leaning against the front desk. I placed the roses on the counter. "A friend of mine is scheduled to set off fireworks right as I ask."

"Aren't fireworks illegal?"

Shit. "I meant the little sparkler ones. It's going to be a flash mob with music and dancing and then they're going to spell out the question in sparklers."

"Oh, that sounds amazing. Do you need someone to record it?"

"No no, we have all of that set up. Do you know if the patios have heated lamps? It's a little chilly tonight."

"I'm not sure, but if there isn't, you can call back down and I can check with housekeeping. Or maintenance. I'm not sure, one of them would know if we have any."

"That sounds excellent," I paused, watching her eyes quickly glance down at her watch. "Will you still be here in about an hour?"

She smiled softly, "Unfortunately no, I'm off in twenty minutes. I can leave a note for Tori, that's who's coming in.

She's," Lindsey searched for a work-appropriate word. "Still learning."

"Thank you, that would be so helpful. I really need everything to run smoothly."

"I wish my husband was that thorough."

Lindsey's proposal was probably very simple, very standard. Her husband acted a little weird for a few days, hiding his phone from her, making sudden doctor's appointments for a mysterious stomach ache that popped up whenever she asked where he was headed.

They both had a Saturday night off, for the first time in weeks, and he plopped down on the couch next to her, switching off the television. He told her to get dressed, they were going to dinner. So they got dressed up. They went to dinner. He couldn't even wait until the final course, sweating and tapping his foot so much that the table next to them asked to be moved.

The black box fell out of his pocket and a passing waiter scooped it up and placed it in center of the table.

Lindsey laughed, that ring now on her finger. I joined her, holding my sides because it felt like my liver was burning. She smiled, sweetly. "So I just need the card you reserved the room under and your ID."

"Oh right, of course." I shuffled the items in my hands, setting the bottle of champagne next to roses and fishing out my wallet.

Getting my father's credit card wasn't hard, especially since he left it on his desk as he worked. The back of his head was the only thing I could see, illuminated by the white light of the computer. His eyes never moved from the text on screen. I almost said goodbye, but he wouldn't hear it.

I had to get a new fake ID with my father's name, so I could use his credit card. Last minute, but I managed to get squeezed in. "Unfortunately, not the most flattering picture," I said, handing the cards over to her.

"You look so young for 22!"

"That could be all the botox."

She laughed, swiping the credit card. Lindsey handed the cards back to me without further investigation. I slipped the wallet back in my pocket as she gathered the room key.

"Ah, thank you—" I missed grabbing the key on the first try. "Thank you, I should get going."

She bid me a good night, pointing me in the direction of the elevator. My room was all the way at the top, even higher than I managed to get last time.

Immediately upon opening the door, I dropped everything except the champagne bottle and headed straight to the balcony. A few stray balloons followed me out.

"Where are the stars?" I asked, but there were no popcorn faces to answer.

My knees slumped to the patio cement, my body slouching against a pole. Well, a heat lamp. The concierge was right. I flipped the switch to what I assumed was on and took a quick thirty second chug of champagne, staring up at the clouds.

I wasn't sure how long I stayed like that.

The space heater was a nice touch.

Blake used to say I had a warm heart. "That's why you can stand the cold!" He would poke me in the center of my chest, and once I looked down, his little frozen fingers would slide up to check my chin.

I swatted his hand away, then shoved my own back in my pockets. "That doesn't even make sense." We were only eleven that particularly night, back when Blake was the teeny tiniest bit taller than me.

Blake leaned his elbow on my shoulder. "Sure it does. Because your heart is warm, that warms the rest of your body. Like a radiator."

"That sentence could have been phrased better."

"You know what I mean." He was wearing three coats on our hike, sweats over his jeans, and at least five pairs of socks plus earmuff some girl gave him. It was only October.

I was wearing a hoodie and jeans, but I didn't feel the cold as we climbed the hill. "So does that mean you have a cold heart?"

"The coldest."

It wasn't a big hill, but it was in the middle of nowhere, past the reach of city lights. It took us a bus ride and almost half an hour of climbing over fallen logs and pulling our shoes out of mud to reach the short summit.

The top was a flat plateau, with thick but short grass. The air smelled of autumn, crisp like a deep red apple. The scent was earthy, but different from Spring. Spring was bright and fresh. Spring was sweet and the air was thick. It smelled like hope. Autumn was an omen. I plopped down in the center of the field.

"So," Blake began, after he circled his spot and sat down next to me. "I was thinking."

"That's a first."

We leaned back at the same time, nestling into our familiar Saturday nights. It was cloudy, but I could imagine the constellations in the sky. Aquarius should be visible in the northern hemisphere. After a beat, Blake said, "What would you think about me moving in?"

I turned to him, but he was looking up. "You're already kind of moved in."

"I mean more than move in."

"You want to put your name on the mortgage?"

"I mean." He sucked air in through his teeth. The moon was so bright that night that it could be seen behind the grey clouds. Blake's cheeks were pinched pink. "I mean permanently."

The stars shifted underneath the veil of clouds. My zodiac sign was Aquarius. Not that I followed horoscopes, but it was a decent constellation. It didn't have any particularly bright stars, but it looked like a lasso.

"Ricky? What do you think?"

"You're already permanent, Blake." I didn't look at him. "You're not going anywhere, okay? You'll never have to worry about that."

"You're not going anywhere either, right?"

Even after stars died, the light lingered around for others to enjoy. No one noticed a star was gone until it was far too late. "Sure."

I clenched my fists on the concrete of the hotel patio. I leaned my face back, all the way to the sky, closing my eyes. The back of my eyelids swirled with speckles of yellow and red. The chilling breeze kissed my neck and I inhaled.

The air smelled hollow. I concentrated on the crispness. Like a glass of refreshing water. It wasn't autumn, but I tasted dried leaves in the air. Around me was silent yet at the same time loud. Cars honking and bare branches rustling and ghosts pulling me closer to the edge of the patio, their teasing lips nipping at my shaky hands. The autumn was inside of me.

"This is so much more fun than prom," I announced to the world, opening my eyes and rising to my feet. The high was wearing thin and my liquor was low. Still in me, but just barely casually drunk. Casually wasted. Maybe a little high. Very high.

It was hard to tell these days.

I climbed up on the balcony ledge. "Let's play a little game." I taunted myself, lifting my leg and letting it hang out over the edge, then quickly hopping onto my other foot. I swayed, from alcohol, from balance, from living. Electricity shot through my arms and pulsed all the way down my spine. It was cocaine, times a hundred.

I read a few of the baby books lying around the nursery, their spines bent and worn from the last few months of preparation. It had been so long since their first pregnancy, both of my parents had forgotten. I skipped the scarring diagrams of vaginas being split open by a twelve pound infant head, but the lullabies caught my attention.

I traced over the soft songs with the pad of my finger, resting my back against the unbuilt crib box. It was reckless to conceive at such an old age, but it was also unexpected, unplanned – at least to my knowledge – and pretty fucking bold. It was a change.

I could respect that.

As the lights danced below me from the balcony, I was laughing. Trembling. "Five little monkeys jumping on the bed." I did a small hop, staggering, but my feet found their footing. "One fell off and bumped his head. Momma called the doctor and the doctor said, no more monkeys jumping on the bed."

I skipped the length of the ledge. I was either agile, or lucky. "Four little monkeys jumping on the bed." I couldn't walk with my feet directly in front of the other, but the edge was wide enough that I was allowed to be off about half a foot before plummeting to my death.

My death.

It had a ring to it.

Exhilarating. "Three little monkeys jumping on the bed." I did a bigger jump to the side, but my foot lost its balance, toppling me backwards onto the patio. Normally, landing flat on my side from three feet in the air would hurt, but the trip was nothing more than an abrupt skip in consciousness. One moment I was up, I blinked, and then I was down.

A thud.

My chest heaved with the bubbling of laughter and anxiety. This was what love felt like. "Momma called the doctor and the doctor said," the back of my head rang the words. "No more monkeys jumping on the bed."

I barely recognized the sound of my phone vibrating against the metal table outside. It was beeping, a steady pulse from behind me.

Climbing to my feet was more of a challenge than I expected because the ground kept moving. My throat felt tense and the pit of my stomach rushed to meet it. I groaned, brain liquid sloshing against my skull as I sat up, then I violently retched into my lap. I couldn't taste the acid as it passed, but I could smell the vapors. Then it poured from my nose as well. I lurched forward, the remaining vomit pooling out in front of me, splattering the floor.

It ruined my nice suit.

I felt lighter, lighter than I had ever been. I used the table to pull myself to my feet, wiping my mouth with the back of my sleeve. Missed calls and texts from various people, mostly Blake, filled my screen. However, this was a time for playing, not reading. Blake would understand.

I sang louder. "Two little monkeys jumping on the bed." I hoisted myself back onto the ledge, my phone dinging like a submarine beacon.

"One fell off and bumped his head." I did a turn, my center of gravity rocking. "Momma called the doctor and the doctor said."

My mother would be sighing to herself right about now, still huddled in her chair, the book rested upside down on her knee. How long would it take her to find the note? She rarely ventured into my room. Would she register my disappearance as trouble, or sum it up to after-prom weekend festivities? Would she register it at all? What would momma say when she called the doctor?

"No more monkeys jumping on the bed."

My father would probably get the first phone call to identify a body since his wallet was in my pocket. Efficient tracking.

Mr. Schenk hadn't experienced a fit in over a year, at least not in public. He had improved on internalizing his frustration and removing himself from stressful situations to unwind in a dark room. The last incident was when he got into a mild paint-scrape car accident on his way to work. He was screaming at the top of his lungs when the cops arrived. His words made no sense to the police and any attempt to reason with him only worked my father up more. My mother picked him up from the station a few hours later. He was still mumbling Estelle.

"One little monkey, jumping all alone on the bed."

I inhaled, throwing my arms out to the open. I had been the leader of my class since 7th grade. I knew how the school board operated better than the board members. If I could lead a misguided band of angsty teenagers, I could lead the nation. I had gotten a perfect score on five separate SAT exams and I had never gotten a grade lower than an A. I could make a living selling people lies that they would willingly eat out of the palm of my hand. I could do anything with no one's permission except my own. If I willed it, so it would be. I was both the morning and the evening stars. I was Christ the Redeemer. I was unstoppable, and only I had the power to control my life.

I was at the top.

God, it felt so good.

I was free.

I finally exhaled, and let myself fall.

No more monkeys jumping on the bed.

-19-

I was vaguely aware my name was being said, but I remained unresponsive. Over and over they called to me. It didn't seem to matter whether I responded or not, the world would keep moving without my consent. They continued to call my name as they dragged my body across the cement.

Someone rolled me onto my side, hands holding my temples, cold as a gun. Bodies talked over me between themselves, occasionally to me, but mostly between themselves. I remained unresponsive, swimming. Treading water. If they shut up long enough then I could sink under forever and it would all end, but their voices kept me afloat.

They told me I was going to be fine. They told me I had fallen from a hotel balcony.

Blake paced back and forth beside me, his dress shoes scuffed with blood. Shit, shit, shit, said the bottom of his bloody shoes. He was running his hands through his hair. I couldn't see it, but I knew. Blake did not deal with stress very well. Ranked top 10 in both personality and looks but 225th in academics, Blake's scholastic career was based largely on following my lead.

Now his lead was lying in a pool of blood and vomit.

Maybe urine.

It wasn't my brightest moment.

Blake pulled out his flip-phone. I could hear the tip tapping of his phone keys. His voice was shaking. Horrified.

Blake, always so worried.

Never the right amount though.

I managed to blink, shifting my eyes to the blurry figure holding my head steady.

"Ricky?" Hana's voice asked, her words reaching me with a two second delay. "Blake told me to hold your head, in case you have a spinal injury. He learned it in Boy Scouts."

He learned it from seeing his mother beaten to unconsciousness in his living room hallway.

Her fingers gripped my scalp, "What happened? Are you okay?"

Blake talked into his phone in a hushed whisper. He looked down at me, eyes wide, then spoke faster.

Hana continued. "Your face is bleeding. Do you feel it?" I couldn't feel anything. "We're taking you to the hospital now."

Blake hung up the phone. "Ricky, what the fu—" he cut himself off with a deep breath. His voice was small, a child again. "You could have died! You're lucky you landed on a balcony a couple floors below instead of—" He stopped, his eyes red. "Can you walk?"

My gaze floated to the clouds.

Why couldn't I fly?

"Hana, scooch over, let me see his chin." Shit, shit, shit, said the bottom of his bloody shoes, my head transferring into Blake's hands. "Definitely going to need stitches, but." He paused and my head slowly tilted in his fingers. "I think he's fine other than that."

"He threw up everywhere."

"And other than that." He placed my head down slowly on the cold cement, "Hana, I talked to Jensen, I told him we are watching a movie at Ricky's house to make him feel better. I'm letting you know in case anyone asks."

Which explained the hushed talking.

"You lied?"

"Stretched the truth. We're still making Ricky feel better, right? Do you mind grabbing some more towels? These are already soaked." Hana hopped to her feet, her two inch heels galloping away.

Then there were just two little monkeys.

Blake pried open my eye with his fingers, his face inches from mine. "You motherfucking—" he heavily emphasized, "—Idiot. How could you be so careless? You could have died."

Could've would've should've.

His lips continued firing off words, but it all blended into the same indistinguishable hum.

"Should you be yelling at him like that?" Hana gasped. She was back, arms bundled with towels.

Blake waved her over, but continued talking. "Can you move? At all? Can you move your toes? Are you paralyzed?" I closed my eyes and imagined a little version of myself pulling the nerve fibers connected to my feet. They twitched. "Oh thank God. Hana's he's going to be okay."

Always so optimistic.

Blake pressed a fresh towel to the bottom of mouth. With another, he wiped down the rest of my face. "At least I hope so," Blake whispered to someone, but it only reached my ears. He pressed yet another towel to my chin, motioning to Hana. "Help me get him up."

With Blake supporting most of my weight, and my other arm slung over Hana's low shoulders, we took one step at a time to the elevator.

One step, two step. My head hung toward my feet, Hana's free hand pressed steady against my chin. My legs dragged all the way down the hallway, all the way to the side exit, all the way through the parking lot. I collapsed in the backseat, Hana joining me, resting my head on her bare thigh.

"Should we be more concerned he's still bleeding?" She carefully lifted the towel to catch a glimpse of the wound.

Blake looked at her in the rearview mirror. "Joke's on him, it's his car."

I either slept or passed out until we arrived at the hospital. Both had the same meaning to me.

Luckily, the ER considered a moderate facial injury and a sprained wrist more important than a kid with a head cold. Blake left to take Hana home, promising to come straight back for me. He would handle everything according to the standard procedure.

The nurses hooked me up to an IV and I was swept back under again. They threaded a tub through my nose.

This was beyond alcohol, or frankly anything I'd ever had.

This was some strong shit.

My vision was a confused void, black, but perhaps it wasn't black. A void where I didn't know if my eyes were closed or if the room was just very dark. The same void that I cried myself to sleep in, ears pooled with warm tears in the middle of the night.

At least they didn't pump my stomach.

A few hours later, long enough for the sun to rise and the hospital to fall into a quiet churning of machine beeps and pager calls, the nurse pushed me out to the lobby in a wheelchair. Blake waited for me with his arms crossed, but wearing jeans and a hoodie. His eyes were still red. The hospital's Care Plan rested in my lap, which listed how to not rip open my wound and how many pills I could take before my stomach lining started eating itself. On top of the pile, a large bag containing my ruined tux. Blake brought a really ugly olive green track suit that I could change into, but the legs were too short and the arms too long.

"How's it going, Blake?" I greeted, my voice hoarse.

"You dick."

The nurse pursed her lips.

I looked down at Blake's shoes, less bloody. "Can you just take me home?" My mouth was still numb from the stitches and anesthesia. And whatever else.

Blake stared at me, but eventually his eyes softened, as usual. He took my chair from the nurse and we drove home, silent. I leaned my head against the window but I didn't sleep.

The lights were off in my house. Blake pulled back my bedsheets and helped me out of my sweatpants, throwing them in the corner instead of in the laundry hamper. I collapsed onto the bed before he could slip my off sweatshirt.

Blake spent the rest of the weekend completing the cleanup procedure.

He informed my parents that I had fallen off my bike and busted my chin, even personally going through the trouble of trashing my bike that I hadn't ridden in three years. Blake called the school, posing as my father, to let them know I had mono and would be out for three weeks. The school didn't notice I had already used that excuse freshmen year. Blake called Samantha back, reassuring her that the mono was a lie and she didn't need to get tested for anything.

"You slept with Samantha?" Blake hung up the phone but continued scrolling through my missed emails and messages, replying to what he could. "When did that happen?"

I couldn't move my eyes away from the wall.

He waited, but I gave him nothing. I didn't have anything to give. Blake sighed, scratching his thigh. "Jesus, dude, you have a lot of messages. Are you ever going to text Hana back? She's really worried about you, by the way." But never the right amount. "Here, I'll do it." He typed something out, then held the phone in front of my face. The screen was blurry. "How's that?"

It didn't matter.

He added an emoji, then sat my phone down on my desk, on top of my suicide note that had been buried, unread, by more college brochures that came in the mail. "Can you at least promise me you won't drink any more alcohol?"

Even on my best of days, I wouldn't promise that.

Blake tried again. "Ricky, is something wrong? Like, seriously wrong?"

Probably, because I couldn't see the faces in the wall anymore. They didn't notice I needed their help. Or maybe they decided I was a lost cause.

"Ricky?"

Hard to tell. I was comatose for the first two days. Not literally, I managed to get to the toilet just fine, but my mind was blank. I had prepared so diligently for flight that I hadn't made a backup plan in the event I crashed back down to the ground. And no one noticed.

Well.

Except Blake.

He lifted the blinds in the morning and closed them at night. He informed me, from a mostly credible website, which stars were visible each night. He sent my tux to the dry cleaners, turned in my homework that I had completed days ahead, and brought soup to me that my mother prepared. Blake told her my new favorite was carrot and sweet pea.

That little shit.

"Ricky."

Vaguely aware, still unresponsive. Here, in an over-chilled office. Stark white, purposely. Light tan hardwood. Two white rugs. The walls were bare, save for a few degrees and certificates. Minimal distractions. A desk separated us, dull pale cream, but he still felt too close. Also, who the fuck had a cream desk?

"Ricky."

I was sentenced to two weeks of counseling after my ER visit. It was too inconvenient for the doctors to ignore a few minor cuts on my arms while administering my IV, even after I insisted they were months old and I definitely didn't do it anymore. One appointment every two days, or until the doctor felt I had made substantial progress. Whatever that meant.

"Do you want to be here?" He asked me again.

I blinked at the question, slowly. I spoke at the same pace, stitches tight on the lower half of my face. "Why exactly would I want to be here?" I thought my voice would sound how I felt. Tired, distant, done. But it was normal, just a little muffled.

You're good at bluffing.

The doctor cocked his head to the side, sliding the notepad in front of him. He wore a lab coat, his last name etched above the breast pocket, as if at any moment he would have to do actual lab work or performer open heart surgery. With his face clean shaven, Dr. Wang landed in the ambiguous age of Asian professional males. Not a wrinkle on the horizon. Dr. Wang lightly chuckled, leaning in toward me. "I suppose that's a good point. Let me rephrase. What brings you in?"

"The ER doctor strongly recommended following through with my appointment with you." I studied his face, then added, "But also, I think it could help. What brings you in?"

He nodded with a smile, "It's my job and I love it. I am a psychiatrist specializing in youth and young adults. I am assigned to certain individuals, like yourself, to make sure they are getting the most suitable treatment for their needs, and if not, make referrals to seek additional support."

"That was very well rehearsed."

"Thank you, it has been a while since someone has asked, I was a little nervous I would trip up." He smiled at me, but wrote something in his notepad. "Do you have any more questions for me?"

Why was his desk such a putrid color? "Nothing relevant." Everything else seemed mundane. "What was your question again?"

"Why do you think you are here?"

"The doctor strongly recommended counseling."

"Why?"

"Legal reasons, probably." I shifted again in my seat, the scars on my body itching. Blake told my parents these sessions were just a checkup on my stitches.

"So, Ricky." The doctor sat his pen down, interlacing his fingers on the table. "Tell me about yourself."

I could hear a ticking sound even though there were no clocks. I was born and raised in a suburb where an HOA ensured everyone's lawn was in order and there was an unnecessary amount of speed bumps to prevent driving over 8mph. My father worked as a lawyer at a tech company in the city. My mother, a housewife. They seemed relatively happy together, but not all that happy individually.

I liked to get blackout drunk so I didn't have to think about the draining feeling in the pit of my stomach that life was ultimately a boring waste of time and it would only get worse into adulthood where I would settle into the routine of working, juggling bill payments, and restless nights counting down until my next brief vacation.

I had the hole in me before I realized all that, but the only other explanation was that there was something wrong with me from the beginning and that didn't sound any better.

However, if I was going to get out of mandated counseling, I couldn't say that. Adults understood accidents. Teenagers had accidents, lots of accidents. Teenagers didn't drown their thoughts and feelings in alcohol or drugs or work or sex or food. Adults wouldn't understand that, even though it was the same methods they used to cope.

Instead, adults rationalized that their children tripped into the wine cabinet and their hand popped open an entire rack by mistake. Their innocent growing minds couldn't comprehend the dangers of drugs. Their daughters were tempted by brainwashing pop media and were only imitating what they saw on television, but none of them could ever decide for themselves if they were ready for sex. Boys were just being boys and shouldn't be held accountable for silly mistakes that could ruin the rest of their lives.

Teenagers were curious and they didn't know any better.

Curiosity almost killed the cat.

I took a breath and pushed everything, the whispers the itching the frantic gnawing at the base of my throat, deep deep down, if only for a minute.

It was an accident.

Or at least, I needed him to believe that the hotel *thing* was just a silly little accidental whoopsies. I answered, “So, a couple nights ago, I got pretty cross-faded and tripped off a hotel balcony.”

He didn’t say anything at first, just nodded along. “Why were you at a hotel?”

It was the only place that seemed fitting at the time. “It was prom night.”

“Ah.” He pulled his pen out, jotting down a bullet point. “Were you supposed to meet someone at the hotel?”

I couldn’t take my eyes off the pen. “Yes.”

“Were you nervous? Is that why you felt the need to use substances?”

Jumping to conclusions. But I nodded along, following his pen’s scratches on the clean paper, ink wounds. I shifted in my chair, “How long are these sessions?” I couldn’t hold it down anymore, it was starting to bubble up through the seal.

“An hour, give or take.”

“How long has it been?”

“About ten minutes.”

Jesus Christ.

Dr. Wang’s eyes were warm, but blank. They gave nothing away. He must have learned that in his PhD program. “Did you have any more questions for me?” He asked.

“What happens now?”

“We still have forty-five minutes.” He checked my file again. “Are you ready to talk about that night?”

The elephant sitting on my chest looked back at me, a warning. My lungs strained to expand. “Not particularly.”

“That’s alright, Ricky. Progress takes time.” We sat in silence for 40 minutes.

The camp counselors used to say I was a natural born leader. My parents sent me to summer camp every year from third to sixth grade, and every year I went home with the title Most Dedicated. It was extremely cheesy, they set up the banquet hall like the Oscars, with tablecloths and a red carpet and interviewers. Really, it was the whole nine yards. All the kids combed their hair and wore their best clothes, which usually equated to whatever didn't have a hole in it yet.

I walked down the red carpet my last year at camp, my jeans notably cleaner than my peers because I spent my summer indoors learning Microsoft Office and improving my typing speed.

Dedicated; adj – exclusively allocated to or intended for a particular service or purpose.

I had never taken the word to heart before, but what purpose was I supposedly so dedicated to? Success was the only answer I could think of, in the most general terms. At my current age, that meant academically. It was the backbone to any rewarding childhood.

Right?

Dedicated; adj – devoted to a task or purpose; having single-minded loyalty or integrity.

There I was, on stage, my plastic trophy in hand and parents clapping and taking pictures with oversized phones. There I was, when I felt it. The hole.

Its location was hard to pinpoint. It felt like the hole was in my chest, but it was deeper, really deep down. Everything else inside of me tittered on the edge of the hole, threatening to tip, to be pulled in.

I tried to gasp for a breath, but my throat tightened, invisible hands around my neck. The trophy fell from my palms and I just stood there, on stage. The director placed her hand on the top of my back, bending down to my level.

Her lips moved silently, with a smile, but the hole pulled my mind. My body was vacant, for just a second, and I don't know where I went.

Then I was off stage, trophy back in hand, and on my way to find my parents in the crowd. Just as quickly as the hole appeared, it was gone. Or maybe just covered up.

I showed my parents my backpack full of projects, though they were mostly print-outs of coding script and spreadsheets. I highlighted the important bits so I wouldn't waste time.

Blake also joined me every year at camp. My parents picked him up and dropped him off at the beginning and end of each camp season, telling his mother that the admission was free and all she had to do was sign a waiver. At camp, Blake rolled around in the fields full of wildflowers, danced in the streams, braided flower crowns, and sang at the top of his lungs. He woke up with stars already in his eyes, he didn't need to look for them somewhere out in the universe. Every year, Blake went home with Most Happy.

As it turned out, however, Dedicated was more useful.

-20-

Day three of self-imposed house arrest provided me with new company. "Ding dong," Jensen entered my bedroom without knocking, seven AP classes worth of material piled in his hands. "I am here to give you this day, your daily bread."

"How gracious your love." I was sitting at my desk, but I was still in my pajamas. But my pajamas were also the same clothes I had worn the day before. But the clothes I had worn the day before were pajamas and those pajamas were the clothes from the day before that day.

Jensen would never know any of that though.

He walked over to me, not making the slightest effort to look away from my jaw, and dropped the assignments on my desk. Jensen's clothes were always pressed and his hair combed back and fingernails polished. When did he find the time? Or the energy? "What are you working on? Art project?" He tapped on the white paper in front of me.

I pulled my eyes up from his suede boots and moved them to the sheet of notebook paper on my desk. It was blank, with the exception of a weak black line scrawled midway through the page. I put down the pen I hadn't realized I was carrying. "I don't know." It felt so normal to sit at my desk, but I didn't have anything to work on. I wasn't normal.

"Kind of looks like one of those heart line things."

"Heart line things?"

"You know, at the hospital."

"An EKG."

"Right!"

"Sure."

He sat down on my grey comforter that hadn't been washed in months. "Anyway, how's your jaw?"

"It hurts."

"Yeah, I bet. That's why I don't ride bikes."

"Do you even have a bike?"

"A couple." He shrugged, "No one to ride with." If he was waiting for an answer, I didn't give one. Jensen slipped off his backpack, turning around to unzip it. "I have more good tidings for you. You didn't specify, so I just brought whatever."

He passed me a bottle of whiskey.

Then a bottle of rum.

Then a bottle of tequila.

They clinked as I sat them on the desk. I wanted to explain how much it meant to me, to have a couple more drinks. How I needed the blanket. To feel normal again, whatever that meant. But instead I said, "Thanks."

"No problem." He waved me off. "Can you come over to my place tonight?"

"Party?"

"Just studying." My attention narrowed in on the bottles. Jensen cleared his throat. "So, Samantha told me you were feeling a little stressed. Like with school or whatever."

"Did she?" Rum would hit me first. I should start with that.

"She diagnosed gifted kid burnout."

"Huh." Rum was warm.

"Yeah, don't listen to her. Nature sucks and yoga is boring." Or maybe I should start with the tequila, just to get it out of the way. Jensen stood, dusting off his ironed jeans. "You should just do what I do."

I looked back to him. "Which is?"

"Buy shit."

By the state of his bedroom, Jensen was practically a new age hoarder. Every inch was filled with junk. Nice and expensive junk, but junk nonetheless. Most of it would be thrown away in a few months and its spot eventually replaced with a new purchase.

I twisted the cork off the Patron. "Yeah? How's that working out for you?"

He smiled, "Alright, I gotta get going, you know, party host and all."

"I thought you were studying."

"Same thing."

I tilted the bottle to my lips.

"Ricky, watch out for that," Jensen lingered at the door. "You know what they say about tequila."

After Jensen left, I took a bath.

Baths were a waste of time, time that I didn't have to sit around in lukewarm water, paddling my feet like a duckling, instead of organizing an elementary school outreach program and enrolling high schoolers to act as academic mentors to underserved communities. For example.

But tonight, I took a bath. I gripped the side of the tub with my good arm as I slid into the water, filled to the brim so that the lower I sank the more water sloshed over onto the tile.

I gritted my teeth against the steaming water that turned my skin red. I had looked at my phone a few hours ago and my messenger app kept crashing from trying to load everything I had missed. There was time to catch up, I would make time, once my mind was erased of all the whispers. They were too loud to cut out.

I sank until my ears were below the water, the voices louder now, submerged along with me. Razors wouldn't do the job, plus, a tub of blood was disgusting. I flipped over, my back floating to the surface. More water spilled onto the floor.

I had a quarter of Jack in me and, even if I managed to sit up, I had poured two cups of vegetable oil in the tub before I filled it. I would pass out and fall back under the water before I even got a leg out.

All I needed to do was inhale. One more breath.

One last breath.

"Ricky!" The bathroom door slammed open, Blake marching into the room like a parade on steroids.

I gasped, underwater, boiling pain shooting up my nose and down the back of my throat.

Shit, shit, shit, Blake was screaming, as loud as a parade conductor's whistle, hands pulling my coughing chest out of the water. He sat on the edge, eyebrows pulled together, slapping me on the back until I could verbally tell him to get the fuck out.

He tilted his head. "Why are you taking a bath?"

"Why did you just walk in?" I coughed again, grabbing my chest. I was sitting on my knees, every muscle aching but mostly the part behind my chest, the part that would have been gone if Blake had waited three more minutes. A shock traveled up my body, to my thighs, my arms, exposed. "Get out!" I snapped again, pushing him off the side of the tub.

"Alright, Diva," he held up his hands in retreat, standing. "I just came to grab some floss. Next time put a sign on the door if you're not going to have the shower curtain closed." He snatched the blue carton of floss off the counter and marched back out.

The time I allotted for a bath had come and gone. Another shot thrown away.

My third appointment with Dr. Wong was more productive. "Ricky, you told me you were taking a little time off so your stitches could recover, correct? How have you been feeling?"

"I mean, it's good. I'm good. Amazing, even. It's a surprising breather. I didn't think I needed time away, but I think everyone needs some time, sometimes." I practiced that line in the mirror every morning as my razor looked for a fresh spot on my upper thigh.

He nodded, making notes. "Great, I think that's a great outlook. Let's try diving in today." During the past week, somewhere between scavenging for prescription pills and selling my study packets to last minute AP crammers, an idea popped into my head on how to get out of therapy early.

I was going to tell him everything he wanted to know.

"How does that sound?" Dr. Wang smiled.

Or at least what he thought he wanted to know.

"Sure! Great!" I replied.

"Great."

Great. I took a deep breath, sitting up straight in my chair. I wasn't in theater or anything, but I could perform when needed. "Where do we start with that?"

"I like to begin fairly general and then narrow the topics down to try to find what could be the root of any distresses or," he glanced briefly down at my file, "Why you feel the need to drink."

"Fun isn't a good enough reason?"

"Humor me."

"Sorry, okay, let's do it." I reassured myself everything would stay deep down. I had practiced. I had prepared. I had studied. "There's probably something deep underneath, who knows." Studying was my strength.

"Tell me about your childhood." He smiled again, pen at the ready.

"My childhood," was average. "Well, nothing traumatic I suppose. I was supported, but not necessarily spoiled. I met my best friend, Blake, when I was five." Those were the highlights.

"Tell me about Blake."

"Oh, okay. Well he is obviously not five anymore." I paused for a laugh, but instead he nodded, encouragingly. "Blake is a male, really thin. He's a runner. He actually got into a decent school on a cross-country scholarship. Shoulder length hair, blue eyes, a couple freckles on his back, he has a weird big toe on his left foot—"

"That's very statistical."

"Isn't everything?"

"Do you have feelings for Blake?"

I took a mental step back. "Romantic feelings?"

He momentarily lifted his pen, "Yes."

I raised my eyebrows, but relaxed back in my seat. Unexpected, but nothing bubbled up. I was still in control. "No, I do not. He's like my brother. He practically lives with us."

"And why is that?"

"He has serious family issues, so it's just easier if he stays with us."

"Do you think this has affected you in anyway? In a stressful or uncomfortable manner?"

"Not really, I like having him over. It's like a permanent sleepover." The conversation needed to be light, cheesy. Innocent.

"Do you have romantic feelings for anyone at the moment?"

"No, I do not."

"Have you ever been in a romantic relationship with anyone?"

I paused, my heart pinching for half a second. "I have, actually." The angle, here it was.

"Tell me about them."

"Well. Her name was—is Andrea."

"When did you meet her?" He saw the hesitation in my eyes. I knew he could see the wall I built. "Ricky?" He prompted again, after I sat there with my mouth parted for two minutes.

I cleared my throat, settling back in my chair, creating as much distance between us as possible. I didn't like talking about it, in fact, I hadn't in almost a year. Andrea didn't even exist to me anymore, the memories of her were barely even a faint mist.

It wasn't like I thought about her when I spent countless hours at my desk that she liked to lean against, or in my truck with her mixtape classic rock CDs still lost under the passenger seat, or when I passed her old locker in the hallway at school, fifty-two steps away from mine. And I definitely didn't waste my time thinking about her god*damn* fucking eyelashes. But she was an angle. A good angle. A believable, innocent angle. The only useful thing about her.

But I digressed.

I cleared my throat again. "Yes, um, Andrea. She was—is a year older than me. We met, wow, I don't even remember actually."

She came up to me, six weeks into my freshmen year, in the cafeteria. She had her hair up in a high ponytail, loose brown waves tumbling down her shoulders. She was in a triangle formation with two other girls, a blonde and a fake redhead. The blond, just like any stereotypical high school movie, led the triangle toward our table.

Blake followed my eyes to the cheerleaders, then turned back to me. "Are we about to get hazed?"

I shrugged, my eyes not leaving Andrea, even though she was concentrated on the back of the blonde's head. When they reached the table, they all just stood there, waiting. "Hello?" I prompted.

"Hi, I'm Kacey," The leader nodded enthusiastically. "The cheerleaders are actually planning a special little thing for the upcoming pep rally and you're the freshman class president, right?"

"Yes, Ricky, nice to meet you."

"Likewise."

"I'm Blake!" He turned his body to face them.

"Hi," she lingered on Blake a second too long before introducing the other two. "This is Andrea and –"

"Robin," the redhead sighed.

Kacey smiled really big again, nodding. "Right. Yeah, we're all talking about it right now, if you guys want to come join us. We're outside near the field." It was sunny, but a little on the chilly side. There wasn't any productive reason someone would willingly chose to sit outside when there were plenty of tables on the warm inside, even near the windows if sunlight was an importance.

Maybe because it was harder to gossip and spread rumors inside.

"Sounds fun, can't wait to hear what you've planned," I said to Andrea, who smiled at me with her summer passionfruit lip tint.

Dr. Wang waited for me to continue, so I threw him a bone. "Three years ago, we were together for two and a half years."

"How would you describe the relationship?"

"At the time, it was amazing. I think—thought, she was perfect for me. I was always pretty confident in myself, but she made me feel," I spoke slowly, choosing my words carefully, trying to picture what he would write about them. "She made me feel invincible."

"How?"

"I think it was the support. She was always interested in what I wanted and she believed I could do it. She really did." I borrowed that line from Samantha, but he'd never know. Dr. Wang didn't say anything, but I needed to continue. To just get it out. "Her eyes lit up when they looked at me. It was like a switch flipped when she thought about me—us, whatever."

"Was it possible that maybe your eyes were the ones that were lit? Perhaps, rose-colored?"

Nothing about my memories of her were rose-colored. "I don't think it was like that. She really was a wonderful girl."

"Was?"

"Is. Sorry. She's not dead or anything."

"How did you feel about her?"

I could fit my hand around her wrist, but not quite to the halfway point of her forearm. We were sprawled out in the back of my truck, nestled in duvets and itchy sweaters.

"Can you stop that," She swatted my hand off of her arm, laughing. Her voice sounded like a basket of kittens.

Shrill.

"Stop what?" I rubbed under her chin.

"Stop!"

I stopped, but pulled her in closer. She turned into me, burying her nose in the side of my neck. "You're so soft," she whispered, lips grazing me.

"Not my favorite compliment, but okay." The sky was sprinkled with stars. We couldn't get too far away from the city because Andrea had planned to catch some reunion special of some reality television show hosted by some celebrity, which was fine and all, but also meant the stars weren't as bright. "Do you see Orion?"

"Mhm," she hummed against my throat, snuggling her face into me.

"Those eyes in the back of your head must get irritated from all your hair."

"Mhmm."

I sighed, watching my breath creep into the night sky. I pulled her in closer for warmth. She shivered, but I didn't feel anything.

"Ricky, how did you feel about her?" Dr. Wang broke through.

I closed my eyes. This was my angle, my way out of this place. But I didn't know if I should tell the truth or lie. "I loved her."

"Loved? Or love?"

Truth or lie, truth or lie. "Loved."

"Why are you no longer in a relationship with Andrea?"

"Oh, it was mutual." I tried to shrug, but I didn't have the strength. I needed all of it to keep talking about her. "She was graduating and going to college. Statistics. You know." The usual.

"I see." He wrote a couple more sentences and I took the moment to catch my breath. "Do you think that the break up could have something to do with the way you're feeling now?"

"I was thinking about that and," I paused, imitating the face of someone deep in reflective thought instead of struggling to keep everything deep deep down. "That's probably it."

He nodded, but didn't speak. He didn't even write anything down, just looked back at me with sympathetic eyes. "You did wonderful, Ricky. You opened up and explored a lot of what you might have bottled up."

Understatement.

"It wasn't a bad breakup. I guess we're still okay even though we don't talk." I looked down. "I didn't know it had affected me so much." I was over the topic, but it was my ticket out. Teenage boy acting out because of heartbreak. Easy. Believable. Relatable. A completely reasonable excuse to feel hollow inside. Totally normal and not crazy.

Dr. Wang folded his hands. "Sometimes the hardest things we experience seep up from the cracks of our self-conscious."

What overrated young adult novel did he get that from? "Yeah," I said, because I didn't know what else to say.

"I think that's a good place to stop for now, you've made amazing progress here. I'll see you in a few days, Ricky."

The worst thing about the whole situation was that everyone needed something to blame it on.

Blake, unsurprisingly, blamed alcohol.

I sat on my bed with my back against the wall and my legs stretched in front of me as Blake rampaged through my room, confiscating mostly empty alcohol bottles. He used a black Hefty trash bag, the one with the red drawstrings, and he lectured the entire time, pulling contraband from my dresser drawers, under the bed, out of my backpack, behind books on the bookshelf, and in shoe boxes, each bottle erupting a new fun fact about the dangers of alcohol abuse.

To which, I half-heartedly offered a comeback. "Alcohol could possibly reduce the risk of diabetes."

"No one in your family has diabetes." He huffed and he puffed, but it was for show. Blake wouldn't tell anyone. It was just the alcohol, and alcohol could be controlled.

Blake of all people should've know that was a lie, but it was a moot point. Alcohol wasn't the problem.

"Blake, have you seen my duffel bag?" I asked. Blake had cleaned my room a few days ago, which was how he found so many of my empty bottles, but my duffel bag was missing.

"What duffel bag?" He plopped himself on my bed, the bottles chinking together as he dropped the bag on the floor. "Ricky, you gotta stop drinking."

"Why?"

"Why?" His mouth hung open, waiting for his brain to catch up. "Because you almost died." Almost, but not quite. Not physically. "What would I do without you?"

"That's a pretty selfish way to think."

"How is it selfish that I want you to be alive?"

"But why do you want me alive?"

"Because you're my best friend!"

"And?" I straightened on the bed, "You wouldn't die with me."

"A piece of me would."

"Don't be dramatic." I looked him in the eye, "You would be fine if I died."

"Don't say things like that."

"Asking people to live is self-centered."

"Do you not want to?" The words were a whisper, but firm.

"That's not what I'm saying," I rolled my eyes away. "I was just pointing out the flaws in your logic."

He scoffed, "Thanks for that." He got off the bed, pulling the drawstrings of the trash bag together. "I'm taking you to an AA meeting. You're a fucking alcoholic."

"What would you do without me?"

He flipped me off and left the room.

My father's blame landed on my coursework. I walked past his office on the way from the kitchen and back to my bed. It was just after dinner, and the dishwasher had started.

"Ricky, could you come in for a second?" When I looked in, he was still staring at his computer screen, typing.

I debated ignoring the call, but he swiveled around to face me before I made my decision. I entered the room, keeping close to the shelf with the amber bottle. "What's up?"

"Take a seat."

I took a seat. The cushion welcomed my weight and I rested against back of the chair.

My father rubbed at the dark circles under his eyes, "Ricky, I am concerned about you." I looked past him to his computer screen, where everything was underlined red. "Are you stressed about school?"

"Are you stressed about work?"

He scratched at the arms on his chair, his fingers razors. "No, no, I'm stressed because of this." He was looking at me, looking for the answer. "What's wrong, Ricky?"

"Nothing." Everything. Potayto potahto.

His fingers reached for his hair. "If it's school, I can help you with that. You are taking so many advanced classes and you are in so many clubs, you need a break."

"That sounds like a good idea."

"Sometimes school was overwhelming for me as well, you need to know what your limits are."

"Of course."

"You've already got into college."

"Right."

"Don't put yourself in the hospital like your mother."

My eyes widened, but he had already swiveled back around to his computer. "What do you mean?"

"Well, she was in the hospital for a long time. It was stressful for me."

My comparison to her was only in relation to the hospital stay, not the cause. "This house doesn't revolve around you," I said.

But his allotted family time was already up. He resumed typing, ignoring run on sentences and misspellings. I stood and left the room, words on the tip of my tongue. They would only fall on deaf ears if I pushed them off.

There was a distant knock on my bedroom door, but it didn't register until my mother's head poked in. "Hey Ricky, are you *resting*?"

I was lying in bed, fully clothed, headphones in my ear but no music playing. She was holding a bowl of cut fruit and a glass of water, waiting for permission.

I tapped on my earbud.

She nodded, putting the fruit and water on my desk. She carefully sat in my chair, watching me. I watched the corner ceiling of the room. After I didn't move, she started anyway. "You know, I accidentally fell off my bike once."

I wasn't sure if I imagined a tone change on the word accident.

There was a long pause before her next sentence. "It was when I was young. I couldn't have been older than nine or ten." Her fingers twisted her wedding ring. "It was a Saturday, but Papa still had to work and Memaw was," she looked up, her lips slightly parted. After a few blinks, she returned, "She was somewhere, I don't remember. But I was riding my bike on the sidewalk, never on the street, just like they said I could."

She didn't ride all that often, but she gripped the handles correctly and could pedal just as well as the next kid. The wind brushed her hair away from her small ears, round gold studs dotted in the middle of each. The air smelled like freshly cut grass. Spring.

The sidewalk was approaching the corner and she had the option to either turn and follow the sidewalk or ride off the sidewalk and cross the street.

"In hindsight," she said with a smile on the edge of her lips. "I should have followed the sidewalk."

The sewer drain grate just off the sidewalk was broken, leaving an exposed hole in the drain. The front wheel of her bike hit the hole and stuck. The rest of her body continued, flinging her small frame into the middle of the street.

Her hands shot out to meet the pavement. They stung, but they weren't bleeding. Just a little red. She sat up, pulling her legs in closer as she lifted her hands to the sky. Soft weightless clouds drifted between her stretched fingers, and if she could only be one of them as well, if only.

I pulled out my earbud. "What is the point of this story?"

Unflinching, she looked me in the eye. "There isn't one. It's just life." She patted the table, "Let me know if you need anything else." And left the room.

I walked into Dr. Wang's office knowing it would be my final visit.

"Good morning Ricky, how are you feeling?"

"Like I'm on top of the world. And yourself?"

"Wonderful to hear, I'm doing alright as well. Have a seat."

I obliged, even going as far to scoot my chair closer to his eye-sore desk. "What should we talk about today?"

He cleared his throat, interlacing his fingers on his desk. "I spoke to your parents this morning. You have made tremendous progress and I think this will be our last session."

Biting my lip was the only way to suppress the obnoxious grin threatening to break through. Blake could do stand-up comedy with his impersonations. “So today,” Dr. Wang continued, “We should wrap up and solidify some areas that might be troubling you and find a regular counselor at home so you can continue to express yourself in a safe and supportive environment.”

“Thank you Doctor, I definitely feel a lot better. I would love to keep talking to someone.” Just nod and agree. Nod and agree. I was a robot at this point, only one last goal programed into my coding. My goal did not involve returning to any more of these dumb unhelpful meetings.

“Great to hear. What do you think are some aspects of your life, past or present, that require more attention or closure?”

“Well, we’ve talked about—Andrea.” I paused. “But also, I think that my family has caused a bit of stress by expecting a lot but not giving support.” I despised every word coming out of my mouth, but I had to sell it.

“What about some parts of your own personality that have caused you hardship?”

“Well, I know I can be a little arrogant,” I shuffled my thumbs, trying to come up with more bullshit. “I think that this experience was very humbling, so if I continue working on that, I would get myself into a lot less trouble.”

“Anything else?”

“I can also be rude to those I’m comfortable with, even though I know they only put up with it because they love me. I’ll make it a personal goal to be more polite, especially to my friends and family.”

“Anything else?”

Okay, asshole. “What do you think?”

He smiled, “My only suggestion is that you should try to find and pursue a hobby.”

“A hobby?” He smiled at my reaction, his eyes crinkling at the corners. “Wait, are you serious? A hobby?”

"Yes, a hobby," his smile only got wider. "Has that never crossed your mind? What do you do for fun?"

"Um." I moved my tongue along the edge of my teeth, scrambling for an answer somewhere in the back of my head. "Hang out with friends."

"Friends that you drink with?" He didn't give me a chance to reply. "You need an activity that you can do alone, that makes you happy, something enjoyable that you can turn to when you don't have friends available to hang out." He reached out his hand towards me. "Think about it, okay?"

I looked at his hand. "Okay."

He pulled his hand back. "For counselors, I have a few suggestions here," he slid a stark white paper toward me, which I pretended to look at while he continued. "Let's go over them real quick and I can tell you a little about each of them and their specialties. The first on this list is Dr. Daniels blah blah blah." I stopped listening and blindly agreed to whatever he was saying for the next forty five minutes.

I wasn't surprised to see Blake's face waiting for me at the facility lobby. I also wasn't surprised his face was the only one waiting. I wasn't sure what I felt, but it wasn't surprised. Mostly exhaustion.

"Hey loser," I offered a small wave.

"Dirtbag." He pulled me into a solid hug, patting my back. I wrapped my arms around him. He pulled away first, holding me at arm's length. "How ya feeling?"

Shitty. I managed a smile and a nod. "I've been better, but I've also been worse."

"Well you look shitty, you want a chalupa on the way back or something?"

"Let's just go."

The outside smelled about what I expected.

The same.

The ground was wet with leftover rain from last night. Spring was a new beginning, a fresh start. The clouds always parted and the rays broke through, if only for a couple days, relighting hope for the coming sun. Animals woke up from their dark hibernation, refreshed and about twenty pounds lighter. They felt as though they could soar to the sky, the baggage dropped from their lives. Weightless and free.

Weak buds poked through the dirt, waking up to the chirpings of baby birds emerging from their porcelain eggs. Children, jumping in the shallow puddles that glistened in their driveway as their parents swept dead leaves and dirt off the front porch.

A new beginning. I lifted my head to the clouds, closing my eyes on the inhale. Spring.

I needed it to end.

A long exhale and I opened my eyes again as the robot. I was walking to the car. I was in the car. We were driving.

Blake tapped his finger against the steering wheel. A country song sauntered between us, humming out the sound of the traffic. "So," Blake finally started, keeping his eyes on the glass. "What did the good doctor say?"

"No more alcohol." Which wasn't a lie. My voice sounded like a sudden unexpected curve in the road.

"Ah, so he learned a thing or two in medical school after all." Blake's laugh was so light, weightless. "What else?" If Blake wanted, he could drive the car straight off the highway.

"I need to find a hobby." Which wasn't a lie. My voice sounded like skidding tires.

Blake rolled his eyes. "I told you that like twelve years ago. All you do is homework, study, and drink. You're basically already in college." His finger tip tapped on the wheel, steering us toward Spring. "What else?" A new beginning.

"Family. Issues." Which wasn't a lie. My voice sounded like the car hurling through the thin metal railing and plummeting off the side of a cliff.

"Mm, don't we all." Blake stared straight at the passenger sitting in my seat, but not really looking at me. If he could see me, he wouldn't have asked, "But, really. How are you feeling?"

"Pretty good."

His eyes were searching for something that wasn't inside of me anymore. "You sure?" Nodding was a lot easier than talking. "I mean, you did fall off a building."

"Right, right. Don't remind me." I imitated a laugh, which made Blake smile. If I were weightless, I wouldn't have fallen. "No more alcohol, I promise."

There was a semi-truck on the other side of traffic, barreling toward us. The steering wheel, not but an arm's reach away, was only guided by the tip tap of a finger and Blake's knee. "So, how are things outside of the psych office?" My voice sounded like a cross highway collision at seventy miles an hour.

"Oh, yanno." Blake signaled, checked over his shoulder, then took the next exit. I closed my eyes, inhaling. "The usual."

Soft rain had started to fall by the time we pulled up to my house. Blake grabbed the fast food and hopped out of the truck before I had even opened my door. "Come on Slowpoke," he opened it for me, handing me the food.

"Sorry, I'm just." Exhale. "Tired." Which wasn't a lie. My muscles were asleep, like I had just finished the world's longest marathon. They were pre-shutting down.

Blake patted my truck, as if that would magically make me move faster. "Don't be mad at me," he warned, leading me to the front door. I could feel the warmth radiating out like an oven, inviting me to stick my head in. "They promised me not to tell you." He turned the key in the knob and opened the door.

"Surprise!" My mother popped out from behind a wall. My father, slowly and awkwardly, slithered out from behind the couch, two beats behind.

I was unsurprised. "Oh, wow, hey." Even at my best, I would have been short for words. "Thanks. I'm quite surprised." And confused. And uncomfortable.

And tired.

My mother rubbed the small of her back, eyebrows raised into her hairline. "Really? I'm glad you liked it." I didn't. "Just thought we should celebrate your stitches coming out!"

My hand immediately shot up to my face. I had completely forgotten about the stitches. They were taken out earlier this morning. I looked to my father, but he looked everywhere but me, ashamed he had been talked into such an idiotic idea. I turned back to Blake, but suddenly his shoes were the most interesting thing in the world.

"So, how are you feeling?" My mother probed, cautiously. "Better?"

"A lot better, thanks."

Both of my parents let out the breath they had been holding for two weeks. "You've been so *upset* since the accident," she continued, rubbing her hands together in front of her.

"Well, it is his face. Of course he'd be upset."

"*Robert.*"

"What? It's his fa—" He shut up when he saw the knives in her eyes. "I mean, it'll heal up just fine. You won't even be able to tell."

"It's already healing just fine!" She took a step toward me. I had to swallow the chills down my spine to stop myself from stepping back. "Does it hurt a lot?"

It was either nothing or unbearable pain. That was my life. I shrugged.

"*How does it feel?*" She asked, her eyes widening with another step in my direction.

"What?" I felt the gun against my temple.

She tilted her head, curls lazily falling over her other shoulder. "I said, how do you feel?"

So tired.

My father patted her shoulder. "Okay, I'm pretty sure he's fed up of hearing that by now. Ricky is going to be fine, let's leave him alone for now."

"Right, right, sorry," She shook her head with a smile, forced. It hurt to watch.

I walked past them and climbed the stairs. A shower would help wash everything away in the hot steam. Fresh, like Spring. Spring never really changed anything though.

"Ricky?" Blake pitter patter tip tapped on my open bedroom door.

I blinked. I was standing over my desk, drawer open and my fingers hovering above the razor. Autopilot. "What's up?" I answered.

"I gotta head to work, but," He waited until I turned around to face him. "Do you need anything before I leave? You're okay, right?"

"Yup." I smiled. "I'm just going to take a shower then rest."

"Good idea. See ya later, and don't have too much fun without me."

"I'll try not to." My fist closed around the razor.

My first day back at school was about as miserable as I imagined, but thankfully not more.

I expected the reactions to my face, thinly veiled shock when they tried not to stare too long. I told them all the same thing, that mono made me really sick and fatigued and I fell down the stairs a week and a half ago.

Teachers talked to me after class, congratulating me for keeping up with my coursework while sick and recovering from – they would always smile so sweetly – the accident. If there was anything they could do, I just needed to let them know. I just had to go out of my way, when I was already so exhausted, to seek out help. They wished for me to get well soon.

As if it were that easy.

I lugged my body between classes, a husk following the usual routine. For most of the time, my mind was elsewhere, though the elsewhere was unknown to me. I would randomly snap back into consciousness, if I ran into someone or my elbow slipped off the desk, but mostly I was absent.

Already gone.

However, in the back of my mind, I heard the distant scuffle of feet behind me, hurrying through the open school quad. I tried to ignore it, to slip back under the thick blankets, but she was calling out to me. My hollow eyes stayed dropped to the floor, unfocused, my blurry feet moving in and out of frame.

The shoes behind me were louder, thick, echoing in the space between my ears. They were boots.

Ignore it. Ignore it.

"Ricky!" The words were recognizable now, her voice ringing. "Hey, wait up!"

Ignore it. Ignore it.

I tried to pull the blanket back over me, but it was ripped away, the voice shaking my arm. I stopped, lifting my eyes to her.

Hana frowned, her fingers looped in her backpack straps. "Hey! I've been trying to get your attention for two minutes! Did you not hear me?"

"Oh," was all I could say.

"Yeah," she looked away from my scar, down to her Nordstrom sale boots. "So how have you been?"

Oh, you know. "The usual."

She mhm'ed under her breath, nodding to herself. Hana looked up to my face, "You haven't talked to me since, you know," she lowered her voice. "The accident."

As if I were clumsy enough to have an accident.

"Was it something I did?" She continued, "Did I make things weird? Why haven't you texted me? Or called me back?" Her hands wrung the backpack straps with increasing intensity.

"Oh."

She was wearing a striped sweater, yellow and white. The lines waved at me. "I've been so worried about you," Her voice was starting to shake.

Never the right amount.

The hole inside of me ached, squeezing my lungs. "What did I do?" Hana snapped at me. Her legs were shaking now too, anxious energy. It was transferring to me, the back of my eyes started to burn.

I struggled for breath, vision fading. The hole was becoming a whirlwind. I closed my eyes, trying to count to thirty, or at least ten, but I couldn't get away. "Hana—"

"Why are you ignoring me?"

I didn't have an answer. How could I explain that I was no longer here? There was no one inside to answer. Hana had raised her voice, so a few students in my peripheral had stopped to listen. "Stop," I could barely get it out, my chest aching. It was going to happen, right here, if I didn't get away.

"It's not fair!"

"What do you want me to say?"

"Say that you're wrong! Or that you've been a complete jerk! Say what's really on your mind instead of sulking around and avoiding me!"

"I'm not—"

She was yelling. "How about you say you're sorry!" She took a step closer to me, her eyes narrowed into darts.

"Oh."

"Oh?" She was fuming. The pressure inside of me was threatening to explode. "That's all you have to say?" Her knuckles turned white. "Oh?"

"I'm not your fucking boyfriend, Hana."

She was visibly taken aback, her mouth open as her head recoiled from the sting. We stared at each other as the dust settled. Her hands unfolded from fists, all the tension seeped out of her body.

Exhale.

Her mouth trembled, struggling to find words. "That's not what I meant. I never thought—"

The pressure inside my head dissipated as the blanket fell back over me. "Just. Leave me alone," I mumbled. She hesitated to reach out, but let her hand fall down to her side at the last moment. I looked away first, down to my shoes, and resumed walking.

I didn't expect her to follow after me, and she didn't. I was alone, again, and my feet walked me to a park instead of my next class. There were monkey bars at this park, but I couldn't climb them.

My knees fell to the sawdust, my body collapsing shortly after. I was too tired of all of it, which was fine. I could accept that. It would be okay, helpful even, for me to stop now than to continue on half-assed. Better to either give all or give nothing. I looked to the trees and I saw what had captivated Aurora.

The answer was nothing.

-21-

Today was the last day, and I was being dressed by my mother.

How far the mighty had fallen.

I watched her slow inaccurate fingers weave my tie around my neck, sloppily, as she smiled blankly at my chest. Her ring finger glinted from my desk lamp. For the big day, she chose for me a light grey collar shirt paired with a dark grey suit, bought for just such an occasion. Apparently, I ripped a hole in the knee of my other suit.

My mother wore a fitted black dress, breathable yet thick enough to hide her spanx underneath, and a black blazer. Dark tights concealed her spider veins, matched with black pumps and a church-worthy hat.

I wasn't sure what my father would wear, probably something along the lines of all black everything. Funeral attire was the most flattering.

And convenient.

She patted my shoulder, "All done, Ricky." She stepped back to admire her work and I glanced to the floor mirror across the room. My reflection pulled the blanket around me, tight enough that I was already gone. I could only see the suit.

I'd redo the tie later. "Thanks." I didn't know why I thanked her, she did a terrible job and only made more work for me. I didn't even know why I let her dress me. But I guess she did it for *me*. It was her well-meaning intention that I was supposed to thank.

Was that the meaning of love?

Senseless inefficiency.

"Wow." She looked me over, inhaling so deeply she could have started floating. Weightless. With the exhale, "Valedictorian."

I couldn't even twitch into a half smile.

It wasn't a surprise. I had been at the top of my class since before I knew how to rig the game. I was pulled into the office a two weeks ago though, just to make everything official. They had streamers and balloons and those annoying little blow horns with the paper tongue. Confetti littered the outdated carpet, it was the only thing I could focus on as the staff congratulated my outstanding achievement. The carpet, it wasn't much softer than asphalt.

Three other students were there as well, for the title of whatever second place was called, and we were all served pizza and apple cider. The pizza, pepperoni and cheese. The apple cider, flat.

Second place, logically given to three different people. Two girls, one boy. The male, Eric Chang. Impromptu Captain of the speech and debate team. He broke up with his girlfriend a few weeks ago, since they had gotten into different universities. For the best, she out-leagued him so they wouldn't have lasted very long anyway. Chang recognized his strengths.

Angela Tanielu was not a stereotype. Unfortunately, she didn't have many friends, but that was the price of being an individual in high school. She was 5'9" and probably close to 175lbs. Beautiful hair, landing mid-back, styled around a very round face. If I could have chosen, Angela would be the rightful second place (she got a B+ in AP Physics last semester, poor girl).

Lastly, and forgettable, Nicole French. In the top 100 for looks, top 20 for grades but 250 for actual intelligence, and top 5 for scarily conservative. Tall, blonde, volleyball captain, president of the Young Republicans club, Nicole spoke loudly, and said excuse me when she walked into people in the hallway but didn't actually mean it. She would make a supportive senator's wife someday.

The principal asked if we had enough time to write our speeches. I didn't tell him I'd written it three years ago.

ASB organized the graduation ceremony in a nearby banquet hall. Big bright windows, clean lines, and a magnificent hand crafted chandelier. I didn't remember any of the other details. I was at the meeting, but I wasn't there.

"We finally made it guys," Jensen beamed, his hair neatly tucked inside of his cap. The ASB group surrounded me, just minutes before the finale. The parents were seated, the principal had given his congratulations, and the counselor was beginning her introduction to the ceremony. It was so close to being over.

Jensen, at the last minute, had decided to attend Cambridge University, majoring in economics. He nearly shat himself when he told his parents.

Katie nodded. "Yeah, it's kind of weird, right? For this to be the end?" In the fall, Katie would be attending UC Davis, majoring in political science and public service. She would still be within a drivable distance to check on her mom.

Samantha, with her cap resting atop her straightened hair, put her hands on her hips, smiling. "What makes you think this is the end? This is just the beginning." Samantha chose Harvard.

Katie said, "Can we please do one of those lame high school goodbyes?" She huddled us into a group hug. They said things about the future and joked about the past and reveled in the excitement of the present. It was too much to keep up. They blamed it on my pain medication.

The school's orchestra began to play the entrance music, signaling us to return to our place in line so we could file into the hall. "See you on the," Jensen paused, shaking the tassel on his cap. "Flip side. Get it? Because the next time we see each other it will be on the other—"

"Shut up and go to your spot." Samantha pushed him away. I tugged on her sleeve before she could leave.

I opened my mouth to say something.

She kissed me.

"Sorry," she apologized, pulling back. She explored my eyes, digging for a response. She only saw her reflection. "I'm so excited too! We're finally done with this place! Can you believe it?"

The words evaporated from my tongue. "Sure."

"Okay, I really have to get to my spot now."

"I think you'll enjoy being in first."

"What? You're such a fucking weirdo." She shot me a wink before finding her spot in line. The graduating class filed out of the back lot and into the building. I joined the other speakers backstage.

It wasn't a long ceremony, but it felt like eternity. I stood in the wings and listened to their speeches, but I couldn't hear. I was underwater, struggling to breathe. After the speeches from the students, they would begin calling everyone for their diplomas. After my speech. The pain in my chest made it hard to inhale. I was drowning.

"Ricky, are you okay?" One of the set crew pulled her headset back from her ear, concern growing on her face.

"Yeah, sorry, I—" Needed to go. Anywhere. "How much time do I have?"

"Um, maybe fifteen minutes?" She took a peak at the script. "Eric is halfway done."

"Great, that's enough time. Do you think I could make a quick bathroom break? I don't think I can wait any longer." My laugh came out as a choked whimper. "I'm literally about to explode."

She nodded, turning back to her clipboard. "Of course, just be quick! I'll let them know so they can prepare to stall in case something happens, like you trip and die or something."

I had a soft spot for irony.

"Sure." I took off.

Only fifteen minutes, no, thirteen just to be safe. Only thirteen minutes to find an exit. Thirteen minutes to leave. I could do that. I could do anything. Easy.

I headed for the stairs. Technically, access to the upper attic was restricted for safety concerns, since the floorboards had been removed to showcase the beautiful original beams holding up the high vaulted roof. However, I tutored the kid whose parents owned the hall and she slipped me the key.

Last night, I made a visit to the attic.

It was slightly dustier than I expected, being that the beams were exposed and it was a fancy event hall and basic upkeep was assumed, but I wasn't there to judge. The ASB committee, along with volunteers, had spent the entire day setting up chairs, testing the projector and sound system, and inflating navy, gold, and white balloons.

For the first time in weeks – or was it months? – I was completely sober. A few reasons, but mostly because I needed a clear head. I had to make sure I calculated everything correctly, because there wasn't going to be a retake.

It wasn't going to be like the hotel *thing*.

I carefully tight-walked along the two foot wide center beam. In my hand I held my life, cold and limp and made of nylon. My father always kept tow rope in the trunk of his car, for emergencies. Hopefully he wouldn't need it back.

In summer camp, they taught us how to tie knots.

I had prepared everything last night, because I knew I wouldn't have much time to set the plan into motion. High above the ballroom of my crime scene, the 350 attendees, plus or minus the handful that didn't graduate, awaited my entrance in their navy blue graduation gowns, their entourage seated in the back. I wouldn't keep them waiting for long.

My entrance, doubling as my exit, was going to be a grand spectacle. Most people tried to be sneaky and leave quietly:

down the alley in a warm bathtub, a closed garage with the car engine running, an empty house and a bullet. For example. But I wasn't most people. I was Ricky Schenk.

I was kind of a big deal.

The chandelier was glowing extra bright today, full of the crowd's hopes and dreams and aspirations. Full of the last of my star's light. My life was tied around the center pole of the chandelier, though it felt outdated to call it my life. It wasn't really there anymore, just a formality.

I took slow steps, following my path from last night, still etched into the dust. I took extra care when lifting my life from the beam, since I had already secured it around the chandelier. I didn't want the attendees to notice the crystals moving, otherwise my entire plan would be ruined. I never thought of myself as creative, but this was one of my finer pieces of work and it would be captured by one of the hundred camcorders aimed toward the stage.

I looped my life around my head, tightening the end until it reached the base of my neck.

I had to let go of my life, but there was a science to it.

A projectile would be launched with an initial horizontal velocity from an elevated ceiling beam and would follow a parabolic path to the ground. Predictable unknowns included the initial speed of the projectile (an anxious stumble), the initial height of the projectile (5'11"), the time of flight (5:18pm, one minute to go), and the length of the rope tied to initial elevation. What was the estimated time required for the projectile to swing from the chandelier before someone called 911?

It was a simple equation, but I would leave it for someone else to solve.

All I needed to do was let go.

But first.

There was one item left on my checklist. The last twinkle before the light faded out. I pulled my phone out of the breast pocket of my suffocating suit and bought Blake's stupid song for him.

I closed my eyes, finally weightless, and inhaled. Everything was dark. I looked down at the crowd below, clapping as my name was announced. It was time. I stepped forward.

Exhale.

There was screaming, but only for the shortest of milliseconds.

If you have enjoyed this novel, please consider leaving a review (either where you purchased the novel or on Goodreads. Or wherever. I'm not picky)

I would greatly appreciate it.

Thanks
K. Kingsman

Made in the USA
Middletown, DE
06 January 2020

82689904R00168